"Some protector you are."

Breathing hard, she pushed against Mike's chest. "Grandmother might as well have sent in a fox to guard the hen house."

"Why don't you tell *her* that? It would get you what you want, which is me ten stories down on the pavement. Your grandmother already warned me that you were off limits, so if you want to get me fired—"

"Off limits?" Georgina repeated. "She told you that?"

"Loud and clear, not that she should have needed to." He shook his head. "I really am sorry. You never stood a chance just now."

Georgina knew of only one reason her grandmother would warn Mike off. He was a very attractive man who had a certain reputation, and Anastasia didn't want to see her hurt.

Georgina was suddenly disgusted with herself. He never would have kissed her if *she* hadn't made the first move.

Dear Reader,

Spellbinders! That's what we're striving for. The editors at Silhouette are determined to capture your imagination and win your heart with every single book we publish. Each month, six Special Editions are chosen with *you* in mind.

Our authors are our inspiration. Writers such as Nora Roberts, Tracy Sinclair, Kathleen Eagle, Carole Halston and Linda Howard—to name but a few—are masters at creating endearing characters and heartrending love stories. Their characters are everyday people—just like you and me—whose lives have been touched by love, whose dreams and desires suddenly come true!

So find a cozy, quiet place to read, and create your own special moment with a Silhouette Special Edition.

Sincerely,

The Editors
SILHOUETTE BOOKS

BROOKE HASTINGS
Forbidden Fruit

Silhouette Special Edition

Published by Silhouette Books New York

America's Publisher of Contemporary Romance

For Leon and Barbara Wolk Stechenberg.

SILHOUETTE BOOKS
300 East 42nd St., New York, N.Y. 10017

Copyright © 1987 by Deborah Gordon

ISBN: 0-373-09385-3

First Silhouette Books printing June 1987

America's Publisher of Contemporary Romance

Printed in the U.S.A.

Books by Brooke Hastings

Silhouette Romance

Playing for Keeps #13
Innocent Fire #26
Desert Fire #44
Island Conquest #67
Winner Take All #101

Silhouette Special Edition

Intimate Strangers #2
Rough Diamond #21
A Matter of Time #49
An Act of Love #79
Tell Me No Lies #156
Hard to Handle #250
As Time Goes By #294
Forward Pass #312
Double Jeopardy #349
Forbidden Fruit #385

Silhouette Intimate Moments

Interested Parties #37
Reasonable Doubts #64

BROOKE HASTINGS

is a transplanted Easterner who now lives in California with her husband and two children. A full-time writer, she won the Romance Writers of America's Golden Medallion Award for her Silhouette Romance *Winner Take All*. She especially enjoys doing the background research for her books and finds it a real challenge to come up with new plot twists and unique characters for her stories.

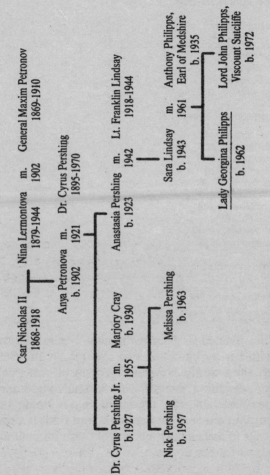

Csar Nicholas II   Nina Lermontova   m.   General Maxim Petronov
1868-1918   1879-1944   1902   1869-1910

                                    Dr. Cyrus Pershing
                                    1895-1970

Anya Petronova   m.   Anastasia Pershing   m.   Lt. Franklin Lindsay
b. 1902   1921   b. 1923   1942   1918-1944

Dr. Cyrus Pershing Jr.   m.   Marjory Cray   Sara Lindsay   m.   Anthony Philipps,
b.1927   1955   b. 1930   b. 1943   1961   Earl of Medshire
                                                                                  b. 1935

Nick Pershing   Melissa Pershing   Lady Georgina Philipps   Lord John Philipps,
b.1957   b. 1963   b. 1962   Viscount Sutcliffe
                                                                                     b. 1972

GEORGINA'S FAMILY TREE

Chapter One

Mike Napoli had no idea why he'd been summoned to Anastasia Lindsay's Fifth Avenue apartment, but it wasn't the sort of invitation you turned down. Not if you were ambitious and close to broke, and not if you had even an ounce of curiosity in your makeup.

Mike slipped his hand into his pocket as he approached the lobby door, feeling for the woman's letter. *Please join me for dinner at seven o'clock on April first,* it read. *I have a confidential matter to discuss with you.* He'd mailed her a formal acceptance just in case the whole thing was somebody's idea of an April Fool's prank, but nobody from her office had called to ask what he was talking about. Obviously the invitation was for real.

A woman in a mink coat preceded him into the building, walked up to a security station manned by a stone-faced guard and told him her name. The guard checked his clipboard and then buzzed her through to the inner lobby.

Mike walked up to the window next. "Michael Napoli to see Mrs. Lindsay."

The guard looked at his list, looked at Mike, and frowned. Mike shifted his weight uneasily from one foot to the other. After six years of rubbing elbows with some of New York's prime movers and shakers, he knew what to say and how to act, but upper-crust millionaires like Anastasia Lindsay were in a category all their own. Even her address intimidated him, although he was trying not to show it.

He was thinking about pulling out Mrs. Lindsay's invitation when the guard snapped his fingers and grinned. "I've got it now. You're Mike Napoli from Boston College."

Mike smiled back, relieved. "You have a good memory."

"Hey, no way. You were the best. If it hadn't been for your knee..." His voice trailed off, as if he was afraid he'd mentioned something he shouldn't.

Mike winked at him and finished the sentence. "I might have been rich enough to buy an apartment in this building, assuming they would have accepted a pro football player. I should probably be getting upstairs now."

The guard nodded and buzzed him inside. As he rode up the elevator he began to hope that seven o'clock really meant seven o'clock. He was exactly on time, not fashionably late.

The butler who answered his knock greeted him by name and took his coat. If the knowledge that he was really expected here reassured him, his surroundings did the exact opposite. The French carpets, the antique furniture, the museum-quality sculpture and paintings... How did you sit down in a place like this? How did you accept a drink when you were sure you would probably spill it?

The butler showed him into a parlor where a slender, blond-haired woman was sitting on a damask-covered sofa, probably Louis something-or-other, probably worth a fortune. Mike recognized Anastasia Lindsay at once and thought to himself that she was an excellent advertisement for the cosmetics she sold. She had to be somewhere in her sixties but didn't look a day over forty-five.

"Mr. Napoli, Madam," the butler said. Mike resisted the compulsion to bow to her and walked forward to accept the hand she was holding out.

"Thank you, Moreland." She patted the spot beside her on the sofa. "Sit down, Mr. Napoli. What will you have to drink?"

Great, Mike thought. *Not only do I get to worry about spilling my drink—I get to worry about spilling it in her lap.* "Nothing just yet," he said aloud.

"Of course you'll have something." There was a hint of Europe in her accent, just enough to sound exotic. Her eyes turned mischievous. "Some Old Sycamore bourbon, perhaps?"

So she knew he'd written the copy for the Old Sycamore advertising campaign. He smiled and sat down beside her, telling her bourbon would be fine.

Not only was she a beautiful woman; her complexion was as flawless as fine English porcelain. Maybe those creams and lotions of hers really worked. Mike knew nothing about her field, even though her company, Corona Cosmetics, used the ad agency he'd left just six months before. Corona hadn't been one of his accounts.

Moreland poured out the bourbon from a crystal decanter and set the glass on a silver coaster. "Give us fifteen minutes and then ask Lady Georgina to come in," Anastasia instructed. Mike sat there wondering who Lady Georgina was as Moreland walked out of the parlor.

"I'd heard you were arrogant and brash, Mr. Napoli," Anastasia said. "I must say, you don't live up to your image."

Never let 'em see you sweat. It was a good line, even if Mike hadn't written it. "I'd heard *you* were beautiful and disarming," he replied with a cocky smile. "You live up to your image exactly."

She threw back her head and laughed. "And charming. They said you could be very charming—when you wanted to be. Thank you for not disappointing me."

"My pleasure," Mike said, reaching for his drink. Anastasia Lindsay had begun to study him intently and he found the experience rather unnerving.

After a few seconds she nodded to herself and murmured, "You really are remarkably good-looking." Her hand darted to his chin, turning his face toward hers. He was so startled he damn near dropped his drink. "Excellent bone structure." She touched the bridge of his nose. "I suppose you broke this playing football. It was football, wasn't it?" Without waiting for an answer, she went on. "Take off your jacket. It doesn't fit properly, but then, ready-to-wear never does, no matter how expertly they alter it."

Mike wasn't just *rather* unnerved by now; he was thoroughly rattled. Anastasia Lindsay was known for three things: her beauty, her business acumen and her social life. So far as he knew she'd always stuck to men her own age, but the way she was staring made him think she was auditioning him for the part of her next lover. Since he couldn't very well ask her about it, he put down his drink, stood up and removed his jacket. It had come from one of New York's finest men's shops and cost more than he could afford, but he wasn't going to argue with her about the way it fit.

To his acute discomfort, her examination went from visual to physical. She touched his neck, ran her fingertips across his shoulders and down his chest, and then, to top it all off, grasped the fabric of his slacks, right at his thighs, and pulled. "You're in good shape," she announced. "If there's anything I can't abide it's a thirty-year-old man with bad muscle tone."

Mike was only twenty-nine, but confined his response to a dry, "I'm glad you approve."

She paid no attention. "Athletes are always a problem, of course, particularly in the shoulders and thighs. I have the most wonderful tailor—an Englishman, naturally. You must have him make you up some suits. And don't bother telling me you can't afford it. Circumstances can change. Go on, put your jacket back on and sit down."

Mike was more than happy to comply. "You seem to know a lot about me," he said, grabbing his drink again.

"Not nearly enough, Mr. Napoli. Why else do you think I invited you?"

Mike took a healthy slug of bourbon. He didn't want to offend the woman but enough was enough. "I can think of three possible reasons, Mrs. Lindsay. Number one, you're thinking about using me as a model in one of your ads. It's a tempting prospect, especially if it means I get to meet that incredible blonde you've been using lately, but I'm afraid I'd have to turn you down. I come from a working-class family in Massachusetts. They think I'm a little weird just for working in the advertising business, but if I turn up in an Anastasia Perfume ad they're going to worry that I'll move to San Francisco and take up with a guy who wears dresses."

She gave him an amused look but didn't comment. Anastasia Lindsay was nothing if not worldly—it would probably take an earthquake to shake her. "Number two," Mike continued, "you heard I'd left Hall & Haywood to start my own agency and you're thinking of giving me some business. Under most circumstances I would prostrate myself in gratitude—"

"I doubt very much that you've ever prostrated yourself, Mr. Napoli, either in gratitude or anything else," she interrupted. "You're not the type."

Mike smiled and shrugged, tacitly conceding the point. "It was poetic license. The point I wanted to make is that Hall & Haywood is your current ad agency. Terry Hall has been exceptionally decent to me over the years and I'm not going to steal away his business. So I can't possibly go to work for you."

"And number three?" she said.

Mike wasn't sure he should mention number three. Then again, the woman had a sense of humor and seemed to like it when he was blunt. The worst she could do was toss him out of her house.

"You took a pretty thorough inventory a minute or two ago," he said. "I felt like a prize stud being sized up by a potential buyer." She was smiling again, in a way that told Mike she'd guessed what he was about to say and was more amused than ever. "You're a beautiful woman and rumor has it that no man has ever walked out of your life by choice, but still, I have this hang-up about sleeping with a woman who knows twice as much as I do about practically everything. I don't see myself in the role of the kept younger man."

Anastasia was laughing openly now. Mike was about to make a self-deprecating joke about his ego having gotten out of hand when a cool, English voice chimed in. "And if she were ignorant and naive? Would the role of the kept younger man appeal to you in that instance, Mr. Napoli?"

He grinned at Anastasia. "Are you kidding me? I'd let her spoil me rotten." Then he turned around to check out the owner of the disapproving voice and almost dropped his drink for the second time that night. It was all he could do to set it on the coffee table and stand up.

The blond hair and green eyes, the exquisite face and coltish body, the aura of class and style—half of New York was talking about this woman. Probably even half of America. She'd first appeared in a Corona ad about six months before and every model agency in town had wanted to sign her up. But Anastasia had refused to say who she was, even keeping Hall & Haywood in the dark. The mystery surrounding her had only added to the campaign's success. Sales had been phenomenal lately.

Unfortunately, she was looking at Mike as if he'd crawled out of a sewer and oozed his way into the apartment. Whoever she was, she didn't have her hostess's sense of humor. Mike would have explained that he was only joking about living off a rich older woman, but her contemptuous stare got under his skin. Snooty English model.

"As always, Georgie, your timing is simply flawless," Anastasia said. "I had accused Mr. Napoli of not living up to his brash, arrogant image and he was doing his best to prove me wrong. Fix yourself a drink and sit down. And do stop frowning. You'll get wrinkles around your mouth."

Georgie—as in Lady Georgina? Mike thought. No wonder she was snooty—her father was some kind of English lord. He stood there watching as she crossed to the bar and poured herself a sherry. Her cashmere dress wasn't especially tight, but it accented her curves in a spectacular way. He continued to watch her as she walked away from the bar, seated herself in a chair, and crossed her legs—long, shapely legs that her photographs didn't do justice to.

"My granddaughter, Georgie Philipps," Anastasia said. "Perhaps you recognize her from our ads."

"Yes." Mike sat down, smiling a warm, interested smile. It was automatic with such an attractive woman, even if she was out of his social and financial league. "Everybody in the business has been wondering who you are. It's a pleasure to meet you, Georgie."

Her expression was so icy it could have frozen an erupting volcano. "The members of my family call me Georgie. My friends call me Georgina. *You* may call me *Lady* Georgina."

Georgina was only in her twenties but had already learned to play the condescending lady of the manor to absolute perfection. Still, this wasn't 1800 and Mike wasn't one of the local peasants. "I think I've just been put in my place," he said to Anastasia, trying to sound as if he'd found Georgina's behavior childish but amusing.

"How perceptive of you to notice," Georgina said. She gave him a sugary smile and proceeded to ignore him. "I love the earrings, Grandmother, especially with this dress. At first I thought they were too big for my face, but you were right as usual. They're perfect. Thank you again."

"You're welcome, darling, I adore you in sapphires and diamonds, but that lipstick..." Anastasia pursed her lips and studied her granddaughter's face. "Royal Elderberry would have been better." She picked up Mike's glass, which was almost empty, and held it out. "Mr. Napoli could use a refill. He's drinking bourbon."

Although Mike didn't want another drink, the prospect of being waited on by Lady Georgina Philipps was too good to pass up. As a well brought-up young woman she couldn't refuse to do as Anastasia wished, but her body was stiff with reproach as she got to her feet. "Of course, Grandmother," she said, and took Mike's glass.

Mike glanced at Anastasia as Georgina marched to the bar. Her eyes were sparkling with unholy glee. She knew Georgina didn't like him, that she hadn't wanted to get the drink. She was deliberately stirring the pot, but why?

Georgina looked so chilly as she approached with the drink that Mike couldn't resist teasing her a little more. He didn't take the glass, but said ingenuously, "Would you mind putting some ice in that—*Lady* Georgina?"

"Of course she wouldn't," Anastasia said. "Hurry up about it, darling, the man looks parched."

Georgina turned on her heel, her face an impassive mask. She probably would have liked to pour the drink over Mike's head. She was just dropping in the ice when her grandmother abruptly stood up. "I'm sure I hear the phone. I'm expecting an important call, but don't worry, I won't be long." She sailed out of the room without a backward glance.

Although Mike had excellent ears, he hadn't heard any ringing. Anastasia had probably left them alone on purpose, maybe because it amused her to picture the two of them coming to blows. He never expected Georgina to actually bring him the drink, but she did, even asking if she could get him anything else. He grinned suggestively and told her no—at least, not at the moment.

She sat down again and picked up her sherry. After half a minute of stony silence Mike decided to try warming her up. No man in his right mind would have wanted to feud with a woman who looked like Georgina Philipps. "So how long have you been in New York?" he asked with a smile.

"Two weeks," she answered, not looking at him.

"And what brought you here? A modeling assignment? Or are you just visiting your grandmother for a while?"

"That, Mr. Napoli, is none of your concern." When it came to sounding haughty, the lady was in a class by herself.

Mike couldn't argue the point—it *wasn't* any of his business. "Okay, then, what brought *me* here? Why does your grandmother want to see me?"

"I suggest you take that up with her. I don't comment on my grandmother's actions."

"How about your own?" Mike was getting a little impatient now. "It's obvious you don't like me—"

"Exactly. If I were to list the attributes I admire in a man, you would possess none of them. However, since you're a guest in my grandmother's home, it would be unpardonably rude of me to pursue the subject." She paused a moment. "Horrible weather we've been having, isn't it?"

Mike gave her a disbelieving stare. Did she really expect him to talk about the weather when she'd just told him what a wretched specimen of humanity he was? He was torn between demanding to know why she disliked him and giving up completely. He still hadn't made up his mind which to do when Anastasia reappeared.

"I hope you've gotten to know each other a bit better," she said, oblivious to the tension in the room. "Trudy is ready to serve. Shall we?"

They made their way to the table in utter silence. Mike helped Anastasia into her chair but didn't have time to do the same for Georgina. She made sure she was already seated.

He had never laid eyes on a dining room like this. Everything looked antique, even the crystal and china, and there was so much silver on the table the meal would probably take forever. He'd attended enough formal dinners in his time to know which fork or spoon to use, but the atmosphere was so elegant and restrained that an ordinary guy off the street probably would have been too intimidated to eat.

He decided then and there that he wasn't going to let it affect him. Anastasia Lindsay had been right about his public image, at least as far as business went. Mike *was* brash and arrogant. He had a talent for knowing how to sell things, and if his clients were too stupid to listen, that was their problem, not his. Besides, Terry Hall had always been around to smooth their ruffled feathers.

He got to the point the minute the first course was on the table—some sort of seafood in pastry. "Mrs. Lindsay, about the letter you sent me—"

She cut him off with a regal sweep of her hand. "It's been such a joy to have Georgie's company for the past several weeks. Did she tell you she'd been ill?"

"I'm afraid not," Mike answered, forcing his impatience under control. "I hope you're feeling better, Lady Georgina." He couldn't quite keep the irony out of his voice when he used her title. Obviously that annoyed her, but the feeling was mutual. Her superior attitude was driving him up the wall.

"I was until I walked into the parlor," she replied.

"Georgie, really!" Anastasia pretended to be scandalized. "It must be the lingering effects of the flu, Mr. Napoli. Unlike me, Georgie usually has perfect manners. They were bred into her, you see. I married off my only daughter to an English earl—the connection did wonders for my business—and Georgie is the result. Unfortunately, she doesn't care for Englishmen—not the ones who would be suitable, in any event—so she's come to America to find herself a rich husband." A hint of sarcasm entered her voice. "Being an earl isn't cheap, you know. Those huge estates cost a fortune to maintain, and Anthony's business interests have suffered a bit of a reverse lately. There's nothing like an advantageous marriage to replenish the family coffers, wouldn't you agree?"

Mike was literally speechless. Why was Anastasia telling him about her granddaughter's marriage plans? He wasn't, to use her term, even remotely suitable—he came from a modest background and barely had a dime to spare. Obviously he wasn't here as a candidate for the lady's hand.

Did she want him to play matchmaker, then? It was unlikely, because she had better social connections in this city than anyone he could think of. It wouldn't have been a problem for her to find her granddaughter a wealthy enough husband to suit the needs of the earl.

Georgina, meanwhile, was red with embarrassment. Mike might have wanted to knock a little of the haughtiness out of her, but he also admired her aplomb. It had to be tough to keep your expression so bland when your cheeks matched the predominant color of the carpet. In the end, gallantry won out over annoyance.

"Once the men in this city hear that your granddaughter is available, you'll have to hire a private cop to control the crowds outside the building," he said to Anastasia. "Now about your letter—"

"Didn't anyone ever tell you it was rude to be so persistent?" she interrupted.

"They tell me that all the time." Mike flashed her a crooked grin. "I don't pay any attention."

"Then I'll have to be equally rude. I don't care to discuss the matter right now. I'll call you into my office when I do. Now tell me about your family, Mr. Napoli. I want to know what sort of background you come from."

Mike couldn't imagine why. "With all due respect, Mrs. Lindsay, you invited me here out of the blue, with no explanation and so little notice I had to cancel another appointment. Now you refuse to tell me why. I don't see why I should answer personal questions."

She squared her shoulders and raised her chin, as imperious as Queen Victoria. Somewhere Mike had read that Anastasia Lindsay claimed to be the illegitimate granddaughter of Czar Nicholas II of Russia. He'd assumed it was Madison Avenue hype, but looking at her now he could well believe it.

"It's not necessary that you should see," she said, "but you might keep in mind that I have the power to make you a very successful man."

"If you're talking about business, I already explained where I'm coming from." Mike was openly exasperated now. "And if you're talking about anything else, I'm not interested."

"Since you have no idea where *I'm* coming from, I would advise you to be more cooperative. But if that's not incentive enough, perhaps you should keep in mind that I have a great many friends in this city. You're in no position to offend me. I believe we were discussing your family."

Family was what kept Mike at the table. He didn't know if Anastasia had the influence to damage his prospects for the future, but it wasn't only *his* prospects they were talking about. He wished to God he'd brought along his brother-in-law. Rich was so much better at handling people than he was—the Terry Hall of Conlin & Napoli.

"Yeah, right," he finally conceded. "What do you want to know?"

He caught Georgina's disdainful glance out of the corner of his eye. She obviously thought he was a toad for allowing her grandmother to browbeat him, but he had no choice.

"You may start with your parents' names and backgrounds," Anastasia said crisply, "and then tell me what sort of work they do."

Mike answered in a stiff monotone. "My parents' names are Marie and Frank. They're both from Cambridge—the working-class part of Cambridge. My mother is a legal secretary at a Boston law firm. Her father was a cop at Harvard until he retired. He and my grandmother live in Florida now. My father is a foreman at an electronics plant. *His* father was a carpenter. He died a few years ago. His mother is in a nursing home. My parents live in Cambridge, in the house my mother grew up in."

"They sound like honest, hard-working people. The salt of the earth." Anastasia nodded at Moreland, indicating that he should serve the next course. Mike had barely touched his seafood and didn't care what came next. His appetite had disappeared. Who the hell was Anastasia Lindsay to make condescending remarks about his family?

"Tell me about your brothers and sisters," she said.

"I have three sisters and one brother. Bianca is married to my business partner, Rich Conlin. They have two little boys. Ellen is a teacher in Newton, Theresa is a law student, and Christopher is in college. Do you want the names of their schools or will that be sufficient?"

She smiled benignly. "It will do for the moment. It must have been a struggle for your parents to send you all to college."

"Education is important to them," Mike answered. He wasn't going to explain that, as the oldest, he'd paid a lot of the bills. It would have been easier if he'd wound up being a rich football player like everyone had expected, but he hadn't sat around crying after that final injury. Not for more than a few months, anyway. He'd come to New York and gotten himself a job.

"That's very admirable." Anastasia paused. "And your personal life? Have you ever been in love? Have you ever been engaged?"

Mike shouldn't have been surprised by anything by now, but he was. There were limits, dammit. "No to both," he said curtly.

"But it doesn't stop you from enjoying the company of the opposite sex—at least not if we can believe what we read in the papers."

He stared at her, unwilling to dignify the comment with a reply. He did his share of running around, but it was mostly business. The more contacts he made, the better the agency's chances. Prospective clients liked to know the men they were thinking of doing business with.

"Tell me," she asked with a sly smile, "do you actually sleep with all those women they link you with?"

If there were limits, Anastasia had just exceeded them. Mike scraped back his chair and started out of the room, but it was a long enough walk to the door for common sense and family loyalty to take over. He was sorry he hadn't turned it into a joke—made some light remark about not even Superman having the energy to satisfy all those women—but it was too late now to back down.

He was nearly at the door when Anastasia's voice slashed across the room, cracking against his ears like a bullwhip. "Come back here, Mr. Napoli!"

Mike instinctively stopped, the same as he would have if one of his coaches had issued the order. He could have kicked himself, but at least there was a way to salvage the situation. He turned around and folded his arms across his chest, silently indicating he was willing to endure another minute of her company if she finally got down to business.

"I'm starting a line of men's products," she said. "Obviously Hall & Haywood won't be able to accept the account. Be in my office at ten o'clock on the fifteenth to make a presentation. I don't expect mock-ups on such short notice, only an indication of the general approach you would take, both in the matter of publicizing the launch and long-term advertising strategy. You may discuss this with Mr. Conlin, but not with anybody else."

Mike was frankly amazed. There hadn't been any rumors about Corona entering the men's field. How had she kept it so quiet? Her product development lab had to have done a great deal of work for her to reach the stage where she was ready to think about advertising, but nobody had breathed a word.

She was right about Hall & Haywood. They couldn't compete for the account because an existing client was in a similar field and Terry Hall was a stickler about avoiding conflicts of interest.

She was offering him a golden opportunity, and his first impulse was to humbly thank her. But humility hadn't gotten him this far—arrogance had. She only seemed to respect a man if he gave as good as he got.

"I would never accept an account that could make me or break me," he said, only half bluffing. It could be dangerous to put too many eggs in one basket, because if your client left you, most of your business would go out the door with him and your company might never recover. "Talk to somebody bigger, Mrs. Lindsay."

She smiled, giving Mike the feeling she could read him like an open book. "Mr. Napoli, do you know how long I've been with Hall & Haywood?"

"You were there when I came," he answered.

"And long before—seventeen years, to be exact. I'm good at spotting winners. I reward loyalty with loyalty. If I decide to use your ideas, it will be the start of a long and mutually profitable relationship. You can count on it."

"I don't count on anything, but I'm willing to talk." Mike gave a polite nod. "Mrs. Lindsay, Lady Georgina...it's been—an interesting evening." He turned and walked away, and this time, nobody tried to stop him.

Chapter Two

If Georgina Philipps hadn't considered Mike Napoli to be one of the lower forms of vertebrate life, she might have admired the way he'd stood up to her grandmother. Very few people tried it, including Georgina herself. Of course, she had seldom had any reason to.

Georgina adored Anastasia Lindsay. Her childhood would have been a misery without her grandmother's letters, phone calls and visits. Anastasia had lavished love and attention on her and she would have done just about anything to return it—even model for Corona Cosmetics ads.

Georgina was too private a person to enjoy having her picture in dozens of newspapers and magazines, but when Anastasia had asked her to pose, she had immediately agreed. It wasn't only a question of paying her grandmother back, but also of family duty. She believed that if your family needed your help, you gave it—to the best of your ability and without complaint.

The past few years were a case in point. Georgina had devoted herself to her sick father for a year and then set about straightening out his business problems. As much as Anastasia had grumbled that Georgina was sacrificing her life on the altar of family duty, she hadn't hesitated to take advantage of that same sense of duty when it came to selling skin creams and lipsticks. Georgina loved her grandmother dearly, but didn't deceive herself about Anastasia's driving ambition and desire for control.

The two of them watched Mike Napoli stride through the door and then turned their attention to the soup. "What incredible gall the man has," Georgina remarked with a sly smile. "Imagine walking off in the middle of dinner that way."

Anastasia sampled the soup. "This is wonderful. Trudy has outdone herself tonight, but Mr. Napoli barely even picked at his food. I can't imagine why, unless those little digs of yours took away his appetite. I take it it was a question of hate at first sight."

Anastasia was being coy, both about what had upset Mike Napoli and why Georgina had been so cutting. Two weeks before, she had breezed into Georgina's sickroom with the latest of her old-country remedies for flu and a copy of a New York tabloid. She had pointed to a photo of Mike Napoli dancing with a hot young actress in New York's newest "in" nightspot and explained that he was a brilliant young advertising man who had just started his own agency. She was thinking of hiring him to handle her new line of men's products. Didn't Georgina think he was gorgeous?

He was gorgeous, all right, and Georgina had admitted as much. They had even joked about hiring him to do more than write advertising copy, but then Georgina had noticed the caption under the photo and her smile had disappeared. She knew more about Mike Napoli than her grandmother could possibly imagine and none of it was good.

Over the next two weeks she had heard more about him and read more about him than she cared to recall. First there were the columnists, who evidently loved to mention him. Then there was Anastasia, who had discussed him with his former boss, Terry Hall, and insisted on telling Georgina about every line of copy he had ever written. Georgina pointed out that Napoli seemed to be an ambitious young man on the make with no morals and fewer scruples, but Anastasia didn't mind in the least. So what if he slept with a different woman every night? So what if he'd walked out on the man who had hired him fresh from college and taught him everything he knew? He was a brilliant advertising man. That was the bottom line.

He'd also caused one of Georgina's dearest friends an intolerable amount of heartache, but Georgina didn't go into that. She never betrayed a confidence, even one from six years before. Besides, it was ancient history now. Jill was happily married and lived in California. She would be coming for a visit in May and Georgina couldn't wait to see her.

She didn't approve of Mike Napoli—of the way he treated his friends, of his lack of loyalty, of his naked ambition— but if her grandmother wanted to hire him, she wasn't going to object. Anastasia was no patsy, to be taken advantage of by the likes of Mike Napoli. She would use his talents to the fullest and sell tons of cosmetics in the process. If Anastasia wanted Georgina to be civil to the man, she would certainly do her best.

It wasn't going to be easy, though. Her back had gone up the moment she'd entered the parlor and realized what he was saying. The man probably *would* agree to an affair, if it meant receiving dozens of expensive presents from his wealthy mistress. He was as discriminating as a tomcat.

Georgina could think of only one thing in his favor—he hadn't let Anastasia push him around, even though a major account was at stake. If there was anything Georgina couldn't abide, it was a bootlicker. As the daughter of an earl and the granddaughter of a world famous cosmetics queen, she had met more than her share of them in her life.

It was a long couple of moments before she answered her grandmother's question about hate at first sight. "I wouldn't say that. It's just that he reminds me of the men I had to tackle when I was straightening out Father's business affairs. Only a few of them were actually stealing from him, you know. The rest were simply running their little fiefdoms in a way that would earn the maximum number of pounds for themselves. If Father lost money in the process..." She shrugged and picked up her soup spoon. Father had lost a bundle.

"Well, darling, there's an old saying that nobody looks after your money like you—unless you have a wonderful, dutiful daughter to do it." Anastasia frowned. "If that mother of yours had had any backbone—"

"She's weak, Grandmother. Both of us know that." Sarah Philipps had barely been able to cope with her husband's illness, much less keep an eye on the family coffers. The thought reminded Georgina of something Anastasia had said earlier, before Napoli had stormed out. "Why did you tell Mr. Napoli that you had married off Mother to Father for business reasons? I was under the impression that she was dying for a title as a girl. Since the only other thing she's ever wanted is to devote herself to a husband, it seems to me that you arranged the perfect match for her."

Anastasia gave her a fond look. "You're far too generous, Georgie, especially for a girl whose parents have practically ignored her all her life. The fact is, it was a perfect match for me, too. I knew that once I had the Countess of Medshire using my products, sooner or later the rest of England would begin to do the same. Even the royal family." She sighed. "What a coup that was!"

Part of Anastasia's genius lay in her ability to give people what they wanted while accomplishing her own ends. Georgina had paid the price, of course, but nobody could have known what miserable parents Sarah and Anthony would turn out to be. And Anastasia had done everything in her power to make up for it.

"The story of your life," she teased. "One coup after another. Tell me, what grade did Mr. Napoli earn on the test you just administered?"

Anastasia laughed. "B, perhaps even a B plus. My estimation of him was much lower at first, but then he mentioned his sister and her family and I realized he would have walked out much sooner if his partner didn't have four mouths to feed. Still, he's young and inexperienced. I'm sure he could have charmed me into telling him what he wanted to know if he'd put his mind to it. Of course, he was very put out with *you*, darling. My cross-examination must have seemed like the last straw."

"You're perverse, Grandmother," Georgina said. "You want everybody to do your bidding, but at the same time, you don't respect them if they let you walk all over them."

"I respect *you*, darling," Anastasia pointed out, "and you always do as I ask."

"Because I love you. And because you love me. You wanted me to come to America a whole year ago but you respected my decision to stay in England and look after Father's business affairs. And you haven't made a fuss about my looking for a rich husband, even though you disapprove. Although I must say, I hope you won't make a habit of mentioning it to any more of your dinner guests." Georgina felt awkward about taking her grandmother to task, but there was such a thing as going too far. "I was dreadfully embarrassed, Grandmother. You made it sound as if I planned to auction myself to the highest bidder."

"And don't you?" Anastasia demanded.

Georgina was embarrassed all over again. "Of course not. I would never marry a man simply because he's rich. He would have to be somebody I like. Somebody I respect."

"Like! Respect!" Anastasia practically spat out the words. "You're too young to be so jaded, Georgie."

Maybe in years, Georgina thought, but not in experience. The more she'd seen of the male half of the human species, the more disenchanted she'd become.

She'd been born with two irresistible assets when it came to the marriage market: a wealthy, doting grandmother and a title. She'd barely been into her teens when the fortune hunters and social climbers had started coming around, and perhaps inevitably, she'd been taken in by a few of them at first. She'd been wary after that, but time had eventually taught her to recognize the phonies and opportunists and avoid them. She had dated some highly respectable men in the years since, and perhaps that was part of the problem. All of them had bored her senseless.

She wanted somebody creative, somebody dynamic, somebody who was curious about a thousand different things. Upper-class Englishmen with generations of family money behind them all seemed so predictable, so tame. The adventurousness had evidently been bred out of them.

She was hoping it would be different in America. For one thing, there were all those self-made millionaires, and for another, you didn't need a title somewhere in your background to break into the highest social circles. She was sure to meet a suitable man, someone who would love her for herself and not just for her family connections.

She wanted to love him back, too, but she had to be realistic about that. She had moved in a mostly male world for the past year and what she had seen hadn't impressed her. Ambition, greed, condescension, selfishness.... Thank heavens her father had recovered enough to assume responsibility for his affairs again. Her little brother John had a good head for business but was only fifteen—their mother had suffered numerous miscarriages—so it would be years before he could take over. Georgina wasn't sure how much longer she could have survived in that environment.

Anastasia was fully aware of her feelings, so she allowed herself to hope the subject would be dropped. It wasn't. "You're not made of diamonds and ice," Anastasia said. "Someone who loves her family as much as you do will never be satisfied to merely like and respect her husband. Good heavens, darling, haven't you ever looked at a man and thought you would melt?"

"Have you?" Georgina asked back, unwilling to give an honest answer.

"Only Franklin," was the soft reply. Anastasia Pershing had met Franklin Lindsay when she was sixteen and married him when she was nineteen. There were still pictures of him all over the apartment, the last of them taken the day before he'd gone overseas during World War II to fight and die for his country.

"With Franklin it was like a bolt of lightning, from the moment we first laid eyes on each other. It was never the same with anyone else, but that doesn't mean I've felt nothing since. I may be in my sixties, but everything is in perfect working order. When Mike Napoli strolled into the parlor..." She gave Georgina a calculating look. "Don't tell me you didn't feel it, too. I don't care what you think of the man's morals."

Georgina had felt it, all right. Napoli had the bluest eyes she'd ever seen and crisp, dark hair that begged to be touched. His broken nose added danger and vulnerability to a strikingly handsome face, but what really did it was the body. American football had always struck Georgina as barbaric, but there was nothing uncivilized about a six-foot frame or broad shoulders, narrow hips, and hard, trim muscles. It was a source of considerable chagrin to Georgina that she could look at a slug like Napoli and feel such a jolt of electricity. Every defensive instinct had immediately slammed into place.

"He's a very attractive man," she said coolly, aware that she was blushing.

"So you're human, after all," Anastasia teased.

Georgina lifted her chin, defiant now. "It was merely a momentary physical reaction. He could look like Robert Redford and I still wouldn't like him."

"Yes, well, I suppose that's for the best. After all, he's so totally unsuitable." Anastasia sighed and took a sip of soup. A few moments later, much to Georgina's relief, she started talking about her newest perfume.

Mike knew it was crazy to go rushing out to Queens when he would see his brother-in-law in the office the next morning, but he also knew he wouldn't be able either to work or sleep until he told Rich about Anastasia Lindsay. Besides, he liked spending time at his sister's place. Unlike his studio apartment in Manhattan, it felt like a real home. There was always plenty to eat and he enjoyed playing with his two nephews.

The younger one, David, was perched on Bianca's hip when she answered the door. Mike had apparently interrupted bathtime, because the kid's hair was still wet. He made a funny face, getting David to giggle, and then sniffed the air. Fried chicken. Manna from heaven. "I'm starved," he said. "You got any leftovers?"

"Fortunately for you, yes. It'll probably be the first decent meal you've had all week." Bianca handed him the baby, who said something approximating "uncle" and giggled again. "You run around too much. I saw your picture in the paper with that French actress—Françoise Dumont." She rolled her eyes. "My brother, the playboy."

Bianca kept up a steady barrage of teasing as they made their way to the kitchen. She knew he didn't have a different woman in his bed every night but enjoyed pretending the opposite.

Rich came in a few minutes later with Adam, their older son, who climbed onto Mike's lap and stole some of his food. They spent the next half hour playing with the kids and talking about the family. If anything happened to one of the Napolis, Bianca seemed to find out about it within hours. The BBC, they called her—the Bianca Broadcasting Company.

"I was talking to Ellen about Mom and Dad's anniversary," she remarked as Mike demolished a piece of chocolate cake, "and she had the most fabulous idea. Thirty years.... It's a special number, you know?—especially since we couldn't do anything big for twenty-five. She thinks we should send them on a cruise—give them the tickets and tell them they're non-refundable so they won't try to return them." She suddenly grinned. "And you know the best part of it? It would get them out of the house for a couple of weeks. We could go through all that junk in the attic while they're gone. Honestly, Mike, if we don't do something soon, they're going to have a fire up there."

The state of the Napolis' attic was a standing family joke. Ellen claimed their mother had saved every bill she'd ever paid, every child's baby tooth, every cancelled check and every piece of clothing. She'd also stored away dribs and drabs of extra paint, half-full bottles of chemicals, and God only knew what other dangerous materials. Their father, an easygoing man by nature, had long ago given up arguing with her. He was a lot less worried about a possible fire than about keeping peace in the family.

Mike thought the cruise was an inspiration—providing they could swing the cost. With Chris and Theresa still in school and Bianca a full-time mother, only he and Ellen had regular incomes. And Mike's salary was at a bare-bones minimum right now.

He'd never lived lavishly, even in the years when he'd made a lot of money. Anything he didn't need for day-to-day living expenses had gone toward the younger kids' educations or been put aside for the day when he went into business for himself. He knew it wouldn't be cheap, especially in a field as competitive as advertising, but he'd always dreamed of being his own boss, the creative director of his own agency.

The one stumbling block had been his total lack of interest in management, but then Rich Conlin had come to H & H. Rich was a born executive with ambitions of his own The two had become close friends, and then, after Mike introduced Rich to his sister, brothers-in-law. They had saved their money, learned everything they could about advertising, and bided their time till they were ready to make the break from H & H.

The six months they'd been in business had eaten into their savings at a ferocious rate. Still, their client list was growing and there was the possibility of getting the Corona account. Mike thought he and Rich could afford to spend a little more freely, so he told Bianca he loved the idea of a cruise.

She offered to check on prices and schedules and ask Ellen to call their parents' employers to find out when they would be able to take time off. With any luck, she could make the reservations next week.

Later, when the boys were in bed and the three adults were having coffee, Bianca admitted that she'd expected more of an argument from Mike about paying for the cruise. "You're always worrying about me and Rich having enough, but I can get a job if I really need to and—"

Rich cut her off. "You're wasting your breath, honey. He's been playing the big brother for twenty-seven years now and he's not about to stop."

"The money might not be a problem," Mike said. "I had dinner tonight—or one course of it—with Anastasia Lindsay. As soon as I get home I'm going to write up one of those profiles for *Reader's Digest*—'My Most Unforgettable Character.'" He pulled out Anastasia's letter. "This is how it began."

Rich and Bianca were alternately incredulous, hysterical and appalled as he described his adventures on Fifth Avenue. "So to make a long story even longer," he concluded, "we have exactly two weeks to come up with a brilliant advertising strategy."

"Brilliance is your department," Rich drawled. "I don't have time to be creative—I'm too busy paying the bills and placating the people you insult. Maybe I should drop in on the fair Lady Georgina."

"The fair Lady Georgina is a spoiled brat," Mike said. "I never had a chance to insult her. She started using me as a verbal punching bag before I could get a word out. I only hope Mrs. Lindsay doesn't pay too much attention to her opinions."

"From what I've heard about Anastasia Lindsay, the only opinions she listens to are her own," Rich said. "Remember my friend Ronny Hoffman, her account executive at H & H? An hour with Anastasia and he was heading for the nearest bar. Once he grabbed a rose from the vase on his table, put it between his teeth and started tangoing around the room, singing, 'Whatever Lindsay wants, Lindsay gets,' to the tune of 'Lola' from *Damn Yankees*. In deference to my wife here, I won't repeat any of the lyrics he made up."

"But he's still handling her account."

Rich nodded. "Yup. It's been five years now. Another year and he'll be checking into the Bellevue psych ward. One thing about Anastasia Lindsay, though. She may drive you crazy with her demands, but she never plays games about the fees. Give her top value and she pays top dollar."

"Top value being defined as your undivided attention, twenty-four hours a day," Mike said.

"Something like that. So what about her new line of products? Have you got any ideas?"

Mike had kicked a few things around in his head but nothing had reached out and grabbed him. He would need to do some research first, to remedy his abysmal ignorance of the cosmetics field. He planned to read everything he could on the subject—thank God for the Public Library—and then stop into a couple of department stores to buy himself whatever Anastasia's competitors had on the market. Brands like Corona weren't sold in drugstores or supermarkets, only in places like Macy's and Saks Fifth Avenue, or in their local counterparts in cities around the country.

Up till now, Mike had used only the usual necessities—shaving cream, deodorant, and so on. The one exception was a combination moisturizer and sunscreen that he'd taken to wearing after his father had had several skin cancers removed, about ten years before. He wasn't about to take chances with a problem that might be hereditary, not when he spent as much time as he could outdoors.

"Nothing definite," he said to Rich, "but there's got to be a way to use our friend Lady Georgina in the campaign. People are curious about who she is. We could build up the mystery even more and then reveal her identity when we launch the new line. It would grab a lot of attention."

"But would she cooperate?" Bianca asked.

"We'll send Mike to her door in a bikini," Rich said, taking a potshot at his brother-in-law's lady-killer reputation. "One look at that body and she'll be his slave for life."

Mike got a sudden mental picture of Georgina kneeling at his feet wearing nothing but harem pants and dozens of gold slave bracelets, pleading for permission to pleasure him. He didn't have to be told where that one came from. She treated him like one of the servants, so it was only natural to fantasize turning the tables.

"No way," he said aloud. "I'd like to be able to father a child someday, and if I give Lady Georgina too obvious a physical target, there's no telling what she'll do. If it's all the same to you, I'll leave her to her grandmother."

Rich began to sing. "Whatever Lindsay wants...Lindsay gets...and Lady G....Mrs. Lindsay...wants you..."

"Exactly," Mike said with a laugh. "Georgina may be arrogant, but I doubt she plays lady of the manor with her grandmother." After all, hadn't she knuckled under about getting him that glass of bourbon? If he could create a campaign that Anastasia loved, Anastasia would sell it to Georgina.

It was ironic, but he'd begun to think of Anastasia Lindsay as an ally. His earlier anger was all but forgotten now. She might have pushed him hard, no doubt to size him up, but he'd learned a valuable lesson from the experience. Your work for her had to be excellent, not merely good. You had to sense when she was bluffing and refuse to give in. And if she wasn't bluffing? If she wouldn't back down and you knew it?

You had two choices. Either you gave her what she wanted or you resigned the account. Mike promised himself then and there that he would never do the first if his personal code of ethics required him to do the second—no matter how much money was at stake.

Then he smiled at his own pretensions. Terry Hall was as straight as they came, and he'd managed to work with the woman for seventeen years. There wouldn't be any problems. He and Anastasia Lindsay were going to make a great team.

Chapter Three

Anastasia Lindsay loved to parade her royal connections. All her products had prominent silver crowns on the front of their packages and an oversized version of that same crown decorated the heavy glass door that led into her executive offices. There was even a painting of Czar Nicholas II himself, one of a number of portraits that lined the hallway down to Anastasia's private office—evidently the descendants of the czar and his mistress. Mike passed by a painting of a beautiful, platinum-haired child and realized it must be Georgina as a little girl, but there was no recent portrait of Anastasia's granddaughter.

If his crash course in the cosmetics industry had taught him anything, it was that the field was an absolute jungle. Anastasia Lindsay and her rivals were fiercely competitive and stole from each other without compunction. Product ideas, sales gimmicks, advertising strategies—nothing was safe for long. If you weren't extremely careful, your competitors could beat you to market with their own versions of *your* new products.

The competitive nature of the industry was problem enough, but there was also the challenge of convincing average American men that taking care of one's appearance wasn't just for actors and wimps. Hair spray and blow dryers might have invaded professional locker rooms, but skin creams were another story. And even though fragrance for men was pretty much accepted nowadays, there was still the problem of grabbing the customer's attention and switching his loyalties from the likes of Polo and Aramis. It wasn't going to be easy.

Mike took a deep, steadying breath and knocked on Anastasia's door. He was always nervous before he made a presentation, but he'd always been nervous before football games, too. He felt the tension gave him an important edge, that it made him perform better.

Anastasia was sitting on an elegant, rose-colored couch behind a coffee table littered with cans and jars from her new men's line. The labels read, Essex for Men.

"Michael, you look terrified," she said as he walked through the door. "Come sit down and have a cup of coffee."

Mike joined her on the couch, setting his portfolio on the floor by his feet. She poured some coffee into a china cup and handed it over, inviting him to help himself to cream and sugar if he liked. He stirred in a tablespoon of sugar and tried to sound brisk and confident.

"I think you'll like what I've come up with," he began, only to have her pat his hand reassuringly.

"I'm in no hurry," she said. "Have your coffee and relax for a minute. You know, Mike, a lot of people think I made up my family history out of whole cloth, but every word is true. I really am Nicholas II's granddaughter. My grandmother Nina was a lady-in-waiting to Czarina Alexandra, and a very valued one, because of her talents as an herbalist. She was always experimenting with the native plants, brewing up all sorts of beauty potions and medicines. Alexandra tolerated her relationship with Nicholas because of her gifts, but then she made the great mistake of becoming pregnant and Alexandra insisted on marrying her off and sending her away. Her husband was an elderly general who was far more interested in young soldiers than in his new wife. According to my mother, their marriage was never even consummated.''

Mike was completely bewildered. Why was Anastasia trying to charm him? If anything, he'd expected more tests, more challenges. Fascinated all the same, he asked her what had brought her grandmother to America.

''The prospect of revolution,'' she replied. ''After the general's death, Nina took everything she could get her hands on—jewelry mostly—and smuggled it out of the country. She opened up a shop in New York and supported herself and my mother by mixing up her beauty products and selling them. Then my mother met my father, who was a doctor and researcher, and my father introduced the concept of scientific formulas. That was the real beginning of Corona Cosmetics.''

Mike knew she was being modest. Maybe Anastasia's mother had given the name Corona to Nina's products and maybe her father had added some science to the Russian voodoo, but Anya Pershing hadn't expanded the business beyond that same small shop in Manhattan. She had considered herself a wife first and a businesswoman second.

''I did some research before I started work on your account,'' he said, ''and according to what I read, *you* were the real beginning of Corona Cosmetics. You were the one who started large-scale manufacturing. You got Corona products into local department stores and then made it into a national brand by traveling all over the country and selling local retailers on it.''

Anastasia was visibly pleased. "Well, Mike, I knew I had to make a new life for myself after my husband was killed in the war, so I took the money he left me and I invested it in my own talents and in my own capacity for hard work. One of the things I like about you is that you've made the same choice. You've invested in yourself. You believe in yourself.''

"One hundred percent," Mike said with a smile, "but I also try to be realistic. The idea I've come up with is—outrageous is as good a term as any. You may love it as much as I do or you may hate it. But if you hate it, I have a couple of good alternatives.''

"I could never hate anything outrageous. In my opinion, dullness is the cardinal sin." Anastasia poured herself a cup of coffee and settled back on the couch. "I'm all ears, Mike.''

Mike knew he would have to lay a little groundwork first. "You made an interesting statement at dinner two weeks ago," he said. "You told me your granddaughter was looking for a rich husband, presumably to pump some money into your son-in-law's business enterprises. I assume that's how he maintains his estates—with money from his outside investments.''

"He could if he paid the slightest attention to his business. Sarah came to him with a very generous dowry, but he didn't make nearly as much of it as he could have." There was obviously no love lost between Anastasia and her aristocratic son-in-law. "So now it's Georgina's turn to shore up the family exchequer. The whole thing is absurd.''

"So you don't approve." Mike only hoped her objections wouldn't prove an insurmountable stumbling block.

"Of course I don't approve. The girl has the most idiotic notions about family duty that I've ever heard of. Imagine selling herself to some wealthy jackass just so Anthony will have the money to live like a king! He's not all that broke, you know. He and Sarah could tighten their belts and cut back on expenses." She cocked her eyebrow at him. "I take it this discussion has some relevance to that outrageous proposal of yours?"

Mike was adding two and two and coming up with three. There were factors here he didn't understand. "Bear with me a little longer, Mrs. Lindsay. Obviously you love your granddaughter very much, so why not just give the earl the money and—"

"Never in a million years!" she interrupted vehemently. "I refuse to support his extravagance."

"And Georgina? She has no money of her own? There's no inheritance she could sign over to him, no trust money she could give him?"

"I wasn't about to set up a trust fund when her father would only have gotten his hands on it and frittered it away. My grandson John has the Pershing head for business, but he's only fifteen. Still, Anthony will no doubt dump the whole mess on him as soon as he can, and then John and Georgie will get what's coming to them. Not a moment before."

Her position only made sense if you ignored her feelings for her granddaughter. "So you're saying you don't want any more of your money to go to your daughter and son-in-law, either directly or through your granddaughter, even though it will mean that she—how did you put it? Sells herself to some wealthy jackass?"

"That's what I'm saying," Anastasia insisted. "I can't stop the girl from marrying, you know. She's twenty-five and she can do as she likes."

Mike didn't believe it for a moment. Anastasia Lindsay could have changed the course of the Hudson River if she'd put her mind to it. She probably planned to sit back and watch developments, and then, if Georgina picked a man she disapproved of, sabotage the whole arrangement.

From Mike's point of view only one thing mattered—that Anastasia was allowing Georgina to proceed with her plans. He gestured toward the bottles on the table. "Those are samples from your new line?"

She nodded. "I took the name from Essex County, where Anthony has his estates. I also liked the air of status it suggests, and then, of course, there's the matter of those final three letters."

Mike smiled and told her he approved. She had already used the Earl of Medshire's country house and grounds in several Corona ads and they could carry through the theme in the new campaign.

Picking up his portfolio, he went on, "Over the past six months, your granddaughter has come to epitomize the Corona woman. The man she marries should epitomize the Essex man. We live in an age when corporate executives pose for Hathaway shirt ads...when former vice presidential candidates do Pepsi-Cola commercials...when bestselling authors hawk the American Express card. I don't have the slightest doubt that most of the men your granddaughter dates will be willing to appear in an Essex ad. But let me back up a couple of steps and start at the beginning."

Mike opened his portfolio and took out a series of sample ads. Although Anastasia hadn't asked for them, he hoped they would sell her on his ideas. They had used Bianca in the artwork, mostly because she was a beautiful woman but also because she'd been willing to work cheap.

The first ad showed her in a garden, staring longingly across the frame. "Picture your granddaughter on her father's estate, just after the trees have come into leaf and the first flowers have bloomed. The Corona woman is fresh and self-assured. Her life has always been perfect—she's never wanted anything she doesn't already have. But suddenly she's restless. Suddenly she's looking for something more." The copy underneath the photo read, *The Corona Woman. Successful and self-assured. Glowing with fresh, healthy beauty. It was always enough—until now.*

Mike proceeded to the next mock-up. The background was the same, but Bianca was looking at something now, something just out of the frame. Her expression was intense—wary and yearning at the same time. The copy was the same, too, except for the final line: *She knows what she wants—but it's just out of reach.*

"She's spotted something here," Mike said, "but she's not sure it's the right something. Which brings us to ad number three."

He showed Anastasia the next photograph. A man had entered the picture, his back to the camera. Bianca was gazing pensively at him. The copy read, *The Corona Woman. Successful and self-assured. Glowing with fresh, healthy beauty. Only one man could match her—but is he the one?* Mike had chuckled as he wrote those words, because he was the man in the photo. Rich had pointed out that his height and build gave him a physical presence that was perfect for the job, and besides, like Bianca, he worked cheap.

He gave Anastasia a moment to look at it and then moved to the fourth and final ad in the series. He and Bianca were facing each other now, but his face was intriguingly shadowed. The copy read simply, *The Corona Woman, Lady Georgina Philipps. Only one man can match her—the Corona Man.* They had used the name "Corona" because they hadn't known the line would be called "Essex" when they'd done the mock-ups.

"*Is he the one?*—that's the hook of the whole campaign," Mike said. "That's how we take something that's just another clever launch and turn it into a continuing story that's going to hold people's attention for months. We tell them your granddaughter is ready to settle down—that she's looking for the man she can share her life with. Who will it be? We take the men she dates, put them in Essex ads and let the public follow along. I came across a study reporting that women buy most of the products in this field for the men in their lives, and the romance of Georgina looking for the one man she can love will captivate that female customer. But we have to appeal to the male customer, too, and convince him the Essex man is a guy he can identify with. I think using the health angle is the way to do that. Once the four launch ads run, we can go to a campaign that features your granddaughter and her dates exercising together, with a couple of paragraphs giving whatever health claims we can legally make. Here's an example using my sister Bianca and myself.''

The photo showed Mike and Bianca jogging in Central Park. The headline read, *Corona for Men. Because you want your hair and skin to be as healthy as the rest of you,* and the copy below dealt with the damaging effects of wind, water and sun and how Corona products could help prevent them. There was also a caption under the photo: *The Corona Woman, Lady Georgina Philipps, with advertising executive Michael Napoli.*

Mike had been doing all the talking so far, going briskly from ad to ad so Anastasia would get the flavor of the campaign as a whole. Now he paused, waiting for her to offer her opinion. It was as bad as sitting with an open mouth while the dentist checked your teeth for cavities.

She looked through the five ads again, studying them with pursed lips. Mike forced himself to relax. If she said no, she said no. It wasn't the end of the world.

"Georgina isn't going to like being put on public display this way,'' she finally murmured.

Mike was alert to every nuance. She hadn't said, "Georgina *wouldn't* like," but, "Georgina *isn't going* to like," as if her granddaughter's participation was a fait accompli. He could probably afford to push her a little.

"Your granddaughter wants to marry somebody rich," he said. "The more publicity she gets, the more men she'll have to choose from. You don't find yourself a husband by hiding in a Fifth Avenue apartment."

"Word would get around," Anastasia said.

"Eventually, yes, at least to men in certain social circles. But why should she limit herself? It's the same as running a personal ad in *New York Magazine*. You tell 'em who you are and you list what you're looking for. Coyness is a waste of time." Mike winked at her. "I'm a firm believer in the power of advertising."

Anastasia thought it over, then nodded in agreement. "The power of advertising. You have a point. After all, she *is* in a bit of a hurry."

"In which case she'll want to meet as many men as possible, in as short a time as possible. She can talk about what she's up to after the fourth ad comes out—the one where we reveal her identity. I'm sure she'll be able to explain why she wants somebody filthy rich without it sounding too crass."

Anastasia smiled at that. "Perhaps we'll have you write the copy."

"Sure. Why not?" Mike began to think out loud. "She comes from the sort of background where family and tradition are important. She feels that England's heritage should be preserved and wants her husband to play a part in that. Naturally that would entail investing some of his money in the earl's enterprises."

"Naturally," Anastasia repeated dryly. "You have a fertile mind, Michael. I have to confess that I find your approach intriguing." She set the ads on the table, suddenly a little troubled. "If only Georgie were more experienced! It's one thing to introduce her to men I know personally, but to expose her to anyone off the street..."

"Any *millionaire* off the street," Mike corrected with a grin.

"All the more reason to worry. Men don't become millionaires by being shy and retiring, and Americans are so much more aggressive than Englishmen. I'm not sure poor Georgie could cope."

Mike was hard-pressed not to laugh. Was Anastasia serious? Poor Georgie could paralyze a wandering hand with one haughty sniff of her beautiful nose.

"Things were so much simpler during the Victorian era," Anastasia continued with a sigh. Then she smiled and snapped her fingers. "Why, of course! Why didn't I think of it sooner? The obvious solution is a chaperon." She gave Mike a level look. "You, Mike."

"Mrs. Lindsay..." The woman had a habit of rendering Mike speechless. "Your granddaughter—in case you didn't notice—she doesn't happen to like me. If you're telling me I should tag along on her dates—"

"It's the perfect solution," Anastasia insisted. "I'll lend you the Cadillac so you can drive her around. After all, if Georgie provides the car, her dates can hardly spirit her up to their apartments and compromise her virtue—not with you waiting down in the street. Whether she likes you or not is beside the point. It's probably better that she doesn't, because she certainly can't afford to become involved with you. I hope you understand that, Mr. Napoli, because I noticed the way you were looking at her—the way most men look at her, if you come right down to it. She's strictly off-limits, is that clear?"

Georgina probably would have scratched his eyes out if he'd gotten within six feet, but it didn't matter because he had no interest in trying. She might be beautiful, but she was also cold and imperious. Mike preferred a sense of humor and a little warmth in a woman, but didn't say so. Anastasia would have been offended.

"All morning long it's been Mike," he said instead, trying to charm her out of her contentious mood. "Why did it suddenly become Mr. Napoli?"

"For the same reason I call Georgie Georgina when I'm put out with her. To underscore my point."

"Your point doesn't need underscoring," Mike replied. "I'm not going to make a pass at Georgina. I know I don't meet her qualifications." He paused and smiled. "But I don't think your suggestion about chauffeuring her—"

Anastasia cut him off. "It was a condition, not a suggestion. If Georgina is to take part in this she must receive adequate protection. My regular chauffeur can't be expected to cope with a young woman's social schedule in addition to my own, you know. You, on the other hand, will be perfect. The account is yours if you agree to personally supervise my granddaughter's hunt for the perfect man. I assure you, you'll be well compensated."

Mike hadn't expected to come face-to-face with one of Anastasia Lindsay's impossible demands so soon. She wasn't bluffing—that much was obvious—so what did he do? Was there really any chance of Georgina agreeing to such an outlandish arrangement?

He had to admit there was. Georgina wouldn't like it, but Anastasia was a hard woman to refuse. If she could talk Georgina into going along with the "Corona woman in search of the Essex man" campaign in real life, she could probably talk her into having Mike as a chauffeur. Maybe she would even like the idea. It would give her endless opportunities to boss him around.

He supposed he could live with the job—providing it didn't take up too much of his time. Trying to be tactful about it, he told Anastasia she had herself a deal and then started talking about the demands made by his other accounts and the need to keep soliciting business. He expected her to insist that he be available twenty-four hours a day, but she was suddenly the soul of understanding.

Naturally she realized he had a business to run, but Georgina would be at the office most of the day so it was only the evenings they were talking about. And Georgina wouldn't be going out every night. Certainly Anastasia didn't expect Mike to do without a private life—she knew he was a busy man. They could discuss the details over dinner this Friday. "Six o'clock, Mike dear, and this time you'll stay for the entire meal. I insist."

Mike felt a little like Alice in Wonderland as he walked out of Anastasia's office. She'd been beaming at the end, all smiling approval and maternal warmth. The world kept shifting under his feet whenever he was with her. What in hell had he gotten himself into?

Chapter Four

Georgina had been irritable for days. Her grandmother had come up with some pretty wild ideas in her time, but Mike Napoli had topped them all. "The Corona woman in search of the Essex man," indeed!

It had started on Wednesday, over lunch in the Russian Tea Room. Anastasia had pulled out some ads with Bianca Conlin in them and asked Georgina what she thought. Of course she had loved them—anyone would have. She'd never even considered refusing Anastasia's request that she fly to England to pose for the actual advertisements. My Lord, she had even agreed to have her name revealed in the fourth and final ad just to help the Essex launch. But had Anastasia been satisfied? Of course not!

She had sprung a fifth mock-up on Georgina, the one with Napoli and his sister jogging, and said casually, "This is only a sample, of course. We'll be using you and some of your gentleman friends in the actual campaign." After a few stunned seconds Georgina had managed to open her mouth, but the only thing that had come out was a hoarse croak: "*My* friends?"

Her grandmother had been utterly blasé. Could Georgina think of a better way to publicize Essex than by combining her real-life search for a rich husband with the Corona woman's search for the Essex man? The public would love it. Essex would become a household word. And best of all from Georgina's point of view, every man in town would know she was available and looking. Think how it would widen her choice of candidates!

Georgina could see Anastasia's logic but still felt shocked to the roots of her proper British teeth. She couldn't possibly take something as personal as choosing a husband and turn it into a public sideshow. She had flatly refused.

Anastasia had shrugged and dropped the subject, but only until they were leaving the restaurant. Then she'd scolded, "I never thought I would see the day when you would act like such a hypocrite. You're perfectly willing to beat the bushes for a suitable husband, but God forbid anybody should find out about it. If you're really so ashamed of the idea perhaps you should forget it."

Looking back on it, Georgina could see that her crucial mistake had been to let Anastasia get her on the defensive. It hadn't done any good to insist that she wasn't ashamed—that she wasn't so much hiding anything as looking for a little privacy. Anastasia kept pounding away on the same two themes: the logic of advertising for what one wanted and Georgina's so-called hypocrisy. If she really meant to go through with this absurd manhunt of hers, she should have the guts to do it in the open.

In the end Georgina had given in, telling herself that the paparazzi would probably record her every movement anyway, so privacy was a vain hope. Besides, there was nothing wrong with wanting to get married and saying so. By

Thursday night she was almost perversely defiant about it. If she had to announce her plans in public to prove she believed they were honorable, she would.

But Anastasia had saved the worst for last. Mike Napoli wasn't content to simply dream up advertising copy; he wanted to select the men who would appear in the Essex ads personally. He claimed that neither Anastasia nor any other woman could know what would appeal to male consumers, and that examining photographs or meeting candidates for a drink would never be enough. He needed to observe them in the course of their daily lives. He needed to see how they interacted with Georgina, because the chemistry that existed in real life always carried over to the printed page. He wanted to chauffeur her around on her dates, for pity's sake. It was the last straw.

Georgina wasn't sure why her grandmother had gone along with his demands, but whatever the reason, she had nagged and cajoled until Georgina, tired of arguing, had agreed. She had no intention of honoring her promise, however. Napoli was coming for dinner that night and she intended to make it clear that this chauffeuring business was going too far. A dynamic young lawyer was taking her to the theater tonight and taxis would do just fine.

Her back got a little straighter and her pace got a little brisker as she walked up Fifth Avenue to Anastasia's apartment. It grated on her to know her grandmother liked Napoli so much. Why couldn't he have come up with something mediocre? And why did he have to photograph so well? She knew without being told that Anastasia would wind up using him in that first series of ads. He would be coming to England, staying in her parents' house, and working beside her for hour after hour. The thought was enough to set her teeth on edge.

And then, as she strode along cursing him out, she saw him in the flesh, standing in front of her grandmother's building. He checked his watch and she did the same. It was twenty before six. He was probably waiting another few minutes before he went inside. Anastasia wouldn't be home yet—she seldom got in till six.

Georgina decided to have it out with him then and there. If ever a man needed to understand his proper place, Napoli did. He noticed her approaching when she was half a block away, and smiled. She was irked by her response to that smile—something flip-flopped inside her stomach. More vexed with him than ever, she marched to his side and gave him her haughtiest look.

"I want to talk to you," she said, and set out for the door. Of course, she was going to feel like a perfect fool if he elected not to follow.

Mike never even considered the possibility—he was much too curious about why Georgina was so bent out of shape. Because she didn't like him and her grandmother did? Because of the campaign he'd dreamed up? Because she didn't want him as a chauffeur?

He followed her inside, bracing himself for a spectacular tirade. She stabbed the elevator button viciously but didn't say a word. Then she stood there, tapping her foot impatiently as they waited for the elevator to come. They were the only ones to get inside.

"So what did you want to talk about?" he asked as the doors slid shut.

Georgina raised her chin a fraction, silently telling him she would get to the point in her own good time. In fact, she found him rather intimidating. He was so damn big and the elevator was so small.

He leaned against the wall and crossed his arms in front of his chest. "I asked you a question, your ladyship."

Georgina pressed her lips together and refused to answer him. Let him cool his heels for a while. And if he called her "your ladyship" in that sarcastic tone again . . .

Mike, meanwhile, was telling himself to be patient, to ignore her high-and-mighty behavior. God, she got under his skin! What was she going to do next? Send him into the apartment through the servants' entrance?

"Why don't you get it off your chest?" he finally drawled. "You're furious about the ad campaign. Somehow or other your grandmother talked you into going along and now you'd like to kill me for thinking it up in the first place."

Her expression went from haughty to disdainful. It was really quite a talent, to silently tell a man he was so contemptible he made Idi Amin look like a humanitarian. Mike wondered if she'd been born with that ability or acquired it in finishing school.

Whichever it was, he began to see the absurdity of it. A few more minutes and she was going to explode. It was a crazy way to deal with life—bottling things up until the pressure sent you flying into orbit.

The elevator doors opened and Georgina stepped outside. She didn't know why, but her emotions were in turmoil. Anger, embarrassment, confusion—she took a deep breath as she walked down the hall. Feelings were the enemy. If you didn't control them, they destroyed you.

"Maybe you'd feel better if you slugged me." Napoli was right behind her, speaking in an intimate, amused voice. "Release all that pent-up aggression, Georgina. Give it a physical outlet."

"Don't tempt me," she snapped, and reached into her purse for her keys.

He continued talking as she opened the door. "I'm completely serious. Hitting me might make you less frustrated. Then maybe we could have a productive conversation, like two civilized human beings."

Meaning that she wasn't civilized, Georgina fumed. She closed the door and glared at him. "Go on," he said with a grin. "It'll make you feel terrific and it won't bother me at all. I'm used to being knocked around—I played a lot of football in college." He looked her up and down with obvious appreciation. "Tall but skinny. You never would have made the team, your ladyship. Too little hitting power."

That sardonic "your ladyship" was what did it—that and his amused appraisal of her body. So he thought it was some kind of joke, did he? He thought she was frustrated and uncivilized, and—and some sort of sex object into the bargain! She drew her hand and swung it against his cheek, slapping him so hard her palm stung. He never even flinched, just watched with a level stare.

The moment it was over she was totally appalled with herself. Losing her temper was bad enough, but striking another human being was unthinkable. What was wrong with her? Her emotions were churning like a rampaging river. Badly shaken, she jerked around and ran down the hall.

Mike barely had time to tell himself what a punch she packed before he noticed how pale she was. As much as he'd enjoyed teasing her, he'd never meant to upset her that way. It was automatic to go after her when she turned and fled— to offer some brotherly comfort. After all, he had three younger sisters.

He caught her by the arm and forced her to stop, but she stiffly refused to look at him. "Take it easy," he said gently. "It's okay. Whatever the problem is, let's just deal with it."

Georgina could feel herself slipping again. The bloody hypocrite! How could he ask what the problem was when he was the one who had caused it? And how dare he use that gentle tone on her? Did he think she'd be taken in by it?

She forced her breathing into a slow, regular pattern and fought down the tears in her eyes. She wasn't going to lose control of herself again—it was playing into his hands.

Taking back her arm, she straightened and turned to face him. "I'm sorry I hit you," she said coolly.

Mike could hear the withdrawal in her voice. She was retreating behind that stiff English upper lip of hers, and he didn't like that a bit. The raging spitfire was a lot more appealing to him than the cool lady of the manor.

"I'll accept your apology on one condition," he said. "I want to know why you're so angry." He also wondered why she'd loathed him on sight but decided it could wait.

"On one condition?" Georgina was livid all over again. "Where do you get off laying down conditions? You goaded me into it!" The moment the words were out she could have bitten her tongue. He'd done it again—irked her into saying something she hadn't meant to.

He laughed. "Very true. Come on, Georgina, admit it felt good."

Uncivilized American roughneck. "Physical violence—" she began, intending to lecture him on American men and their brutal ways, but he quickly cut her off.

"Be serious. You're what? Five-nine or -ten, a hundred twenty-five or so? I'm six-three, two-ten. There's no way you were going to hurt me or I never would have let you hit me. I may be the scum of the earth, your ladyship, but I'm not stupid."

Georgina struggled not to notice his teasing tone and lazy smile. When he said "your ladyship" in that certain special way she didn't even mind. Why were the biggest cads so often the most charming?

"In that case," she answered, "I'm not sorry I hit you at all." And yes, it *had* felt good, for a second anyway. "We can talk in the parlor. If you'll come with me?"

Georgina started down the hall again, thinking she didn't understand herself at all. Where had her anger and embarrassment gone? She hadn't repressed them—they had simply vanished. The only things left were irritation over the ad campaign and a lingering dislike of Mike Napoli.

She wasn't even especially annoyed when he strolled to the bar and helped himself to a drink. Obviously she'd grown accustomed to the man's presumption. She was about to ask for a sherry when she noticed he was already pouring her one. Presumptuous, she thought, but well mannered.

He handed her the drink and then settled himself on the couch. She knew it would be useless to rage at him—the trick was to be calm but firm.

"I'll come straight to the point," she said. "I'm not having you as a chauffeur. That business about checking out all my dates and choosing the right ones for the Essex ads is the most absurd thing I've ever heard. I refuse to be examined like a bug under a microscope."

He gave her a puzzled look. "What are you talking about?"

Was the man deaf? She forced down the urge to yell at him. "I want to be reasonable about this, Mr. Napoli. Perhaps you're right that you should choose the men for the Essex ads, but surely you don't have to actually see them with me. I'll simply tell you which ones I've clicked with."

Mike understood now. He'd fallen into a rabbit hole the other day in Anastasia's office and this was where he'd landed. Wonderland on Fifth Avenue.

"The only reason I'm driving you is because your grandmother insisted on it," he said. "We never even discussed who would choose the men in the ads, or how."

Georgina didn't believe it for a moment. Her grandmother wouldn't have lied to her about having him chauffeur her. "I don't know why you're denying it was your idea," she said, "but—"

"But nothing. Your grandmother gave me an ultimatum. If I wanted the account, I had to agree to play chauffeur. She seemed to think you needed protection from all the big bad wolves out there.'' He rubbed his cheek, wincing with pretended pain. "Personally I tend to doubt it."

Never once in the past seven years had Anastasia expressed any doubts about Georgina's ability to look after herself. It was odd, but she was suddenly disappointed in Mike Napoli. A handsome face and a dash of wit shouldn't have made her forget what he was really like, but they had.

She was about to answer him back in the iciest possible terms when Anastasia herself breezed into the room. She kissed Georgina hello, and then, much to Georgina's astonishment, did the same to Mike. When had they gotten so chummy?

"Mike dear, get me a glass of sherry," she said as she seated herself on the couch. "I'm absolutely frazzled."

While Mike was at the bar, Georgina repeated the conversation she had just had with him. Not surprisingly, Anastasia began taking him to task the moment he handed her her sherry. Georgina sat there feeling vindicated while Mike had the nerve to look bewildered.

The longer Mike listened, the less bewildered and the more irritated he became. *No way, lady!* he thought. It's not my problem if you don't want your granddaughter to know your real motives. I'm not taking the rap.

He stood there in silence until she finished lecturing him and then said evenly, "Mrs. Lindsay, do I really have to walk out on another one of your dinners?"

"Why should you do that?" she asked. "I'm not angry with you, Mike. It's perfectly understandable that you didn't want Georgie to be any more cross with you than she already is, but you mustn't compound your sins by lying about the whole business. Now sit down and let's put this incident behind us."

Mike stayed right where he was. "I'm not going to go for it, Anastasia. Tell her what really happened."

Georgina was half fascinated, half appalled. Nobody but Anastasia's closest friends called her by her first name, much less used that heavy-handed manner with her. "Young man," she said, "I will warn you once and only once not to push me too far." Georgina fought down a smile. Mike was about to get flailed alive.

But before Anastasia could remove so much as a bit of skin, he was calmly answering her back. "I'll be glad to give you the names of two or three agencies that could pick up on my ideas and do a good job with them, or you could talk to Terry Hall about a replacement. Let me know what you decide." He turned on his heel, and, without another word, started out of the room.

Whatever Georgina expected, it wasn't that her grandmother would burst out laughing and call him back. "Don't you dare leave here, you miserable scoundrel! I'll tell her the truth if it's all that important. Just keep in mind that now she'll be angry with me, and I have to live with her."

He looked back over his shoulder, a half smile on his face. "And I have to drive her around."

"Nobody has to drive me anywhere," Georgina said plaintively, trying to make sense of what was happening. "This is New York City. People take taxis everywhere."

"You're not just people, you're my granddaughter," Anastasia replied. "And if you're going to be running around New York with God only knows who, I want you to have some protection."

Georgina followed Mike with her eyes as he crossed back to the couch. Good grief, he'd been telling her the truth. Her grandmother had actually lied to her. Was she going dotty, to suddenly start worrying about Georgina's virtue?

She reminded Anastasia that she was a grown woman, fully capable of coping with a pair of wandering hands. "Besides," she added, "I doubt if anyone is going to assault me in the back seat of a cab."

Mike seemed to find Anastasia's statements as funny as Georgina did. "How about luring you into his apartment and doing unspeakable things to your body?" he asked.

"Not that, either," she said.

Anastasia put down her sherry and glowered at the pair of them. "I'm glad you find this so amusing, but let me tell you, Georgina, Manhattan isn't England. You'll be moving outside the tight little world you're used to and it makes a difference. A few drinks too many and before you know it, you're naked in some man's bed. If you think your innocence will protect you, think again."

Georgina didn't know whether to blush or laugh. The reference to her virginity was a little embarrassing, but Anastasia's worries were perfectly absurd. She ignored the slyly speculative look on Mike's face and said, "Really, Grandmother, I have more sense than to get into a spot like that."

There was a dramatic sigh. "Very well, then, you've backed me into a corner. The fact is, you're the granddaughter of a wealthy woman and this is a dangerous world."

"Are you suggesting somebody might try to kidnap me?" Georgina asked in disbelief.

"It's possible, especially late at night, when you're getting out of a taxi."

Now Mike put in his two cents' worth. "If that's your real concern, you should hire a professional bodyguard."

"Bodyguards can be bribed. I prefer to trust *you*."

Georgina had seldom known her grandmother to be either so adamant or so irrational, but she loved Anastasia dearly and that decided the matter. She looked at Mike and shrugged. "If it would set her mind at ease, I suppose I could live with the arrangement."

Mike thought both of them were nutty. Anastasia's screwy demands, Georgina's outraged refusal and abrupt capitulation—none of it made sense. Then again, he thought resignedly, he'd been warned. Now he understood why Anastasia's account executive at H & H was talking about checking into Bellevue. Maybe Hoffman could save him the next bed.

Chapter Five

As Mike finished his second cup of coffee after a splendid meal, he told himself he could get used to Anastasia's brand of luxury. Dinner had been so relaxing that he wasn't even nervous around the fifty-dollar glasses anymore. He and Anastasia had started things off by trading a couple of stories about oddball New Yorkers and then Georgina had topped them both with a series of tales featuring a cast of English eccentrics straight out of Gilbert and Sullivan. Mike hadn't laughed so hard in months. He didn't know which surprised him more—that Georgina could be so funny or that she could also be warm and informal.

She'd gone off to change immediately after dinner, leaving him and Anastasia to talk business. Mike thought about asking why she *really* wanted him to play chauffeur but decided it would be a waste of time. She wasn't going to level with him now when she hadn't before.

After about ten minutes she sent her chauffeur to bring around the Cadillac, and then, when another ten minutes went by with no sign of Georgina, looked at her watch and frowned. "They'll miss the opening curtain at this rate. Go light a fire under Georgie, will you, Mike? Her room is down the corridor off the main hallway."

Mike was about to knock on Georgina's door when she opened it up. He sucked in his breath at how sensational she looked. She was wearing an emerald-colored silk jump suit with long sleeves, a deep V neckline and a wide choker necklace that sent his imagination into places it didn't belong—like nineteenth-century pleasure domes. Her hair was up except for a couple of loosened tendrils that made him want to free all the rest of it and bury his hands in it. Maybe Anastasia wasn't so crazy after all. If he'd been Kenny Sarazin—Georgina's date that night—he never could have kept his mind on the theater.

"Your grandmother sent me to see if you were ready," he said. "By the way, I like your jump suit."

Georgina thanked him and closed the door. She was used to having men look at her the way Mike had just looked at her, but it had never made her so uncomfortable before. She was acutely aware of her own body—of the way it would probably respond if a skillful enough lover kissed and caressed her. Mike Napoli, for example.

Why not just admit it? she thought. He was handsome, funny and smart. She'd enjoyed his company at dinner. And yes, she was physically attracted to him.

But none of that changed his essential character. He was an ambitious womanizer with absolutely no money—the last man she should want. If she had any brains, she would give him the widest possible berth.

The Cadillac, unfortunately, was an ordinary sedan that lacked a smoked window between the front and back to give her the privacy she would have liked. It turned out not to matter, though, because she might as well have been a department-store mannequin for all the attention Mike paid her.

It never occurred to her that Mike might be as eager to keep his distance as she was. Anastasia's warning was as fresh in his mind as ever—Georgina was off-limits—but even more important, he knew he was all wrong for her. She was what his mother would have called "a nice girl," the kind you only slept with once you'd put a ring on her finger. For the next few years he needed to concentrate on his business. There was no room in his life for marriage.

Kenny was waiting on the sidewalk in front of his building when Mike got out to open the door. The two of them weren't good friends, but they'd known each other for years. Kenny was puzzled to see Mike with Georgina and then curious about the reason. Tongue firmly in cheek, he asked Mike if the advertising business was so slow he'd had to hire himself out as a chauffeur.

Kenny was one of Anastasia's lawyers, so he understood Mike's answer about her impossible demands. More curious than ever, he started firing out questions. Mike was conscious of Georgina watching them from inside the car, apparently growing more and more impatient as the minutes dragged on. Mike couldn't blame her. If he had been Kenny Sarazin, he wouldn't have wasted his time grilling the chauffeur.

Georgina *was* impatient, especially after Kenny shook Mike's hand and walked back into his building. "Don't tell me," she said as Mike slid behind the wheel. "Grandmother's given you instructions to sabotage all my dates."

Mike laughed and shook his head. "He'll be back in a minute. He's going out to his parents' place on the island tonight, but his car is in the shop. He asked me if I could give him a ride. He went upstairs to get his suitcase."

"You're friends, then."

"More like acquaintances. We go to a lot of the same places."

Georgina smiled knowingly. "Meaning that he gets around as much as you do."

Her teasing tone had a dramatic effect on Mike's blood pressure. He suddenly felt sorry for the men who took her out, many of whom were doomed to suffer the agonies of unrequited love. "*Almost* as much," he corrected with a grin.

Her smile gave way to cool disapproval. "I'm surprised you're willing to admit it. Don't you think it's a little adolescent to need one conquest after another in order to reassure yourself of your masculinity?"

Mike told himself she had some strange ideas about how he spent his time. It sounded as if she'd been talking to his sister Bianca and had believed every word. "Is that what you think?" he asked.

"I read the papers, Mr. Napoli. You don't exactly keep a low profile. You go through women the way other men go through shaving cream."

"And you believe everything you read?"

"Of course I don't. Why? Are you denying you have a Don Juan complex?"

Mike ignored the question. "Is that why you don't like me? Because you think my major interest in life is seeing how many women I can seduce?"

"Well, isn't it?" she demanded.

"No. My advertising agency is." Mike had assumed she knew that, but since she didn't he pointed out the obvious. "If you want to be successful in this town you have to get to know the right people. You don't do that by staying in your apartment every night."

She gave him a skeptical look. "So it's strictly business. All those women you've been seen with—you haven't taken a single one to bed."

"It's none of your business, your ladyship." Did she expect him to be a monk, for God's sake? Of course he'd had occasional love affairs. Next she'd be ordering him to name names.

Georgina couldn't decide if Mike was being gallant or evasive. A gentleman would never discuss the ladies he'd known intimately, but Mike wasn't exactly a gentleman. The truth, she decided, must be somewhere in the middle. Perhaps he wasn't the playboy the papers made him out to be, but he'd still been around the track too often for her personal taste.

Her thoughts turned to Kenny Sarazin, whom she'd met in Anastasia's office one day. His family had been in this country for centuries, he was one of the youngest partners in his firm, and he had tons of money. Excellent husband material, in short.

He was also a charming escort. The play they attended was a fascinating avant-garde drama and the restaurant where they had dessert afterward was one of her favorites. They were arguing about one of the characters in the play when Mike pulled up in the Cadillac. Kenny had made some telling points, but then, he was very intelligent.

He put his arm around her once they were in the car and then pulled her close. Georgina wasn't strongly attracted to him but knew that a woman could be indifferent to a man when they first met and wind up adoring him. It happened all the time.

When he asked her to keep him company on the drive to Long Island, she readily agreed. She enjoyed talking to him. As they continued their conversation, laughing and arguing about the play, he slid his hand to the back of her neck and fondled a tendril of hair. Georgina yawned, finding the physical contact neither pleasant nor distasteful. Mostly she was just very tired.

"I'm sorry, Kenny," she said with another yawn. "I was up awfully early and it's hit me all at once."

"It's okay." His arm tightened around her shoulders. "You smell great. What's that perfume you're wearing?"

"Anastasia," Georgina said sleepily. "What else?" She nestled against his chest and closed her eyes.

Up in the front seat, Mike's hands tightened on the steering wheel. What was going on back there? Why was it suddenly so quiet?

He cursed under his breath. He wasn't supposed to care about things like that. If Georgina's dates wanted to tell her she smelled fantastic or confess that it drove them crazy to have her in their arms and not make love to her, it was none of his concern. Kenny Sarazin was a bit of a womanizer, but he wasn't a bad guy. She could have done a lot worse.

He heard Kenny take a deep breath and then moan Georgina's name. Georgina, sounding cranky, reminded him how tired she was. There was another period of silence, punctuated only by Kenny's heavy breathing. Mike felt like punching out the windshield.

It was a complication he hadn't counted on—that he would mind it when another guy touched her. He tried to dismiss it as brotherly protectiveness but knew he was kidding himself. At that moment, he would have given anything to change places with Kenny Sarazin. Like most human beings, he wanted what he couldn't have. It was the only possible explanation for the tightness in his gut.

He spent the rest of the trip brooding about what was going on behind him. Probably very little, because Kenny gave him directions from time to time in a perfectly level voice, but his imagination filled up the silences in between.

By the time the trip was over he was almost afraid to turn around. If Georgina was half-undressed...if Kenny had his hands all over her body...if their faces had the pleasure-drunk look of two people aching to make love... But she wasn't and he didn't and they didn't. An immaculate Georgina was asleep on Kenny's shoulder, and Kenny was sitting there looking disappointed.

Kenny gently freed his arm and reached for the door. Mike felt a sense of satisfaction he had no right to feel as he got out to unlock the trunk. "Tell her I said good-night," Kenny muttered as he took his suitcase. "And thanks for the ride."

Mike managed a polite "You're welcome" and returned to the car. Georgina was lying down now, all curled up and dead to the world. He took off his coat, folded it into a pillow, and slipped it under her head. She murmured something in her sleep but didn't open her eyes.

There was very little traffic on the way home—almost nobody was heading into the city so late at night. Every now and then Mike glanced back at Georgina, but she never stirred. The sleep of the innocent, he thought with a smile. Was Anastasia right about that, or had Georgina been less than honest? Probably the first, if the way she'd blushed was anything to go by. That cool English reserve of hers evidently went very deep.

Too deep to penetrate? he wondered. Could any man arouse her? Could he? The thought of teasing her into forgetting her inhibitions and losing herself in passion was too damn appealing. It did uncomfortable things to his body. He forced his thoughts onto more productive topics, like the copy he needed to write that weekend.

Georgina was still sleeping when he pulled up in front of her building. He'd be taking the Cadillac home—Anastasia was paying for the garage—but first he needed to get Georgina upstairs. He opened the back door and lightly touched her shoulder, but she didn't stir. He was lifting her out of the car when the doorman walked over.

"Fast asleep, huh?" he said.

Mike nodded. "Could you grab her purse?"

"No problem. That grandmother of hers could wear anybody out. Runs around like a kid." He picked up the purse. "She only got in about an hour ago herself."

The doorman opened all the doors so Mike could carry Georgina inside and then offered, "I could come upstairs and unlock the apartment if you want. It looks like you've got your hands full."

Mike did, but he wasn't complaining. After all the weights he'd lifted, Georgina wasn't much of a burden, and she felt warm and cuddly in his arms. She'd curled herself close against his chest and moaned in contentment, but he doubted she knew where she was. It was probably pure instinct.

In fact, Georgina knew exactly where she was—floating in Mike's arms, feeling relaxed and secure. A couple of times she'd drifted awake, but she'd known she was safe so she'd always dozed right off again.

The lights in the elevator were so much brighter than the ones in the lobby that they roused her into opening her eyes. She saw the doorman smiling at her and smiled back. Then she looked at Mike's face, and sleepily studied his features. His lips, his nose, his eyes. Sensual, crooked and beautiful, in that order. He stared back, his mouth so close he could have bent his head and kissed her. The thought wasn't at all unpleasant, except that she probably would have bored him after all the worldly women he'd known. And those beautiful blue eyes—were they always so intense? What did they see? She closed her own eyes again, worrying about the blemish that was threatening to break out on her chin. Did it show? .

Mike swallowed hard as the elevator doors opened. He hadn't noticed any blemishes. As far as he could tell, Georgina was perfect. Fully awake she was both beautiful and challenging and his ego as well as his body longed to possess her—both for the sheer physical pleasure of it and for the satisfaction of proving he could arouse her into giving herself. But half asleep...half asleep she was soft, shy and vulnerable, and the desire he felt was tangled up with gentleness and protectiveness. The second set of emotions was far more powerful than the first.

The doorman unlocked the apartment and handed him Georgina's purse. Everything was still and quiet inside, but the lights were on in the side hallway, illuminating a path to Georgina's room. Mike carried her inside and laid her on the bed. Just enough light filtered in from the hall that he didn't have to turn on a lamp to see what he was doing.

He didn't plan to undress her, just take off her coat and jewelry and get her under the covers. She shifted to make herself more comfortable as he unbuttoned her coat and mumbled a protest as he worked her arms out of the sleeves. Finally she woke up enough to say something intelligible: "Does your nose mind?"

He lifted her up and slid the coat out from under her. "Mind what?"

She opened her eyes and stared at him. The impact of that stare was like a torch along his nerve endings. He sat down on the bed, still holding the coat, and reminded himself that he wasn't supposed to touch her. But when his gaze dropped to her mouth just in time to see her tongue peek out to moisten her lips, what he was or wasn't supposed to do began to seem irrelevant.

The necklace, he thought doggedly, and laid her coat across the foot of the bed. Her eyes were closed when he looked back again. The necklace was a four-stranded pearl choker with a diamond and emerald clasp that was sharp enough to scratch her if he didn't get it off. His hand was shaking as he fiddled with the catch. In the fifteen years since his first kiss, he'd never had anything like this happen. *You want what you can't have,* he reminded himself. Nothing was as tempting as forbidden fruit.

Georgina felt gentle fingers against her neck, but she was still thinking about Mike's nose. Technically it was his worst feature, but she considered it the best thing about his face. There was something so human about it, so sweet and vulnerable. She opened her eyes for another look. The scars of battle. She knew there were others—Jill had told her about his knee operations. Had the disappointment hardened him? Was that why he'd behaved so badly all those years before?

For some reason he was trying to tickle her. No, not tickle, she realized. Tickling didn't make your face heat up or cause that lovely tingling sensation clear down to your toes. She heard his soft, "Dammit, who made this thing? Houdini?" and finally understood what he was up to.

"Tiffany's," she murmured, and added teasingly, "Are you trying to steal it?"

"I'm trying to get it off before it pierces your jugular vein," he answered, sounding as if he meant to *rip* it off in another few seconds.

Georgina didn't care about the necklace. She wanted to know about Mike Napoli, about what made him tick. She lifted her hand and ran a fingertip across the bridge of his nose. "Did it hurt when you did this?"

He stiffened under her touch. "Yes."

"And your knee?" She groped for it, but couldn't quite reach it and had to settle for his thigh instead. "Did it hurt when you injured it?"

He pushed away her hand. "Some times were worse than others. That's probably why I kept hoping..." His voice died out.

Georgina yawned and closed her eyes, thinking that she understood everything now. "Umm. I supposed as much."

He went back to fiddling with the necklace, coming so close she could feel his warm, quick breaths against her neck. "You have to press and pull at the same time," she mumbled. "The button is on the back of the clasp."

The calluses on his fingers rubbed against her skin as he worked and she wondered how it would feel if he caressed the softest parts of her. Probably wildly exciting. There was something so physical about him, so tough and masculine. The other men she'd known weren't like that.

As she came more fully awake, the scent of him began to tease at her nostrils. Bottle it, she thought dizzily, and women everywhere would go mad. Without stopping to think, she raised her arms and put them around his neck. She wanted him closer. At almost the same moment he pressed the button and pulled at the catch, and the clasp came undone. She heard him take a sharp, quick breath as she tightened her grip. "Georgina, for God's sake..." he muttered.

She giggled, feeling as if she were floating near a warm, lovely flame. She knew about the husky tension in his voice, knew how to make it explode out of control. "That's *Lady* Georgina to you, Napoli. You're just the chauffeur around here. *I* give the orders."

His mouth was suddenly on her neck, hot and urgent against her skin. His lips slowly worked their way higher, finally finding her mouth and kissing each corner in turn. When he slipped his finger between her lips, she obediently parted them. Then she sucked the finger farther into her mouth and playfully nipped it. She might as well have bitten the pin out of a grenade. His hand was suddenly grasping her chin and putting her mouth exactly where he wanted it—a fraction of an inch under his.

His lips brushed hers, hovered for a long, teasing moment and then settled in for a firm, mobile kiss full of erotic promise. Georgina felt herself tense as his lips caressed and explored. She needed more than he was giving. She opened her mouth to offer it but the kiss never changed. He was deliberately holding back, deliberately making her wait.

She moaned a husky "Please..." then felt the first taste of his tongue, and shuddered convulsively. She longed to feel him in her mouth. She wanted him to fill her up, to demand everything she had to give and more, to take her into a world of pure, wild sensation.

The reality was even more intoxicating than the fantasy. Those deep, moist kisses—real lovemaking must be like that. As the seconds stretched into minutes it was no longer enough to give—she wanted to submit. Her body was hot, restless and pliant. Oh God, when was he going to touch her? Her breasts were aching. Her mouth grew frantic under his, her fingers dug into his shoulders. His teeth and tongue were making her need more and more, but he wasn't giving it. What did she have to do, beg him?

And then, with shattering abruptness, it all fell apart. For the first time in hours, Georgina was fully awake. She knew exactly what she was doing and exactly whom she was doing it with. Breathing hard, she yanked away her hands and pushed against Mike's chest. He had a dazed look on his face as he straightened up.

Her initial reaction was anger—white-hot, irrational anger. How dare he make love to her that way? Had he gotten a kick out of torturing her? "Do you always take advantage of women when they're half asleep?" she demanded.

He ran his hand through his hair and took a deep breath. "I'm sorry, Georgina."

"That's all you're going to say? You're sorry?" After he'd driven her so crazy she'd all but begged him to put her out of her misery? "I barely knew where I was." An exaggeration. "I barely knew who I was with." An outright lie. She'd known, all right. Nobody had ever had that effect on her.

He was suddenly as angry as she. "You started touching me, dammit. That business about my being the chauffeur and what I was supposed to call you—you know what that sort of stuff does to me."

"And Don Juan that you are, you lacked the self-control to restrain yourself when a defenseless female who was half asleep teased you a little?"

"I didn't think it was necessary. You seemed to be enjoying it as much as I was. In fact, I made damn sure you were."

He'd been yelling at her through clenched teeth, looking as if he wanted to throttle her, but the anger drained out of him as quickly as it had come. Georgina watched in confusion as he slumped forward and looked at the floor. "You're right," he said. "I should have kept my hands to myself but all I could think about was not scaring you off, not going too fast. I must have been out of my mind. I've never seduced a virgin in my life."

Georgina was more embarrassed than angry now. So he hadn't meant to tease her at all, just to give her as much pleasure as possible. She blushed at how well he'd succeeded. His previous lovers had taught him a damn sight too much.

She tried to make a joke out of it but wound up sounding touchy rather than worldly. "Some protector you are. Grandmother might as well have sent in a fox to guard the henhouse."

It was a long couple of seconds before he replied. "Why don't you tell her that? It would get you what you seem to want, which is my ass ten stories down on the pavement. Your grandmother already warned me you were off-limits, so if you want to get me fired—"

"Off-limits?" Georgina repeated. "She told you that?"

"Loud and clear, not that she should have needed to." He shook his head. "I really am sorry. You never stood a chance just now."

Georgina knew of only one reason why her grandmother would warn Mike off. He was a very attractive man who had a certain reputation and Anastasia didn't want to see her hurt. She'd meant well, but Georgina wasn't exactly innocent when it came to men. Nobody had ever seduced her into doing anything she didn't want to.

She was suddenly disgusted with herself. She was usually more honest than to assign blame where it didn't belong. She might have been sleepy before, but not so sleepy she hadn't known how provocative she was being. He never would have touched her if she hadn't made the first move.

She knew she owed him an apology but couldn't bring herself to look at him as she made it. "I'm a big girl, Mike. It was as much my fault as yours. I'm sorry I was so rude." She swallowed hard, wishing she had a glass of water. Her throat was horribly dry. "Thank you for carrying me upstairs. It was thoughtful of you not to wake me. I'm going out again tomorrow night so I suppose I'll see you then— about six."

If Mike was surprised by the apology, he was also rather amused. Georgina had sounded so polite, so English, like a nervous schoolgirl reciting a prepared speech. He found it both endearing and enchanting. He'd never met a woman with more class.

"Your future husband is a lucky guy," he said as he got off the bed. "I'd better warn you right now, if any of the candidates gets out of line, I'm going to have a hard time not throwing him out of the car. You need protection from guys like me."

She raised her eyes, clearly startled, but didn't answer. That was fine with Mike, who still had more to say. "I realize you don't like me—that you think my brains are somewhere in the vicinity of my belt buckle. You could have run to grandma when I handed you the right ammunition, but obviously that's not your style. You're too honest. And maybe that's why I need you to believe that whatever you've heard or read about me—it's just not true. My life is ninety-nine percent business. Almost every dime I have is tied up in my agency. If it fails, I lose everything—and so do my sister and brother-in-law. With pressures like that, women aren't much of a priority. If you want the truth, I enjoy working more than I would have enjoyed going to bed with any of the women I've met lately.'' He couldn't stop himself from smiling. ''Present company definitely excluded. Good night, Georgina.''

For the life of her, Georgina couldn't manage an answer. Mike had a talent for throwing her into a tailspin. She was ashamed of misjudging him so badly—obviously he was no Don Juan. He'd proved that tonight. And his ambition was probably understandable given how much was on the line.

Still, he should have been more honest with his former boss. And no matter what inner demons had plagued him, his behavior toward Jill Eliott had been unforgivable. His personality had its dark side, that much was certain.

She started to undress as soon as he'd left the room but doubted she'd be able to sleep. That last, smiling remark about not picking work over her... How was she supposed to forget the way he could make her feel?

She punched down her pillow. She would forget it because it was irrelevant. She needed more than sex from a man. She needed someone decent and upstanding.

She thought about her parents. And rich. Most of all, somebody rich.

Chapter Six

Bianca Conlin gave her husband a startled glance when the security guard in Anastasia Lindsay's building waved at Mike and immediately buzzed them through. She hadn't realized her brother was such a fixture around this place. A few seconds later a legendary anchorman and a former first lady passed by in the lobby, and both Rich and Bianca gaped. A feeling of awe was beginning to set in.

Mike had been the same way three and a half weeks ago, but he barely noticed the famous faces anymore. Bianca listened in fascination as two society types in the elevator discussed a ball the next night in honor of an English prince, but balls were old hat to Mike, too. "I've got the night off thanks to that party," he remarked as they made their way down the hall. "Anastasia and Georgina are going to the same place for once. They'll be taking the limo."

"You mean they actually know the prince?" Bianca asked.

Mike felt around in his pocket for the keys. "They know everyone. Anastasia's date is an English diplomat and Georgina's going with some viscount. He and the prince were in school together."

Bianca watched in bemusement as Mike unlocked the door. "Mike—those keys—"

"Anastasia thought I should have a set. Georgina keeps falling asleep in the Cadillac, and I usually wind up carrying her upstairs. Having the keys saves me from excavating in her purse. I told Anastasia that Georgina might be less tired if she didn't drag her to the office every morning at an hour when sane people are in bed, and then work her like a damn draft horse all day, but you know Anastasia. She wants Georgina to learn the business. She only sleeps five or six hours a night herself and she thinks anyone who can't keep up must need vitamins."

Bianca gave him a distracted smile, her attention now fixed on the entryway. "This place is incredible," she hissed. "Those paintings…" She shook her head. "You don't even notice them anymore, do you!"

"You get used to it," Mike answered. Anastasia had taken to asking him to dinner most nights, saying he had to come here anyway to pick up Georgina. He enjoyed the food, of course, but the company was the main attraction. He no longer had to club-hop to meet potential clients. All he had to do was sit down to dinner.

It was typical of Anastasia that when she decided to meet Mike's partner, she would bluntly add that she wanted to look over his wife at the same time. Mike had asked a little sarcastically if the Conlins should bring around his two nephews for approval, too, but she'd only laughed. He was beginning to realize that she allowed him to speak to her in a way that few other people dared to, but he didn't waste his time wondering why. She was a law unto herself.

Several people were seated in the parlor when Mike led the Conlins inside, among them Anastasia's nephew Nick Pershing, a biochemist who ran Corona's research lab. He was about Mike's age, with dark hair and a well-trimmed beard that brought his famous namesake, Czar Nicholas II, to mind.

A round of introductions followed. The other guests were Nick's fiancée, a magazine editor; the artistic director of a New York ballet company; and the president of International Flavors and Fragrances, the huge perfume and flavor development company, and his wife. Anastasia walked in about ten minutes later accompanied by Georgina, Mike's old boss Terry Hall and his wife, and an elderly woman with the carriage and bearing of a queen.

Anastasia said a general hello and then walked over to Mike and the Conlins. "Mama, this is Mike Napoli. Mike, my mother, Anya Pershing."

Not a queen, Mike thought as he shook Mrs. Pershing's hand, but the daughter of a king. "And this must be your sister and brother-in-law," Anastasia continued. Mike was about to introduce them when she went on, "Royal blue is a wonderful color for you, Bianca dear, but with your dark hair and fair skin you need more dramatic makeup. Come with me—I'll show you." She took Bianca's arm and led her away, oblivious to the confusion on her face.

Anastasia's inspections were another thing Mike had gotten used to. She had a habit of commenting on everybody's appearance, and since she had a brilliant eye for color people tended to accept her advice. As far as Mike knew, however, he was the only one she'd ever told to undress.

He introduced Mrs. Pershing to Rich and then shook hands with Terry, whose wife Marcia was laughing about the first time *she'd* met Anastasia. "She told me I should never wear yellow again, and it was always my favorite color. To this day I can't face the prospect of seeing her without agonizing about my clothes and makeup."

"You look beautiful, as always." Mike kissed her hello and turned to Georgina. "Your ladyship," he said with a teasing smile, "permit me to introduce my brother-in-law, Richard Conlin. Rich, Lady Georgina Philipps."

Georgina felt a little disoriented as she shook Rich's hand. She'd expected a moment of awkward silence when Mike saw his former boss again, but the two of them acted like the best of friends. Why weren't the Halls cooler? Were they really so forgiving?

Putting the matter aside for the moment, she gave Rich a dazzling smile. The smile was actually directed at Mike, the first part of the revenge she meant to take for the way he'd teased her. "Please, call me Georgina," she said. "All my *friends* do."

Mike picked up on her meaning right away. "Hold it a minute, your ladyship. You've never invited *me* to do that."

"Of course not. You're only the chauffeur." She arched her eyebrow at him. "Not that the lack of an invitation seems to matter to you, Mr. Napoli. You've never understood your proper place."

"I'll do my best to keep it in mind next time I take you to bed," he retorted with a laugh.

Georgina blushed a little, but she was also determined not to let him get the better of her. "Mr. Napoli is referring to my habit of falling asleep in the car. I'm rather hard to wake, so he's carried me upstairs once or twice." She felt his biceps and then winked at her great-grandmother. "He has splendid muscles, Babushka. That's undoubtedly why Grandmother chose him as my chauffeur."

Anya laughed at that. "I, too, would fall asleep in my car, if I had such a handsome man to carry me in his arms. Tell me, Terry dear, do your women clients miss him?"

"He was only an asset as long as he stood there looking pretty and kept his mouth shut," Terry answered. "He and your daughter are two of a kind, Mrs. Pershing. When it comes to choosing between tact and bluntness, bluntness will win every time."

Marcia Hall linked her arm through Mike's. "Mike wasn't really that bad, except perhaps for the time an airline president complained that the ads he'd written hadn't helped their ticket sales and Mike told him the ads would have worked better if their employees weren't so surly and their food didn't stink."

"Terry was thinking about resigning the account anyway," Mike said with a shrug. "I saved him the trouble by getting us fired."

Terry looked at Rich. "Has he improved any?"

"Definitely," Rich replied. "He hasn't offended anyone in over a week."

"What is this, open season on Mike Napoli?" Mike made a show of peering into the hall. "Where's my sister? She's the only ally I've got around here."

Georgina would have said that all of them were his allies. Much to her amazement, there wasn't a trace of animosity in the room. She couldn't understand it.

Bianca returned a few minutes later looking glamorous and sophisticated, a gift pack of Corona samples tucked under her arm. Anastasia was always handing them out, both to personal guests and to charities for use as party favors. She insisted there were only two kinds of women in the world, customers and potential customers, and was determined that everyone from the second group would move into the first.

They had barely sat down to dinner before Anastasia began to subject Rich and Bianca to the same kind of cross-examination Mike had once endured. When she was finally finished grilling them, she remarked that Mike and Bianca were fortunate in their choice of parents. Sighing, she added that long and happy marriages such as the Napolis' were sadly rare these days.

Bianca nodded and smiled. "Mom and Dad are celebrating their thirtieth anniversary next month. It's like pulling teeth to get them to take a vacation, so we all chipped in to buy them a cruise and told them the tickets were nonrefundable." She looked at Mike. "Did I mention that Mom called the travel agent with a story about needing surgery? Thank God I warned him about her. He told her she would need a hospital receipt to get any money back. Dad finally admitted he was looking forward to the trip, but he doubts Mom will come around until she's convinced she can't get out of it."

"Actually, we had an ulterior motive for sending them on a cruise," Mike explained to Anastasia, and told everyone about his parents' attic. Anastasia's mother promptly invited the whole Napoli clan to come to her country estate some weekend and clean out *her* attic.

"Only the attic?" Georgina teased. "What about the cellar and storage room? Really, Babushka, there's so much family history in all those cartons that you owe it to posterity to sort through them."

"Who has the time?" Anya winked at her. "My stocks and bonds keep me too busy, darling."

"Babushka discovered the stock market about ten years ago," Georgina explained, "after she'd retired as Corona's chairwoman. She's done amazingly well at it, too. Personally I think she has the soul of a robber baron."

"Nonsense!" Anya scoffed. "I work very hard. I read. I analyze. And of course I have a talent for it, too. So you see, that brother of yours comes by it honestly. If only your mother had been more of a woman and produced an heir more quickly, John would control everything now and you would not be in the position of needing a wealthy husband,

Georgina. The Romanov women have always married for love."

Georgina stifled a sigh. Anya was as outspoken as Anastasia and just as illogical. She refrained from pointing out that Sarah's repeated miscarriages didn't make her "less of a woman," and that if she *had* produced a son more quickly he wouldn't have been John. Then again, to have said that wouldn't have helped, and besides, she wanted to get Anya off the subject of her personal life.

"Speaking of John," she said, "I was thinking he might like to come to America during his holidays. He's always enjoyed Connecticut, Babushka. Why don't I speak to Mother and Father when I see them next week?"

Anya permitted herself to be diverted, saying she would love to have the boy's company over the summer. Then Yuri Balnikov, the ballet director, asked if the earl and countess were expected in New York soon and Anastasia explained that she and Georgina were going to England to shoot a series of ads at the earl's estate. All of her guests were old and trusted friends who already knew about her Essex line.

She filled them in on the projected ad campaign, then pursed her lips in pretended dismay. "I've been through pages and pages of photographs from every agency in town and nobody is right for those two final ads! Every single model looks as if he should be tripping through a field of daisies. Where are the real men these days?" She looked around the table, her gaze coming to rest on Yuri Balnikov. "If only you were ten years younger, Yuri! You would be perfect."

Georgina knew darn well what her grandmother had in mind and it wasn't using Yuri's younger brother. Resigned to the inevitable, she coyly played along. "Ten years younger? Then you want somebody about thirty?"

Anastasia shrugged. "Thirty or a little older."

"And his hair and eye color?"

"Blue eyes because they photograph best, dark hair to contrast with yours, and a good strong face."

"And his build?" Georgina asked, struggling to keep a straight face.

"These slender aesthetic types leave me cold. I want an athlete."

Everyone at the table was staring at Mike now. He leaned back in his chair, none too pleased to be the center of attention. Georgina saw Bianca bite her lip to keep from laughing, but it was Rich who delivered the next blow.

"Mrs. Lindsay, Conlin & Napoli yields to no one in its determination to satisfy its clients. You have before you my partner, a dark-haired, blue-eyed former jock whose looks are the envy of men and the delight of women. While it's true that he won't be thirty until October, the vicissitudes of life have etched a dynamic masculinity into his face. Such sensitivity! Such suffering! Such—"

"Such a bunch of bull," Mike interrupted dryly. "Forget it, Anastasia. I'm not going to do it."

Anastasia pretended he'd never spoken. "Why, Richard, what a splendid idea! Do you know it never occurred to me? Ah, well, we do tend to overlook the treasures in our own backyards."

"This particular treasure—and I use the term loosely—intends to stay in New York," Mike said. "I'm an advertising man, not a model. We've got two deadlines coming up, not to mention a bunch of bills that won't get paid if the boss is off powdering his nose for the camera."

Now Bianca got into the act. "But I'm sure Mrs. Lindsay will pay you for your time, Mike. Rich can supervise the rest of the work on the two accounts and handle the presentations."

Mike's only response was a mumbled, *"Et tu, Brute?"*

"But it's such an *interesting* nose," Georgina drawled. "Powdered or not, the camera will adore it." Much to her amusement, Mike was looking more out of sorts by the moment. The prospect of having him in England would have given her fits once, but now it struck her as simply hilarious. God, how he would hate being treated as a sex object!

"And don't forget how wonderful you looked in the mock-ups," she went on. "What do you say, everyone? Wouldn't the men out there identify with a big, strong football player as the Essex man? And think what a promotion it would be, Mike! From chauffeur to pin-up boy in a few short weeks."

Even as Mike told himself he wasn't going to do it, everyone at the table insisted he should. Georgina's teasing, meanwhile, was doing disastrous things to his concentration. Only one possible strategy came to mind. He named such an exorbitant sum as his fee that Anastasia was sure to refuse to pay.

But she never batted an eyelash. "The success of the campaign depends upon your participation. If you don't agree, we'll have to think up a different approach. You're worth double what you've asked and I'm happy to pay it."

Double? Mike thought, and said aloud, "In all of New York there's nobody else you can use?"

She gave him a level look. "Nobody as right for the job. I want *you*, and Terry can tell you I always get what I want."

The strains of "Lola" flitted through Mike's mind. "I don't have a passport," he said, beginning to grasp at straws.

"I have connections who can expedite your application. We'll take care of it first thing in the morning."

Mike looked at Rich, who was grinning from ear to ear. With even his partner against him, his chances of refusing were nil. He finally agreed to think about it, knowing he was going to cave in. The money was great, and besides, if Jim

Palmer could pose in his Jockey shorts, Mike Napoli could probably survive a few cosmetics ads.

Anastasia must have sensed her victory because she changed the subject back to the papers in Anya's attic. Anya began talking about her childhood, and was telling everybody a story about her famous father when Anastasia looked at Mike with a wicked smile that set off alarm bells in his head.

He figured she was going to say something outrageous and she didn't disappoint him. "It appears that you and Mama have something in common. Mama was born five months after her parents' marriage and so were you, if my arithmetic is correct. Have your sister and brother-in-law inadvertently revealed a skeleton in the family closet?"

Mike simply smiled. The circumstances surrounding his birth were no great secret. "My parents like to bill themselves as the most romantic couple since Rhett and Scarlett. The way they tell it, they were sweethearts from the age of twelve who got carried away during a power failure one night."

"A claim I've always doubted," Bianca said. "They were crazy about each other from the day they met. Their houses were only a block apart. You can't tell me they had so much willpower that they only slipped just that once."

Mike agreed. "I've never bought that power-failure story either, but Mom will never admit the truth. She would have to stop lecturing Ellen and Theresa about saving themselves for marriage."

"Only your sisters?" Georgina asked. "Not you and your brother?"

Mike managed to look bewildered. "Of course not. We're men, not women. Do you have a problem with that?"

"Of course I do! It's a double standard. The same rules should apply—" Georgina suddenly realized Mike was putting her on and cut herself off. "Very funny, Mr. Napoli. Go on, tell us the rest of the story. We're waiting with bated breath.''

Mike laughed and obliged. ''When my mother realized she was pregnant she took off for Philadelphia to live with a married cousin of hers. She left her parents a note saying *why* she'd gone but not where. Apparently she had some crazy idea that she'd wreck my father's life if he had to take responsibility for a wife and child. It took him about a month to track her down, and then he drove to Philadelphia and talked her into marrying him. They had a civil ceremony and came back up to Cambridge so Mom could finish high school. Apparently they didn't get the warmest of receptions, but my mother's parents eventually agreed to take them in.''

''And only started to forgive them after Father O'Reilly had given them a proper wedding in the Church,'' Bianca said. ''Then Mike came along and his four grandparents were so crazy about him that Mom and Dad were suddenly in everyone's good graces again. They spoiled him so badly he's been stubborn and arrogant ever since.''

''His stubbornness is a facet of his personality I've gotten to know quite well,'' Anastasia said, ''not that it will do him any good. I promise you, Michael, you've met your match in me.'' She paused, then asked her mother, ''What did you think of his story, Mama? Are the two of you soulmates?''

''It was a grave disappointment,'' Anya answered, her eyes sparkling. ''I, at least, have a czar to my credit, not to mention a homosexual general and an accomplished smuggler. Forgive me, Mike dear, but parents who were sweethearts and went a little too far one night cannot begin to compare. I see I shall have to rely on my grandson for intriguing gossip. Nicky, what have you heard about the Endicotts' divorce? Is it true she deceived him with the boy who walks their dogs?''

Nick Pershing proved a fount of information. He kept the assembled guests entertained through the rest of dinner.

Georgina was relieved when the evening ended early. After all the running around she'd done lately, she needed some extra sleep.

"So what do you think? Is my fish well and truly hooked?" Anastasia asked after they had closed the door on the last of their guests.

Georgina didn't have to ask what she meant. "You know perfectly well he is. You flattered him so shamelessly after dinner he's probably convinced he's indispensable."

"I told him the truth. He fits my image of the Essex man exactly, even his broken nose."

Especially his broken nose, Georgina thought as they walked down the hall. Lord, the man was attractive! And when he teased her, the most extraordinary hot and cold sensations rippled through her body.

When she didn't make any response, Anastasia gave her a speculative look. "Aren't you going to make a fuss about it? I thought I was risking the wrath of God by insisting he should come to England, although I must say you were surprisingly friendly to him tonight."

She'd been more than friendly and both of them knew it. The more she saw of him, the less he fit her preconceived notions. He and Bianca were so close, and he had such a sense of humor about his shortcomings. How selfish and insensitive could he really be?

"Naturally I was friendly," she replied. "He's your guest and your business associate. I'm sure he's as right for the Essex ads as you say he is. I've never known you to be wrong about what would sell your products."

She stopped by the door to her room. As tired as she was, she was never going to be able to sleep without asking a few questions. "Grandmother, I couldn't help noticing how well

Mike got on with Terry and Marcia Hall. After the way he stabbed Terry in the back, I should think they would barely speak. Are you sure about what happened?''

"Oh, quite sure," Anastasia answered. "Terry was very specific about it. Mike is a charming man who obviously has deep affection for his family, but none of that has anything to do with how he treats everyone else. Terry made it clear that Mike was in line for a partnership and Mike took full advantage of it. He squeezed Terry's mind dry as a bone, all under the pretext of learning the business, and then blithely turned his back on him and went off on his own. I suppose you're puzzled about why Terry would recommend him to me after that, but that's the way business works. Terry knew Mike would do a wonderful job, and above all, Terry is a realist. He understands the ambitiousness and selfishness of youth. He decided it was wisest to accept what had happened and maintain a cordial working relationship. After all, it's a small world. People run into each other all the time, and you never know when you'll need a favor."

Georgina nodded and said good-night, thinking that Terry hadn't been merely cordial, but warm and . . . and almost fatherly. He seemed to look upon Mike as a sort of protégé, despite how unpleasant their initial parting had been. Perhaps he'd decided he could afford to be generous about Mike's success. After all, Conlin & Napoli was a small fish indeed compared to Hall & Haywood. Besides, Terry had to be patient and forgiving by nature or he never could have put up with Anastasia all these years.

Georgina thought about Mike for a full half hour before she realized what she was doing and stopped. Even if Mike had had money, he wouldn't have been the right sort for her. Terry's experience with him proved it, and then there was the way he had treated Jill.

She had to put him out of her mind and make a greater effort to get interested in somebody else. She couldn't compare every man she met to him, or wonder why she didn't feel the same jolt of electricity when somebody else touched her. Otherwise she would never survive five full days in England working by his side, dining at the same table, and sleeping only a few doors down the hall.

Chapter Seven

Lady Georgina Philipps and Roger LaSalle. Mike considered it a total mismatch, but the earl's daughter and the playboy hockey star didn't seem to agree. They'd been talking and laughing all the way from midtown Manhattan to Chinatown.

Mike tried not to listen to their conversation as he wove his way through the narrow streets. LaSalle was a household name in New York these days—his brilliant passing and shooting had led his team to the playoffs and then to a quick victory in the Patrick Division finals. Mike had often wished his blazing talent belonged to the Boston Bruins instead of the New York Rangers, but never so much as he wished it now. If LaSalle had lived in Boston he wouldn't have been in the backseat of the Cadillac with Georgina, charming her senseless.

Shaking his head in disgust, Mike pulled up in front of the restaurant and got out to open LaSalle's door. As Georgina delighted in reminding him, he was only her chauffeur, not her protector or lover. He had no business caring about who she saw or what she did, much less hoping that Roger La-Salle would get a sudden urge to move to Tibet or give up hockey in favor of the priesthood.

She gave LaSalle a smitten smile as he helped her out of the car. "What time should Mike pick us up? About nine-thirty?"

"We'll take a taxi." LaSalle gave Mike a dismissive glance and put his arm around Georgina's shoulders. "Should I call your grandmother and promise her I have no intention of kidnapping you?"

"It wouldn't help," Mike said. "If you value your hide, you'll play by Mrs. Lindsay's rules."

"What she doesn't find out—"

"She *always* finds out. She can read Georgina like an open book."

LaSalle turned around, frowning. But his annoyance turned into puzzlement when he looked at Mike—really *looked* at him—for the first time that night. "Aren't you Mike Napoli?" he asked.

Mike nodded. "Right. We met a few times at school." Both of them had gone to Boston College, but Mike had been a big man on campus when LaSalle was only an obscure freshman. A lot had changed since then.

"Sure, I remember," LaSalle said with a smile. "When I saw you on a football field I wanted to forget hockey and become a wide receiver. Football seemed..." He paused and shrugged. "I don't know. More exciting to people. Sexier, maybe."

"Not in New York City, at least not this year. You guys have been great." Mike checked his watch. "I need to get going—I'm meeting a client in fifteen minutes. Will nine-thirty be okay?"

"A client? You mean you don't work for Georgie's grandmother?" LaSalle asked.

So it was "Georgie" already, was it? "Actually it's a prospective client," Mike said. "Georgina can tell you about it. Enjoy your dinner."

"We will," Georgina replied, "and don't worry if your meeting with Sealy runs a little long. We'll go for a walk after dinner."

The two men shook hands as Georgina stood and watched. She was beginning to think Mike knew most everyone in New York, or at least that they knew him. "Was he well known in college?" she asked Roger as they walked into the restaurant. "So many people seem to recognize his name."

"Anyone who followed college football would know him. He would have gone in the first or second round if it hadn't been for his knee."

Georgina had no idea what he was talking about. "The first or second round?"

"Of the draft. The Pats took him in the eighth round instead, and a few weeks later he blew out his knee at a mini-camp."

When Georgina's expression remained just as blank, Roger laughed and said he would explain everything. "Our marriage is never going to work if you don't learn more about sports," he teased.

Georgina didn't doubt he'd used that line before, probably to excellent effect. According to her cousin Nicky, who had arranged the date, when his pal LaSalle wasn't playing hockey, he was wining and dining one beautiful woman after another. Nicky had even cautioned her not to lose her head over him.

It wouldn't have been hard to, because Roger was handsome, charming, and totally unimpressed with himself. He was also a good teacher. Georgina learned about the Heisman Trophy and the pro football draft. She found out what could go wrong with athletes' knees and came to understand that Mike's physical problems must have dealt him a crushing psychological blow. She learned that hockey was more physically demanding than football and required more skill to play well, but Roger delivered these so-called facts with a wink and a grin. Then he asked Georgina where Mike fit into her life and they got into a discussion about grandmothers and how eccentric they could be. All in all, it was the most enjoyable evening she'd spent since arriving in New York.

It was only about eight-thirty when they finished eating, so they strolled through Chinatown together, occasionally stopping to chat with one of Roger's fans. By the time they got back to the restaurant, Mike was waiting out front. Georgina felt a stab of anxiety. It was only nine-fifteen. Why was he early? Had things gone badly?

She told herself it was none of her business but the need to find out what had happened quickly got the better of her. "I thought you'd be longer," she said. "How did everything go?"

"Fine," he answered.

In other words, he didn't care to talk about it. He must have done poorly, or thought that he had. But the fellow he'd met was a friend of Anastasia's, and she had mentioned how wishy-washy he could be. "Sealy takes forever to make up his mind," Georgina said. "Don't worry if he was noncommittal. I thought your ideas were fabulous, and once he has a chance to mull them over, he'll think so, too."

Up in the front seat, Mike told himself he must have committed some dastardly sin because God was surely punishing him. It wasn't enough that Georgina was beautiful or that her initial hostility was only a distant memory. It wasn't enough that she enjoyed teasing him and thought nothing of casually touching him. Oh, no. She had to start worrying about him. She had to show the concern a good friend would show. She had to make herself doubly attractive so she would be doubly hard to resist.

He stopped for a red light and looked back over his shoulder. LaSalle had his arm around her and was playing with a lock of her hair. Mike fought down the ache in his gut, but his answer still came out curter than he really meant it to. "My only problem was that Sealy liked *everything*. I'll be meeting with him again after we get back from England."

Georgina all but shrank back in her seat. She was sure Mike was angry with her, sure she'd antagonized him by pressing him for personal information. "I'm glad things went well," she murmured, but he'd already turned around and was pulling into traffic again.

The feel of Roger's fingers against her neck reminded her who she was with. She didn't *want* to keep thinking about Mike, but his presence was impossible to ignore. She promised herself she would tackle Anastasia about getting a different chauffeur—after they returned from England, at any rate.

"You're very quiet," she said to Roger after a few minutes, and then teased, "Are you bloated from too much food or just bored with my company?"

"I was thinking about who you are," he answered. "It hit me when Mike mentioned England. I saw the Queen once, when she visited Quebec, and I suddenly realized you've probably met her. You probably know all of them."

Georgina was back on comfortable ground now. She didn't really "know" the royals, but she'd met them a few times and was able to entertain Roger with some choice gossip about them. He listened avidly all the way back to his apartment.

Like most of her dates, he invited her up for a nightcap before he got out of the car. She had always said no in the past, but it was still quite early and she knew that sooner or later she would have to make a greater effort to get interested in someone other than Mike. She was even prepared to risk Anastasia's wrath by taking a taxi home, but Roger never even suggested it. Instead, he asked Mike if he would mind coming back in an hour, and since Mike lived only fifteen blocks away, he didn't mind at all.

Roger was much too smooth to make a pass right away. First he fixed some espresso and then he put a jazz tape on the stereo. They sat side by side on the couch, not touching, and talked about their childhoods. When Georgina mentioned her student days in Paris, Roger switched to his native French. He was visibly pleased when Georgina was able to answer in the same language.

A few minutes later, while he was getting them more coffee, she walked to the window to check on the view of Central Park. She wasn't surprised when Roger came up behind her, put his arms around her, and nuzzled the back of her neck.

She wanted to respond. Certainly she had never envisioned a passionless marriage, no matter how practical a choice she made. So when Roger turned her around and took her in his arms, she smiled up at him and offered her lips.

He was very good at kissing, but her appreciation was oddly detached. There was no fire in his lips, no magic in his tongue. Mike could have aroused her more with a single glance from across a crowded room.

Roger was the one who broke things off, easing her out of his arms and turning toward the window. After a long few seconds of silence, he asked, "Why did you come up here?"

Embarrassment made Georgina evasive. "You asked me to."

There was another period of awkward silence. Finally Roger said, "I heard a lot about Mike Napoli tonight. In fact, now that I think about it, it didn't even matter what we were talking about. One way or another you managed to bring him into the conversation.''

"I'm sure I didn't," Georgina said, afraid she probably had.

He gave her the denial the credence it deserved—exactly none. "And now that I think some more, it isn't a one-way street. In the car before, when you asked him about his meeting and he turned around to answer—he didn't like me touching you. What's the story with you two? Are you playing some kind of game with each other?"

Georgina felt simply awful now—guilty, ashamed and embarrassed. She didn't use people. She didn't put them in the middle of other relationships. Why on earth had she come here?

"It's not a game," she said. "That is, if you're thinking I was trying to make him jealous, it's nothing like that at all. Really, I'd rather not go into it."

He nodded. "In that case, our coffee is getting cold."

She liked Roger more than ever then. A painful childhood had taught her to bury her emotions, or at least not to discuss them, so she couldn't bring herself to explain about Mike or thank Roger for his understanding. But she did tell him she was glad she had met him and would be rooting for the Rangers in the playoffs, and he seemed to understand what she was really saying.

Mike pulled up just seconds after they got downstairs. Georgina always sat in back, but Roger happened to open the front passenger door and it would have been unpardonably rude to point out the mistake. She was about to thank him for dinner when he leaned into the car and took hold of her unfastened seat belt. Without a word, he drew it slowly across her chest and buckled it. Then he murmured in French, "Good night, my darling. I will count the hours until you return from England and I can make love to you again." The next thing a stunned Georgina knew, he was kissing her with searing passion.

By the time he finally released her, all she wanted was to close the door so the overhead light would go out. Her face had to be hot pink. But he wasn't done yet. "I told Georgie I'd get her a couple of tickets to the conference finals, if we're still playing when you get home," he said to Mike. "Will you bring her to watch me and fill her in on what's going on?"

Mike was a seething mass of emotions by then. He kept telling himself it was good that Georgina had found somebody she liked, but basically he wanted to mash the guy's face in. He didn't speak French, but he thought he knew what *"Bonsoir, ma chérie,"* meant, and it wasn't the kind of language you used if all you'd done for the past hour was watch the TV news. He managed to unclench his teeth long enough to tell LaSalle he would be glad to take Georgina to a game, but it wasn't easy.

LaSalle bent close to Georgina's ear. "Think of me while you're away, chérie. I'll call you when I get back."

Georgina stared into her lap, blushing like a teenager. "Yes. All right. Good night, Roger."

LaSalle grinned and closed the door, not a moment too soon as far as Mike was concerned. As for Georgina, she sat there wishing she had told Roger the truth. He'd probably thought he was doing her a favor by trying to make Mike jealous, but he'd only made things worse. She felt torn in two. Obviously it was best for Mike to think she was serious about somebody else, but every inch of her wanted to confess the opposite.

As usual, she forced herself to do what was sensible and practical. "Roger is very nice," she said. "We had a pleasant time together."

"Only pleasant?" Mike smiled at her. "Whatever he said, it sounded as romantic as hell."

"Well, that's French for you," Georgina said lamely. "Everything sounds romantic in French."

Mike told himself to drop the subject. Georgina's personal life was none of his business. He had no right to cross-examine her about what she'd done on her dates. But he could still picture LaSalle kissing her and smell the bastard's cologne on her skin. Reasonable or not, he wanted to take her in his arms and destroy every last vestige of the other man's presence.

The thought, of course, was ludicrous. He wasn't some wild animal, to go around marking his territory or fighting over a desirable female. What in hell was wrong with him? He hadn't felt this shaken since his last time on a football field, when his knee had suddenly given way and he'd collapsed onto the turf.

He couldn't think of anything to say, but Georgina seemed to be lost in a world of her own anyway. She probably had a lot to remember and savor. She and LaSalle had been alone for over an hour. What had they done during all that time? Had he made love to her? Was she wishing she was back in his apartment, locked in his arms?

He ordered himself to drop the gratuitous masochism and show a little common sense. He was intensely attracted to Georgina but knew he couldn't have her. All these crazy feelings were the result of ordinary frustration. He was spoiled, that was all. He was used to getting what he wanted when it came to women, and getting it fast. If he had even an ounce of decency, even a gram of sensitivity, he would stop being so selfish and think about what was best for Georgina. Didn't he want her to find a man with a fat bank account and fall madly in love? Of course he did.

By the time he pulled up in front of her building he'd managed to convince himself that all he cared about was her happiness. As he walked her inside, he kidded her about how wide awake she was and said that LaSalle must be as exciting off the ice as on it. She looked at the floor and re-peated that he was "very nice." That was the English for you. They considered anything stronger than "very nice" to be a fulsome compliment.

Mike was totally oblivious to the real truth of the situa-tion—that Georgina's nerves, which had been strained to begin with, were now all but shot. First the intimacy of the darkened car and now the silence of the empty elevator—she couldn't get upstairs fast enough. An attractive man had kissed her tonight and how had she reacted? By thinking about what she hadn't felt. No hot confusion, the way she had with Mike. No restless passion, the way she had with Mike. No burning need to give herself, the way she had with Mike.

And what had Mike felt? A quick burst of jealousy, per-haps, but he'd long ago gotten over it. She wanted to re-treat to a distant corner of the elevator but forced herself to stand by his side and act as if nothing were wrong. Geor-gina had always prided herself on her poise and wasn't going to let it desert her.

They were standing by her door, about to say good-night, when she made the mistake of looking into his eyes and felt desire slash through her like a stiletto. The intensity of it took her by surprise, smashing her composure to bits. God, she wanted him to kiss her. It was madness.

Mike saw the look in her eyes, read it for what it was, and learned that all the logic in the world didn't stand a chance against raw emotion. But even if he couldn't help his feel-ings, he didn't have to act on them. "About tomorrow night..." he began, knowing his willpower could only take him so far. Another night of this and he'd be a basket case. "If you plan to go out—"

"I don't. I thought I'd pack and turn in early." She moistened her lips. "I'll, uh, I'll see you Thursday morn-ing."

Georgina told herself to go inside, but instead she simply stood there, gazing up at Mike with blind yearning. It was an open invitation and in the end he couldn't bring himself to ignore it. He lifted her chin to kiss her, but at the last moment some remnant of common sense broke through and he brushed his lips against her forehead instead.

"Rest up tomorrow, honey," he said, and took a jerky step backward. "We want you to look beautiful for the camera."

Georgina felt like sinking through the floor. She'd practically thrown herself at the man, and what had she gotten in return? A platonic kiss and some brotherly advice! What a total idiot she'd made of herself! She managed a saucy, "I'll do my best, Mr. Napoli," and fled into the apartment.

Mike watched the door snap shut and then leaned against the wall, emotionally drained. How was he supposed to cope with almost a week in England with Georgina in the same house? What was he going to do if something like this happened again?

But it wouldn't. After the way he'd rejected her she'd avoid him like the plague. Besides, he'd heard about these English estates. The houses were huge. She'd probably be two floors away and so busy with her family that the only time they would see each other was when they were working. And when they got back to New York... This chauffeuring business had to go. He was only human, and he wasn't putting himself through another night like this one.

He straightened abruptly at the clicking of spike heels on the floor and looked down the corridor. Anastasia. Thank God he'd kept his hands to himself, because he wasn't in the mood to tolerate one of her lectures.

"Tough night?" she asked, giving him a coy smile.

"Actually things went very well, if you're asking about your friend Sealy. And Roger LaSalle made a big hit with your granddaughter."

"Did he really? How could you tell?"

Mike smiled and shook his head. "No comment, Anastasia. I'll see you Thursday. Good night."

Anastasia calmly watched him go, knowing better than to try and detain him. Besides, she thought to herself, she'd seen as much as she needed to see—Mike Napoli, collapsed against the wall as if all the torments of hell had come crashing down on his head. Jealousy was obviously eating him alive. She should have had Nicky introduce Georgie to LaSalle weeks ago.

Chapter Eight

It was raining steadily when Mike, Georgina and Anastasia arrived in England, not an unusual turn of events from what Mike had heard. It *did* strike him as unusual that they would be met by a chauffeured Bentley belonging to Corona International. He had expected the earl to send somebody.

It wasn't a long trip to the earl's house in Essex, only about an hour, but it drizzled every mile of the way. Mike would eventually realize how appropriate that gray, depressing weather was. If the Bentley was the first clue, the second came when nobody appeared to greet them except the butler, who explained that the earl and countess had retired for the night.

Georgina didn't seem especially surprised, but Mike was utterly baffled. It wasn't even eleven o'clock yet. His own parents would have been awake and waiting even at one or two, probably with enough food to feed an army. The butler hadn't even offered a snack.

At first glance the main house, Shanley Hall, had more than met Mike's expectations. He had seen it looming in the darkness as they passed by the gatehouse, a large stone fortress of a place surrounded by acres of park. The entry hall was magnificent, two stories high with checkered marble floors, muraled walls and a double staircase flanked by carved banisters. But then Mike noticed the murals were dark with age and needed professional restoration, that the carved plaster ceiling needed cleaning and repair, and that the banisters had nicks and scratches that not even the gleaming polish could hide. The place was spotless, but fine old houses like Shanley required more than soap and wax to keep them in shape. A century or two ago the master of this home might have employed a dozen artists and craftsmen in addition to an army of ordinary servants, but the days of the resident earl being able to afford a staff like that were evidently long past.

As far as the sleeping arrangements went, Mike had been partly right and partly wrong. The house had two towered wings in addition to the main building, but one of them hadn't been used in years and was closed off while the other, which contained the kitchen and servants' quarters, was occupied only on the main floor. In an earlier era Mike might well have found himself in a different wing from Georgina, but the late twentieth century offered only one building, the main one, and only one floor, the second. The sole saving grace was that he and Georgina were on opposite sides of the hall.

Studying his room, Mike noticed the same pattern of neglect as downstairs. The wooden floors needed sanding and refinishing. The embroidered curtains around the four-poster bed were seriously frayed in spots. The fireplace needed cleaning and the intricate plaster moldings on the walls and ceiling needed the hand of an expert restorer.

Mike suddenly wondered exactly how extravagant the earl and countess really were. Anastasia had characterized them as frivolous people who frittered their money away on nothing, but she wasn't one to let the facts interfere with her opinions. Maybe Georgina's determination to marry a wealthy man wasn't as quixotic as Anastasia had insisted.

Georgina woke with a start, looked at the clock, and grimaced. It was almost ten-thirty. Her parents hated it when she got down to breakfast late. The minute a pill for jet lag came on the market she would be first in line to buy it.

Although she bathed and dressed in minutes, she was still the last one downstairs. She could hear talking and laughter as she approached the morning room, which was where breakfast was always set out. Mike was telling her parents about his first meeting with Anastasia.

"My ego got a little out of hand," he was saying, "and I started to think she was checking me out as a prospective lover. When I realized how wrong I was I made a joke about it—something about finding your mother too intimidating for me to play the role of the kept younger man, Lady Medshire—and who should walk in but your daughter."

He noticed Georgina in the doorway and began to mimic her accent to perfection. "'And if my grandmother weren't so intimidating? Would the role of the kept younger man appeal to you then?' So naturally I said yes, which convinced her I was total scum, and she put me in my place about as crushingly as I've ever been put. I made the mistake of calling her Georgie and she informed me it was Lady Georgina and I'd better not forget it." Laughing, he got to his feet and pulled out an empty chair. "Good morning, your ladyship. Can I get you something to eat?"

"Just some coffee and toast, thank you." Georgina passed by the chair and walked to the head of the table to kiss her father hello. He didn't kiss her back. "Your color is good this morning," she said. "Are you feeling a bit better?"

"It's a slow business," he replied. "Give your mother a kiss, darling. She's been wondering when you would come down."

Georgina walked around the table and kissed her mother on the cheek. Sarah never moved. "I'm sorry if I held you up. The time difference—"

"Of course, dear. We understand." Lady Medshire looked her daughter up and down, frowning. "You've lost weight. What have you been doing to yourself in New York? Not trying to keep up with Mother, surely."

Georgina smiled. "Both of us know that would be impossible."

Mike had set a cup of coffee and a plate of toast by her place and was waiting to seat her. He gave her shoulder a gentle squeeze after he'd pushed in her chair. Embarrassed, she took a sip of coffee. Her family probably struck him as cold, coming as he did from such a vastly different background. That quick gesture of sympathy at her parents' behavior had been sweet, but he didn't understand that formality was a way of life here.

"John should be home this evening," her mother said. "He's dying to see you, Georgie. He's missed you terribly."

Georgina could hear the reproach in Sarah's voice but knew it wasn't on John's behalf at all. Sarah wasn't pleased that Georgina had gone to New York.

"And I've missed him," she replied. Her brother attended Eton, just as every other male in the Philipps family had. "We were thinking that perhaps he could visit Babushka during his summer holidays. You and Father will probably be able to go to Aunt Elizabeth's once again this year—''

"I doubt he'll be up to it. It's a long trip to the south of France and the villa has too many steps. You seem to think your father's health is much more improved than it really is, dear. We'll need John at Shanley."

Georgina smiled apologetically. "If I do think that about Father, it's only because I wish it so strongly. I'm sorry if I was being selfish about John, Mother."

Mike listened to their conversation with a growing sense of bewilderment. He'd liked Sarah Philipps, at least at first. She was lovely and feminine, not the least bit condescending, and unmistakably devoted to the earl.

Mike didn't know a lot about the potentially fatal disease that had struck him down, Guillain-Barré syndrome, only that it caused extensive to total paralysis that receded with agonizing slowness. Rehabilitation took years, and even the luckiest victims seldom regained the full use of their faculties. The earl walked with a slight but noticeable shuffle, had difficulty saying certain letters, and had to chew and swallow carefully. He seemed to speak very little, but whether that was due to his illness or to a natural reserve, Mike didn't know.

A lot of women in Sarah's circumstances would have left their husbands to professional nurses, but she hadn't done that. She had looked after him herself instead, and was constantly encouraging him to do as much as he could on his own. Mike didn't understand how she could be so loving with her husband yet so cool to her daughter. At first he wondered if she was still angry with Georgina for going to New York, but as the day wore on he realized it went a lot deeper. Sarah might have loved Georgina, but she didn't seem to either like her or approve of her.

The rain never stopped, so the photography session had to be postponed. Other than a trip to the nearest village while the earl was in London, they spent the entire day at Shanley. The earl returned home about three and promptly went off to bed, while Mike played bridge with the three women. Afterward Georgina played the piano for everyone, superbly, Mike thought.

Her mother, he learned, was an expert at backhanded compliments: "You played that hand well, dear, but of course, it was stupid of me to lead the spade," or "The Chopin sounded lovely, Georgie, but think what you could have accomplished if you'd practiced more as a child." Sarah was even better at doling out guilt: "Your father has been wonderful about doing his exercises, but I'm afraid nobody can partner him as well as you can," and "Trayne was dying to see you so I invited him for dinner tomorrow night. Do try to take more of an interest in him, for your father's sake if nothing else." The remarks that followed told Mike that "Trayne" was a wealthy marquess who'd been besotted with Georgina for years, and that Sarah would have killed to see them married.

Georgina deflected her mother's comments with smiles and apologies, but Mike could see how much they hurt. She wanted Sarah's approval, but approval was something she would probably never get. It didn't seem to be in Sarah's nature.

By the time dinner came around, Mike had decided that Sarah was one of those women who resented her daughter's youth and beauty so much that she couldn't feel the love and warmth most mothers did. It was a nice theory, but the arrival of Georgina's brother John sank it like a lead anchor. He walked into the dining room in the middle of dinner, hugged his grandmother and sister, and greeted Mike with a warm handshake. Then he pecked his mother on the cheek and shook his father's hand. He'd barely sat down before Sarah began to scold him. Why was he so late? Didn't he know he had inconvenienced them? And couldn't he have dressed more suitably?

"Really, darling," she said, "you look like something the cat dragged in." John was wearing slacks, an oxford cloth shirt and a sweater. If Mike's brother Chris had ever looked that nice, their mother would have run to the church and lit a candle in thanksgiving.

"I'm sorry, Mother," he said. "I got tied up with some last-minute studying. Shall I go upstairs and change?"

"You would only hold us up even more," Sarah answered. "Go on, John, eat your dinner."

At that point John slid a look of amused resignation across the table at Georgina, who coughed suspiciously. Mike suddenly understood that Sarah hadn't singled out her daughter for special disapproval—she treated her son the same way. The difference was that John seemed to let it roll off his back. He'd had one great advantage Georgina had lacked—an older sister to love and support him. The woman Mike had once called a spoiled brat looked finer and more giving with every day he knew her.

Within twenty-four hours of arriving at Shanley, Georgina began to wonder how she would survive the next several days. Had it always been this bad, or had her parents gotten more difficult? Sarah's continual criticism was no less hurtful for being softly spoken, and the earl's detachment, so much worse since he'd been struck down, showed no signs of reversing itself. Anastasia, who usually kept Sarah in line, hadn't interfered at all. And worst of all, there was nothing to do here, nothing to keep her busy enough to brush aside the pain.

No matter how hard she tried, she couldn't get past the feeling that she should have been able to make her parents love her more. It wasn't impossible—she knew that from personal experience. She remembered her mother's gratitude when she'd gotten the best man in London to take her father's case, and the smiles of triumph she and her father had exchanged when, after hours of working together, he had finally accomplished some small physical task. Her parents might have been difficult to please, but every now and then she'd succeeded, and they had rewarded her with a few shining moments of affection and approval.

In the meantime, she was grateful that John was here to keep her company. She had always adored him for his sunny, imperturbable nature, but it didn't occur to her that she was part of the reason for it. Naturally she'd given him tons of love and attention—he was her little brother and she owed him her protection.

Lying in bed that night she realized that Mike had tried to protect her in the same way she'd always protected John. When Sarah had chided her for not practicing enough as a child, Mike had laughed and said if she'd practiced more she might have become a concert pianist who never would have inspired the ad campaign he'd created, and he would have had one fewer account. There had been three or four such incidents. Protectiveness probably came naturally to him, since he was the big brother to four siblings. But as much as Georgina appreciated his concern, she was also rather embarrassed by it. He saw too much, including the pain she tried so hard to hide.

With John around, Saturday should have been easier, but it wasn't. The rain kept coming, but even worse, Sarah insisted on giving Mike a thorough tour of the house, complete with overobvious commentary. The third earl, she told him, had married a banker's daughter and added the two wings. The fourth earl had wed a brewer's daughter and installed modern plumbing, electricity and heating. The fifth earl had taken a shipbuilder's daughter as his wife, using her dowry to pay the death duties and restore artwork and furnishings. Anthony was the sixth earl, and Sarah's dowry had gone toward the death duties and the gardens, which had grown almost wild in places by then. Naturally, Sarah said, the daughters of the house had done their share as well. Shanley Hall was a treasure and a joy, but it was also a terrible burden. There was never enough money to do everything one wanted.

In other words, Georgina silently translated, if you've got any designs on my daughter, you can bloody well forget them. She was mortified, but then John jabbed an elbow into her ribs and rolled his eyes, and she couldn't help giggling.

Sarah wouldn't hear of them leaving the house—Anthony was entitled to have his children about on weekends—so Saturday was much like Friday. Georgina played bridge with her parents and grandmother while Mike was off somewhere with John, entertained at the piano, and tried to look forward to seeing Geoffrey Barrett, the Marquess of Trayne. It had been three months since their last date and she was hoping he had improved.

One look and she knew he hadn't. Geoffrey was a nice fellow, but the thought of going to bed with him made Georgina as queasy as an expectant mother. She had tried to overcome her aversion, dating him for several months last winter and spring, but Geoffrey had a dreadful complexion and a body the consistency of marshmallow. Even closing her eyes hadn't helped.

It was just her rotten luck that the rain would let up as they were finishing dinner. Sarah promptly told her to take Geoffrey outside and show him the newly relandscaped back garden. Georgina didn't want to be alone with him but couldn't see a polite way to refuse.

Geoffrey had always been rather shy, so she was startled when he pulled her into his arms and tried to kiss her the moment they reached the shadows. He was gentle but insistent, and openly annoyed when she refused to go along.

"Dammit, Georgie, why did you invite me if this is the way you're going to act? You know how I feel about you. I've waited, I've been patient . . ." Further words seemed to elude him.

Georgina understood now. Her mother must have told him she wanted to see him and he'd assumed what any man would assume. Since she didn't want to hurt him, she resorted to a little white lie. "I thought I was ready but I'm not. I'm sorry, Geoffrey."

"That's all you're going to say? After I flew back from Rome just to see you?"

From *Rome*? Dear God, how could her mother have done it? "You have every right to be angry," she said. "You know I value your friendship, but I—I'm simply not ready to settle down."

"It's Napoli, isn't it!" he said. "He's the real problem."

Georgina didn't deny it. Mike suddenly seemed like a gift from the gods. "I know he's all wrong for me, but I have to get him out of my system. Maybe in a few years—"

"A few years? You expect me to wait a few years?"

"Of course not. Tons of women are interested in you, and I expect you'll pick one of them to marry."

Georgina hoped that would be the end of it, and as far as she could tell, it was. Geoffrey's patience had been sorely tried, but he put the best possible face on things when they got back to the house. Unfortunately, he also began to drink and he had never held his liquor very well.

Georgina breathed a sigh of relief when he finally got up to leave, but her relief was premature. Geoffrey's last goodbye was to Mike, and the brandy did the talking.

"I understand she's your mistress, Napoli. Enjoy her. I certainly would in your shoes," he said, and weaved his way out of the room.

There was a moment of appalled silence during which everyone wondered if they could possibly have heard him correctly. It didn't take Mike long to figure out what had happened. Georgina's mother was trying to marry her off to Trayne, but the guy was short and round with a complexion like the surface of the moon. Now, as if two days of being either ignored or criticized weren't enough, she'd had to fight off Trayne in the garden.

He gave her a cocky smile. "I'm honored, Lady Georgina. I've never been used as an excuse to get rid of a marquess before. Too bad it wasn't true."

Georgina was so grateful her eyes filled up, but she managed a light-hearted answer. "If only he had your looks or you had his money! I have to admit I let him assume what he wanted—it was so much easier that way."

"Coward," her brother teased.

Sarah was looking exceedingly perturbed. "Really, Georgina, he's a lovely man. He would be a kind and faithful husband. Most women would jump at the chance to marry him."

"And on her wedding night, Georgie can close her eyes and think of England," John drawled.

The earl, who'd barely said a word all evening, suddenly came to life. "Is that what they teach you in school, young man? To make smart remarks to your mother? Apologize at once and go to your room!"

Anastasia had stayed above the fray so far, but her son-in-law's lecture was evidently more than she could stomach. "Yes, John, do say you're sorry. You made an unforgivable mistake. It's Shanley Hall Georgie would have to think of, not England."

"Mother—"

"Yes, Sarah, I know. I'm a bad influence on the boy. I'll apologize and go to my room." Anastasia stood up, waiting for her grandson to carry out his marching orders so she could join him on the trek into exile.

In the end, all of them retired except Mike, who went off to the library to browse. Georgina felt confused and disoriented as she changed for bed, perhaps because she had never had so many people support her before. John had never been so outspoken in the past and Anastasia had never been so sarcastic. And then, of course, there was Mike.

She was lying in bed with a book when her mother's ladies' maid entered the room to inform her that Lady Medshire wished to see her. Sighing, she pulled on her robe and went downstairs. Sarah was sitting on the couch in her sitting room, but the earl had gone to sleep. The rest of her parents' apartment was dark and quiet.

Far from looking angry, Sarah was subdued and a little teary. "Come sit down, darling." She patted the couch. "I couldn't sleep. I had to talk to you."

Georgina started to worry. "What's wrong, Mother? You look terribly upset."

Sarah took her hand the moment she was seated. The physical contact was a rarity. "You know I only want what's best for all of us. I'm sorry about inviting Geoffrey, but I've always thought he was perfect for you. And he does adore you, Georgie."

"I know. I do like him, Mother, but marriage..." Georgina shook her head. She and her mother had never discussed the more intimate aspects of the subject.

"Naturally, given your lack of experience..." Sarah paused, choosing her words carefully. "You mustn't judge by movies and books. Real people don't always have such feelings. What I'm trying to say is that you're not—you might not be—a warm girl, darling. And if you wait for bells to go off..." She gave a helpless shrug.

There was a time when Georgina would have believed her, but not now. Not since Mike. "I'm not expecting bells, just that it won't be—repulsive. I'm not cold, Mother. I know how it can be."

"Do you?" Sarah asked, openly skeptical.

Embarrassed or not, Georgina wasn't going to back down. "As a matter of fact I do, and I also know you and Father were mad for each other in the beginning, because Grandmother told me so. *You* wouldn't have taken Geoffrey so I don't see why *I* should."

"I had money," Sarah snapped. "You don't." The gloves were off now. "As far as bells go... Who was it, Georgina? No, never mind, I can see what's in front of my own nose. You're infatuated with Mother's latest housepet, and why not? He's a very handsome man."

Georgina stiffened. "He happens to be a very talented advertising executive, which is the only reason she hired him."

"And a talented lover? Is he that, too?"

"I wouldn't know," Georgina mumbled.

"Wouldn't you? God only knows what goes on in this house once I'm in bed! But let me tell you something, Georgina. We'll never accept him, never. He's not one of *us*."

Georgina could tolerate a lot from people, but not social snobbery or religious bigotry. She couldn't remember ever being so angry with her mother. "And if he had tons of money? Would you accept him then? It so happens there's nothing between us, but don't you dare try to tell me that my husband has to come from a certain type of background or practice a certain religion or you won't accept him. If he's a good man you damn well *will* accept him, because I know you would accept his money!"

Sarah burst into tears, throwing her arms around Georgina's waist and sobbing against her chest. Even during the worst moments of the earl's illness, Sarah had never broken down so completely, and the sight left Georgina stunned.

Sarah's apology came out in choppy fragments. "I'm so sorry—I didn't mean... You know I'm not like that—not a prejudiced person... I want you to be happy. But your father—I've been so worried—he frets and frets. He loves this house so and he agonizes that nothing will be left for John..."

Georgina patted her mother's back, feeling awkward and ineffectual. "It's all right, Mother. Please, don't cry."

"But you don't know what it's been like. He goes to the city and comes home exhausted. The house is in his blood—it's everything to him—and he sees all the things he can't afford to do... He sits for hours on end, just looking around, not saying a word. Oh, Georgie, it's pulling all the life out of him, all the will to recover."

"You know I want to help," Georgina murmured. "You know I'll do all I can."

Sarah slowly straightened, still sniffing. "Yes, I know. You've always been a good girl." She managed a watery smile. "But you can't marry Trayne. He's much too homely." She sniffed again and giggled. "Even closing your eyes and thinking of Shanley wouldn't help. And if it did—I couldn't bear to have such ugly grandchildren!"

Georgina smiled, loving her mother more at that moment than she ever had before.

Chapter Nine

The main building at Shanley had two back staircases in addition to the grand double stairway in the entry hall, a remnant of the days when the servants' quarters had been located in the basement story of the house. One of them was just off Sarah's sitting room, so Georgina took it upstairs. Had she gone the way she'd come—down the grand stairway, past the parlor and library—she would have run into Mike, who was listening outside Sarah's door. He didn't make a habit of eavesdroping, but when he'd heard somebody pass the library so late at night, his curiosity had gotten the better of him and he'd followed. In the end, he hadn't been able to tear himself away from Sarah's door.

He wasn't sure what to make of what she'd said. Could a mere house be so important to these people? Maybe so, given the English attachment to land. He was even willing to believe that Sarah was worried about the earl's progress, but her behavior also smacked of out-and-out manipulation.

First she'd tried to tell Georgina she was sexually repressed, and when that hadn't worked, she'd gone on the attack. Mike had felt warm all over when Georgina had defended him so vehemently, but he'd dismissed it as pleasure that she was standing up for herself so well. He didn't want to admit that it might be something more.

Attacking Georgina hadn't worked either, so Sarah had tried tears and apologies next. Her theatrics had done the trick—Georgina was back in line now. She would find herself a wealthy husband because to do anything else was to consign her father to a deathly decline and rob her brother of his birthright. Mike cynically told himself that Sarah couldn't possibly care that a fat-cat son-in-law would also provide her with a more comfortable life.

After such a heartwarming scene of reconciliation he expected things to be warmer on Sunday, but it kept on raining and Sarah kept pointing out her children's shortcomings. At times Mike wanted to take Anastasia aside and tell her to shut her daughter up, but he knew it was none of his business. He told himself to stay out of it.

Of course, Mike had never been very good at that. His silence took its toll in the form of anger and frustration. He was sensitive to Georgina's moods now, and he could tell how disappointed she was that her mother wasn't being kinder. Every little remark seemed to hit her twice as hard, until even John's sardonic comments couldn't get a smile out of her.

She was poignantly subdued after he'd left to return to school. Mike sensed their relationship had changed during the weekend. The little brother Georgina had loved and protected was growing up, and now that he was bigger and stronger than she was, he'd started protecting *her*. John was a good kid, bright and responsible, and the fierce love

Georgina felt for him put additional pressure on her. She didn't want him to inherit a pile of rubble.

It was ironic how much pointless worrying Mike had done. Georgina was much too busy fighting her own private battles to chase after *him*. The earlier sexual tension between them had all but disappeared.

He didn't realize that something far more dangerous was happening. He and Georgina were inching their way into each other's emotions. But Anastasia could see it clearly, and she was very satisfied indeed. The trip to England was turning out even better than she'd hoped.

On Monday morning, Georgina looked out the window, saw the bright sunshine, and sighed in relief. They could finally get down to work. But the relief turned to dismay when she looked in the mirror. The tension showed in her face. So did the pain. So did the restless nights. She looked a mess.

Fortunately she had Anastasia to do her makeup, and nobody was better with makeup than her grandmother. By the time everyone trooped out to the meadow where they would be shooting the artwork, Georgina had convinced herself that Jeremy would manage to hide the lines and shadows. He was a wonderful photographer, and besides, Mike had told her she looked beautiful.

Actually Mike thought she looked exquisite, not simply beautiful. He loved it when she wore her hair loose. He loved her dress, too, a soft yellow shift trimmed in feminine white lace. She would have been the picture of innocence if it hadn't been for the way the fabric clung when she was still and rustled when she moved. The combination of purity and sensuality took his breath away.

Still, the picture would be a bear to shoot. They wanted her hair and dress to billow in the breeze, but breezes didn't always cooperate. They wanted a special expression on her face—expectant but wary, with all the restless yearning of a woman with a bad case of spring fever. The setting was glorious, a fresh green meadow scattered with wildflowers, but the setting couldn't be allowed to overshadow their model. Everything about Georgina had to be so evocative that the customer would take one look at her and understand how she felt.

She had to be in the proper mood. She had to be able to block out the camera and become the Corona woman. Distractions were the last thing she needed, but with her mother fussing over her father and commenting on everything from Georgina's hips to her hair, distractions were inevitable.

Mike hadn't wanted her parents to come, but they had insisted. They had been there the last time, they said, and things had gone just fine. But Georgina hadn't suffered through three days of rain the last time. Mike knew there would be problems within the first minute, when Sarah turned to Jeremy and said sweetly, "Can you do anything about the smudges under her eyes, dear?"

Jeremy had assured her he could, but a few minutes later she was at it again. "Her mouth is tight. Don't you think so, Mother?" She raised her voice. "Jeremy, there's no point fussing with her hair if she's going to grimace that way. Really, darling, you look as if you're thinking about Geoffrey Barrett, not the Essex man."

Georgina closed her eyes for a second and then pleaded with Anastasia to help. "This is very difficult, Grandmother."

Anastasia brushed the complaint aside. "Everything will be fine, Georgie. Just do as Jeremy says."

"If you could all be a little quieter—"

"We're only trying to help," Sarah said. "Am I annoying you, Jeremy?"

The photographer smiled. "How could you annoy me, Lady Medshire? You're like a rare diamond, set amidst the splendor of Shanley. You light up the meadow with your loveliness.''

Mike could understand why Jeremy wouldn't want to offend the countess, but what was Anastasia's excuse? Sarah's comments were getting on Georgina's nerves—anyone could see that. At the rate they were going she would never be able to relax.

Jeremy started shooting again, sprinkling his instructions with flowery compliments intended to loosen his model up. Although Sarah's interruptions came less often, Georgina got tenser than ever. Mike started to think they were wasting their time. The Corona woman looked as if she was ready to have a nervous breakdown, not fall in love.

Georgina was trying her best, but she had a miserable headache and was so vexed with Anastasia she could have throttled her. Why wasn't she shutting Sarah up? She had the last time, and that earlier series of pictures hadn't been nearly so difficult to shoot.

She winced when her mother came out with another negative comment, reacting as much to Sarah's critical tone as to her words. ''You're slouching, Georgina. Jeremy, can't you see she's slouching?''

''I would do better if I only had to listen to one person,'' Georgina pointed out.

Sarah pursed her lips. ''But Jeremy didn't tell you what you were doing wrong. Somebody had to.''

''But not you, Mother.'' Georgina struggled to keep her temper. ''Please, let Jeremy do his job. Your criticism isn't helping. It only makes me nervous.''

''Criticism? Good heavens, dear, don't be so sensitive. If we don't explain what you're doing wrong—''

''I know what I'm doing wrong,'' Georgina interrupted. ''I don't need you to tell me. Please, just be quiet.''

The earl, who had been his usual taciturn self, coughed and frowned. "You have no cause to talk to your mother that way," he said sternly. "She was only trying to help."

Georgina had been raised to show respect for her parents, but she could only take so much. "She can help by either leaving or keeping her mouth closed," she snapped.

The earl reddened. "I'll remind you where you are, miss. On my property. This is no longer your home, and if you wish to be welcome here, you will behave in a proper manner. Tell your mother you're sorry."

No longer her home? The words hit Georgina like a slap in the face. Hadn't her father heard the things her mother had said or the tone she'd repeatedly used? Didn't he care what was fair or who was right?

Her throat was so tight with hurt and outrage it was hard to speak. "I didn't realize it wasn't my home any longer. I suppose I'm not your daughter, either, if I say something you don't agree with."

He dismissed her statement with a wave of his hand. "I told you to apologize."

Georgina bit her lip. She didn't see why she should apologize. She wasn't in the wrong here.

"I'm waiting," her father said.

Georgina had spent a lifetime placating her parents, hoping they would love her if only she was good enough, and it was a hard habit to break. She felt herself weaken, then cursed herself for being spineless. She might have been rude but her mother had started it.

She stared at the earl, challenging him for the first time in years. "And if I don't do what you want, Father? Am I still your daughter?"

She'd never seen him look so angry. "No."

She suddenly felt very cold, all except for her eyes, which were hot with unshed tears. For the life of her, she couldn't manage a word. And then, before she could quite take it in,

Mike was standing with his arm around her, talking to her father in an icily sarcastic voice. "With all due respect, your lordship, if it isn't Georgina's home and she's not your daughter, why the hell is she chasing after a rich husband to pump a fortune into the place?"

The earl didn't answer. He suddenly looked gray and exhausted. But Sarah came charging to the rescue with the fury of an enraged tornado. "You impertinent bastard! You're not a member of this family and we have absolutely no interest in your opinions. Get your hands off my daughter and get out of here."

"*You're* neither a director of Corona Cosmetics nor an employee of Conlin & Napoli," Mike retorted, "so *I* have no interest in *your* opinions—or in your orders."

Sarah's outraged, "You arrogant swine!" was drowned out by Anastasia's laughter. "Don't waste your breath, Sarah. He may be an arrogant swine, but he has a point."

The earl visibly collected himself. "Perhaps so, but I won't have him insulting my wife. He happens to be a guest in my home, and if he wants to stay there—"

"Your wife happens to be a beneficiary in my will," Anastasia said, "and if *she* wants to stay there she'll admit that none of us has behaved especially well. Take Georgie for a walk, Mike, and see if you can calm her down. We'll try again after lunch."

Georgina was relieved to escape. She started toward a round stone temple that had always been a favorite spot of hers. It was quiet and private inside, and unlike most of the other follies and buildings in the park, still contained a few pieces of furniture. It wasn't far from where they'd been shooting, but instinct probably would have led her there anyway.

"I used to come here as a child," she said as she led Mike inside.

"To lick your wounds?" he asked.

Georgina felt a rush of conflicting emotions—pain, anger, guilt, shock. She couldn't begin to deal with them, not after years of ignoring or repressing them, so she changed the subject. "I never believed all those stories about how rude you were to your clients, but after the things you said to my parents..." She smiled as they sat down on a loveseat. "Your brother-in-law must have his hands full mending fences."

"Tact isn't my strong suit," he admitted. "Three days of keeping my mouth shut while your mother chiseled away at your ego was as much as I could stomach."

"I'm sure she doesn't mean to be cruel," Georgina said. "She just doesn't realize how she sounds. And my father is very old-fashioned, so naturally if anybody raises their voice to her, even John or I, he rushes to protect her."

The look Mike gave her cut through her rationalizations. "Are you always so forgiving?"

Georgina dropped her eyes. "I have to be. They're the only parents I've got."

"And you think that if you could only be perfect enough they would love you. You're afraid to challenge them because they might reject you. So you've killed yourself all these years trying to please them, and when you don't succeed you blame yourself, even though it's obvious who has the real problem."

Georgina started to tremble. He hadn't said anything she hadn't secretly thought, but it was devastating to hear it spoken aloud. "I suppose you think I'm a fool," she said hoarsely, "or a weakling, at least, to keep caring, to keep trying, to tell myself it can be better...."

"What I think is that your parents have done an expert head job on you." He put a finger under her chin and coaxed her to meet his eyes. There was anger on his face, but she knew it wasn't for her. He really cared, just as he did about his sisters.

"I overheard the conversation you had with your mother the other night," he continued. "I was still in the library when you went by. Maybe I shouldn't have followed and listened, but I did. And I could tell that your mother knew exactly what strings to pull to get you to do what she wants. Your parents seem to have one overriding concern, Georgina—each other—and it's made them incredibly insensitive to anyone else's rights or feelings. They've apparently convinced you you were put on this earth to serve them, that as their child it's your solemn duty to do what they want, but in my opinion that's bull. Love and loyalty should be a two-way street. If they want it from you, they should damn well give it back."

"But they're not monsters," Georgina said defensively. "They always bought me the nicest clothes and sent me to the best schools—"

"Sure they did. How could they have held up their heads in polite society otherwise?" He paused, then added gently, "Your family is supposed to be there for you, honey. When life knocks you down, they're supposed to lift you back up. When things go wrong, you should be able to call them, even in the middle of the night, and know they'll drop everything to listen and sympathize. Who took care of you when you hurt yourself as a kid? Whose shoulder did you cry on when your teacher did something that wasn't fair, or you and your best friend got into a terrible fight, or you lost when you had your heart set on winning?"

Not Georgina's parents. Not even once. "My first nanny, at least until she died. My grandmother, of course. My brother, when he was old enough. And a special friend or two." Deep down Georgina had always known that, but she'd never permitted herself to acknowledge it before. "My parents have always found it hard to—to relate to me and John, but I'm sure they love us in their way."

"Why shouldn't they? You're always giving and they're always taking. Your mother uses emotional blackmail to get what she wants—your father's health, your brother's future, your duty to English history, and God knows what else. If you want to help your parents, fine, but you're entitled to get something in return. *Entitled* to it, Georgina. If you've never gotten it in all these years, maybe you should take a long hard look at whether you want to keep giving."

"But they're my parents," Georgina said plaintively. "How can I just write them off? I love them."

Mike sighed and put his arm around her. "Yeah, honey, I know. But they cause you a lot of pain. There's an old saying—if you lie down on the floor, people are going to use you as a doormat. Assert yourself and the results may surprise you. But if the worst happens and your parents cut you off, maybe you need to ask yourself exactly how much you've lost."

He was right, of course. Logically Georgina knew that, but logic had little to do with human emotions. How could she risk so much? Suppose she lost the gamble? The pain would crush her. She would have to face the fact that she'd wasted twenty-five years seeking what she could never have, that she didn't matter to the two people whose approval she most yearned for. The thought was too threatening to bear.

"I envy you," she said. "You have such a close family. Do you have any idea how lucky you are?"

"I never forget it," he answered.

Georgina sighed and leaned against his shoulder. He was such a complicated man! He spoke so feelingly about families and what they should do for each other, but it didn't occur to him that the same rules should apply to other relationships. It was mystifying.

"I don't understand you," she said. "If you really believe the things you've said about giving and taking, how could you have treated Terry Hall so shabbily? He was your friend, your mentor. Didn't he deserve better?"

"Better than what?" Mike sounded totally baffled. "Are you saying it was wrong to leave his agency?"

"No, but you should have been honest with him. It wasn't fair—"

"Wait a minute. Just hold it." He frowned in annoyance and straightened up. "Exactly what am I supposed to have done?"

"I heard he was planning to make you a partner. You led him to think you would accept, then learned everything you could from him and walked out."

"And you believed that?"

"My grandmother said—"

"Your grandmother says a lot of things. I asked you if you believed it."

Georgina felt very unsure of herself. Mike wasn't curt with her very often, but when he was, her stomach always started to churn. "Well, I did wonder, especially after you and Terry were so friendly to each other, but she told me the story twice and I knew how ambitious you were and it didn't seem so terribly out of character—based on what I knew about you, that is."

"Based on what you knew," he repeated. "You can tell me what you *think* you knew in a minute, but first..." He rubbed the back of his neck, looking so angry she shrank away from him.

Her withdrawal made Mike even angrier, but at himself, not at her. He had no right to attack her. Of course she'd believed Anastasia. It was only natural to trust someone she loved.

"I told Terry Hall I wanted to start my own agency within six months of the day he hired me," he said evenly. "And you know what he answered? That he'd be one of my investors. He meant it, too. He repeated the offer when Rich and I made our move, but we decided not to accept. We wanted to do things our own way, to maintain our independence. Once we're firmly established, we'll talk to him again. Terry likes the idea of owning a piece of a small, creative shop and we could use his investment money to expand into some areas that would have to wait much longer without it. We were friendly at your grandmother's house because we're still very close. I don't deny being ambitious, but success at any price..." He paused and shook his head. "That's not me, Georgina. I don't stab my friends in the back."

Georgina knew Mike was telling the truth. His story fit the facts and Anastasia's didn't. But why had her grandmother lied? Why did she persist in giving Georgina the worst possible impression of him? It was almost as if she wanted her to dislike him.

"It's odd," she said, "but my grandmother never lies to me except where you're concerned. Why do you suppose that is?"

Mike shrugged. "Maybe because we're together so much. Don't forget, she told me to keep away from you. She's probably afraid something will happen."

Georgina couldn't imagine why Anastasia would object. "But she likes you."

"As a copywriter and a dinner guest, maybe. Not as someone to take you out." Now that Mike thought about it, the pieces fit perfectly. "She obviously has my number, Georgina. My agency is my first priority. I'm not interested in marriage, but even if I were, I'd be a terrible husband— a workaholic with no money. Your grandmother didn't trust me not to make a pass at you so she tried to convince you I wasn't the kind of guy you wanted to get mixed up with. That happens to be true, but not for the reasons she gave."

Georgina supposed it made a crazy kind of sense, especially given Anastasia's devious turn of mind. "She wants us to be friends, though. She must think you'll encourage me to stand up to my parents more—that some of your legendary arrogance will rub off on me.''

Mike broke into a grin. "*My* arrogance? Hell, lady, you can be as imperious as the queen when you want to be. You could give *me* lessons.''

He was obviously referring to how cold she'd been at first, but she was reluctant to go into that just then. She'd had enough confrontations that day.

"I suppose we should go," she said, and started to get up. "Lunch will be waiting."

Mike caught her by the wrist and pulled her back down. "Not so fast, your ladyship. A minute ago you said it wouldn't be out of character for me to screw one of my best friends—based on what you knew about me. What did you mean?"

One look at the determination on his face and Georgina knew she wouldn't escape without answering. "We have a mutual friend," she murmured. "It's not important. We should really get up to lunch . . ."

"Obviously it *is* important. What friend? What did he tell you?"

"She," Georgina corrected. "Her name is Jill Eliott—actually, Jill Stafford now. She lives in California, but we still keep up."

His reaction was immediate and dramatic. He stiffened and turned a dull red. Not only hadn't he forgotten what had happened six years before; he was still deeply affected by it. But how? Was he angry? Embarrassed? Guilty?

"I hope she's happy," he mumbled.

There was no backing away from it. Mike had forced the issue and he was going to have to explain. "She is now," Georgina said. "She wasn't six years ago."

"You met her in Paris?"

She nodded. "We were in school together. We shared an apartment for three years. She told me everything."

"And you've kept in touch? You're still close?"

"Very close."

She and Jill had been in several of the same classes at the University of Paris six years ago, but they hadn't been friends. Jill had barely spoken to other people in those days. Then Georgina had moved into her own apartment and started looking around for a roommate, and much to her surprise, Jill had timidly expressed an interest.

She was a polite, quiet girl who took her studies seriously, as did Georgina. She was also a wonderful tennis player, much too good for Georgina, really, but Georgina loved the game and hoped Jill would help her improve. So the two of them had gotten together, and little by little Jill's barriers began to drop.

Georgina got to know the real Jill Eliott, a girl who was as warm and generous as any she'd met. The deep sadness in Jill, the impression she gave that her life was a constant struggle, had been put there by a man named Mike Napoli.

Jill had met him in a doctor's office, but it hadn't been an ordinary doctor. Mike was a football player with a knee problem, Jill was a tennis player with a shoulder problem, and the doctor was a famous sports medicine specialist. He saw each of them regularly, on Thursday afternoons, so they kept running into each other in his waiting room. Within weeks they had struck up a friendship.

Jill had admitted to Georgina that she'd immediately hoped for more, but she knew there wasn't much of a chance of it. She was an eighteen-year-old Radcliffe freshman with very little worldly experience while Mike was twenty-two and in his fifth year at Boston College. He'd missed an entire football season due to a knee injury and was playing out his eligibility. As a star athlete he had dozens of girls chasing him, and Jill knew he took full advantage of it. She also knew he'd put her in a different category than those other women—she was an honorary little sister, a fellow jock, a pal. She and Mike could talk to each other. Both had the same sorts of problems, the same frustrations, and it gave them a common bond that drew them very close.

Then, that May, Mike had made a sudden cut upfield during a football scrimmage and wound up prostrate on the turf. He'd known at once that it was worse than the ligament and cartilage problems that had plagued him in the past; this time his lower left leg was paralyzed. The next morning, the doctor opened up his knee and found total chaos inside. Not only was there extensive joint damage; the nerve that controlled his foot had been stretched so badly that the doctor doubted he would ever walk normally again. But even if some miracle occurred and he made an exceptional recovery, he would still never be fast enough to play professional football. Even to try it was to invite a permanent disability.

He was so depressed at first that Jill worried he might try to harm himself. She even stayed in Boston once school was out just so she could drag him to movies and ball games. His leg was still paralyzed and encased in a cast from toe to thigh, but Jill kept telling him not to worry. The nerve would regenerate and he would walk again.

As the summer wore on, something special began to develop between them—or so Jill hoped. There were very few people Mike cared to see—just Jill, his closest friends from the team and his sister Bianca. Of all the family, only Bianca had the knack of saying the right thing and getting him to laugh, so she came more often than the others. As a result, Jill got to know her fairly well.

It took time, but Mike finally accepted the fact that he would never play professional football. And then, in late July, he moved his left little toe for the first time. Jill and

Bianca were both there to see it, and decided a celebration was in order. They held the party at Mike's parents' house and invited every friend and relative they could think of.

At that party, the thing Jill had prayed for finally happened. Mike woke up and realized she was a woman, not just one of the guys. Midway through the evening, he pulled her down on his lap in full view of everyone and smiled in a way that was anything but brotherly, and later that night, after the party broke up, he took her in his arms and kissed her for the first time.

She was so giddy with happiness she could hardly sleep. But Mike was alternately distant and impatient over the next several days, and less than a week later called her and told her not to come over anymore—he didn't want to see her again. He refused to give her an explanation over the phone and wouldn't let her inside when she came to see him in person. Her letters were returned unopened. Miserable and distraught, she asked Bianca what was wrong, but Bianca had no idea. Mike wouldn't discuss it with her, either.

For Jill, the rejection was doubly devastating. She had lost the man she loved and her best friend, all at the same time. She had nobody to turn to for support and comfort. Her parents were divorced and their parting had been so bitter that her father had either walked out of her life or been thrown out by her mother, she wasn't sure which. She'd finally gotten back in touch with him again, but the relationship was new and fragile.

As for her mother, the two of them had never gotten along, especially after Dina's remarriage to a man Jill disliked. And then, to make matters worse, her stepfather's bank had failed and the authorities began an investigation. Jill was falling apart, and now she had to cope with hysterical phone calls from Dina two and three times a day. So, not knowing where else to turn, she blindly reached out to her father.

She was terrified he was going to reject her. She was nothing to him, really, except perhaps biologically. She longed to be close to him but the reverse wasn't true, and she was afraid if she asked too much she might lose him forever.

But William Eliott had come through for her with flying colors. His company had scheduled him for a transfer to Paris and at first he wasn't going to go, but then he decided to go ahead with the move and take Jill along. He felt the change of scene would do her good. It would also take her away from the man who had hurt her and put a stop to her mother's phone calls.

Jill had been badly wounded when Georgina had first met her, but she'd gradually picked up the pieces of her life. Eventually her father had introduced her to a young executive at his company and they had fallen in love and married. Her husband worked in Los Angeles now, and both he and Jill loved California. In the end, things had worked out wonderfully.

Still, Mike's behavior had been unforgivable. Knowing how sweet Jill was, Georgina had found it inexplicable that this man Mike Napoli could have been so cruel, so callous. He owed Jill his life but he hadn't even had the decency to explain why he'd cut her off so viciously.

Knowing Mike as she did now, Georgina understood it even less. "You nearly destroyed her," she said. "She loved you more than you can imagine, and what you did to her haunted her for years. I thought you must be the wickedest man in the world, to behave as badly as you did. Why, Mike? What happened?"

Mike was literally shaking. He felt sick to his stomach. Of all the crazy coincidences, Georgina had to know Jill Eliott. No, not just know her—the two of them were close friends. How in hell did he handle this?

He knew Jill. She was sweet and warm—and also incredibly tenacious. If she even suspected Georgina knew anything about six years ago, she would press and press until she got the details. And Georgina—Georgina was one of the most transparent liars he'd ever met. He couldn't possibly tell her the truth because as sure as he was sitting here, Jill would worm it out of her.

He had no choice. The truth could only cause Jill more pain, and she didn't need that. She was more than entitled to the happiness she'd apparently found.

"I'm not going to answer that," he said. "I can't." He swallowed hard, finding the memories incredibly painful. The guilt would never go away—never. Neither would the sense of helplessness, of misery and confusion. "I know how much I hurt her. I didn't want to but I didn't know what else to do. Please believe that, Georgina."

Georgina stared at him, openly shocked. He was in agony. The events of six years ago had hurt him as much as they'd hurt Jill. She couldn't begin to imagine what had compelled him to behave the way he had, but obviously he'd felt there was no choice.

She reached out a tentative hand and lightly touched his face. "I do," she said softly. The pain in his eyes tore at her heart.

Chapter Ten

Mike had sometimes wondered if Sarah Philipps was even capable of controlling her tongue, and at lunch he got his answer. Even though he and Georgina showed up during dessert, Sarah merely smiled and invited them to sit down, saying they must be famished. She and the earl proceeded to act as if the argument in the meadow had never taken place.

They might have been afraid Anastasia would cut them out of her will if they didn't toe the mark, or they might have recognized Georgina's growing independence and decided she would rebel completely if they couldn't win her back. Whatever the reason, their behavior showed a marked improvement. They even had the good sense to go to their apartment after lunch rather than returning to the shoot.

Without her parents there, Georgina was able to relax and concentrate. By the time they lost the light, Jeremy was sure they had the first ad in the can. He promised to develop the film that evening and bring the proofs along the next morning for Anastasia to look through.

Mike had noticed the first morning that Sarah could charm everyone's socks off when she wanted to. After an hour of playing the high-society hostess to perfection, she led everyone into the drawing room for music and more conversation. When Georgina finished playing she was the first to applaud. "That was wonderful, darling. I only wish John had your talent—not that I'm criticizing, you understand, because he has talents of his own, but it's such a joy to have a musical child." Mike caught Georgina's eye, saw the twinkle there, and coughed to cover his laughter. Sarah was incredible. Even when she tried her hardest, she couldn't help complaining.

"Music," Anastasia said with a nod. "Remember the ad with the pianist and the violinist, where the accompanist's perfume drives the soloist so mad he all but assaults the poor woman?" She looked at Mike. "I don't suppose you play the violin?"

Mike laughed and shook his head. "I'm afraid not."

"A pity, but on to more practical matters. We've got to come up with something for the third and fourth ads. Your mock-ups were adequate, but not—extraordinary. You were simply standing there. It was boring."

"Mother, really!" Sarah scolded. "I'm sure they weren't boring."

"Yes, they were," Anastasia insisted. "It would take more to captivate the Corona woman than some man in a sweater trespassing in her meadow."

"That depends on the man," Georgina said with a wink.

Anastasia looked Mike up and down in a way he was all too familiar with. He wasn't an advertising man in her eyes anymore; he was a hunk of Essex beefcake. "Well, yes," she said, "I suppose there's a certain amount of truth in that, but still, it's not dramatic enough. I wish I could think of something more interesting.''

She sighed disconsolately, but then, in a lightning change of mood, bolted up and darted over to Mike. "Get up." Her hand traced impatient circles in the air. "Turn around. That's it. Hmm, yes, that might do nicely."

The next thing Mike knew, she was grabbing him by the shoulders. "Your jacket. Let me have it."

"Talk about déjà vu," he drawled as he handed it over. "If you're going to complain about my tailoring again—"

"It's hopeless. We've already established that." She tossed the jacket onto a chair. "Now the shirt."

"You want me to take it off?" he asked.

"Of course I do. What else would I mean? That you should prance around the drawing room modeling it?"

With Anastasia you never knew, but if she wanted Mike to take off the shirt, he would take off the shirt. Georgina promptly rushed back to the piano and started to pound out a honky-tonk striptease tune.

He'd barely gotten the shirt unbuttoned when Anastasia prodded him to continue. "Keep going, Michael, that's it, the undershirt, too." The music got louder and more raucous and the pianist began to giggle.

Blushing, Mike pulled off his undershirt and tossed it aside. When Georgina called out, "More! More!" even the earl cracked a smile. Mike folded his arms across his chest and tried to look dignified. "That's as far as I go. Now do you mind telling me what this is all about?"

"Make him take off his trousers, too, Grandmother!" Georgina begged. "I'm sure he has marvelous legs."

The dirty look Mike gave her rolled right off her back. She was enjoying the show immensely, and her laughter and teasing had the usual effect on Mike's blood pressure. He couldn't have taken off his pants even if he'd wanted to— not in mixed company, anyway.

"I haven't decided about his legs," Anastasia said, deadpan. "That might be going too far. Come over here, Georgie, I want to see the two of you together."

Georgina obediently got up. She thought Mike was adorable when he blushed, although *adorable* was probably too tame a word. Lord, what a splendid body he had! Broad shoulders and a muscular chest and arms, but still lean enough not to look like an overbuilt caveman. He didn't bulge; he rippled. It was a good thing he *hadn't* removed his trousers, because she could only bear so much.

There had been long stretches during the past several days when she had forgotten how attractive he was, but she doubted she would forget it again. Things were going too well, both with her modeling and her parents. With her private hurts and disappointments no longer preoccupying her, the door had been opened to thoughts and feelings she'd been too upset to notice before.

She had first realized it when she and Mike were in the temple. It should have depressed her to confront so many hard truths about her life, but all she'd been able to think about afterward was him. He hadn't double-crossed Terry Hall. He hadn't wanted to hurt Jill. He wasn't a selfish, callous man with no regard for anyone but his family. She'd suspected as much from the way he'd treated her, but it was still a relief to have it confirmed. She didn't want to think she had chosen an utter bounder as a friend.

Friend. What a fraud she was! She had felt far more than friendship when Mike had put his arm around her to comfort her this afternoon. She had never teased a male *friend* the way she'd teased him tonight, or found that her thoughts about a male *friend* were drifting into embarrassing fantasies. Somehow she had to channel her emotions in a more productive direction.

Her head snapped up at the sound of her grandmother's voice. "Don't daydream, Georgina. Hurry and get over here. Inspiration isn't something to trifle with."

"And that's why I'm standing here half-naked?" Mike asked. "Because you're inspired?"

"You know perfectly well what I have in mind," she retorted.

Mike didn't bother to deny it. "You're damn right I do, and in my opinion, you've seen too many Obsession ads."

"Don't be ridiculous. I'm not going to strip you down to your underwear and tangle you up until nobody can tell whose legs are whose." She gave a disapproving sniff. "The Corona woman is not a trollop. That's far enough, Georgie. Now stare at his mouth as if you're wondering if he could be the one you want."

"Under the circumstances, Mother, I doubt she'd be looking at his *mouth*," Sarah drawled.

Georgina had to agree—she could barely tear her eyes from Mike's chest. Anastasia conceded the point and began moving Georgina and Mike around. She couldn't seem to decide which pose was best—Mike stroking Georgina's cheek, Georgina caressing his arm, or the two of them holding each other lightly and gazing into each other's eyes. Georgina had never known her to be so ambivalent.

In the meantime, Georgina and Mike were getting hot enough for spontaneous combustion to take place. Mike didn't know which was more exciting—the aching pleasure of touching and being touched or the knowledge that he was helpless to ease the pain. Wanting Georgina so badly and denying himself was the most arousing kind of torture he'd ever endured.

As for Georgina, she was so dizzy from the scent and feel of Mike that she could barely take in Anastasia's instructions. Her mind was a million miles away, or perhaps only upstairs in Mike's bedroom, tangled up with him on the bed like the model in those Obsession perfume ads.

Anastasia suddenly snapped her fingers. "I've got it! I don't mean to offend you, Mike dear, but the Essex man has to be larger than life and you, alas, are only ordinary flesh and blood. It's not dramatic enough to have you simply stand there, but if we put you on a horse..." She looked at her son-in-law. "Anthony, is Hellfire in the stables?"

The earl, taciturn as usual, nodded. "He'll be cross, though. The rain, you know. Wants riding."

Mike now knew the meaning of the phrase, "It was like looking into your own coffin." He'd had a run-in with a horse once and had kept his distance ever since. "Wait a minute," he said. "I've never been on a horse in my life. You're not putting me on an animal named Hellfire who's in a bad mood because he's been stuck in his stall lately. No way."

"Never been on a horse?" Anastasia said. "Don't be absurd. Everybody rides."

"Not where I come from." Mike reached for his clothing and started to put it on. "Horses are something you bet on, not something you chase around after foxes on."

Anastasia wasn't one to give up. "We'll just have to teach you, then. You'll pick it up in no time. After all, you're a superb athlete."

"I played baseball and football. I stayed on the ground where people belong. If God had meant us to ride horses, he would have given us saddles instead of, uh..."

"Derrières?" Georgina suggested.

"Whatever," he muttered.

Anastasia sighed and told him not to be difficult. Surely he could see what a splendid picture it would make—the Corona woman gazing upward at a shirtless hunk of beefcake astride a magnificent stallion? Could anything be more quintessentially male? It was the Essex man to a tee.

Mike would have loved to disagree, but the professional in him could see she was right. A tough-looking stranger on a horse appearing out of nowhere and captivating a wary but susceptible woman—it was a very erotic image. As Anastasia's advertising man, he had to be in favor of whatever would sell her products.

"Okay, you win," he said. "We'll go with the horse, but somebody else will have to ride him. There's no way I can learn—"

"But of course you can," Anastasia insisted. "Georgie is a wonderful horsewoman and a splendid teacher. A few lessons and you'll be all set. Georgie should put him on Buttercup to begin with, don't you think so, Anthony?"

"She's gentle," the earl agreed. "Wouldn't hurt a fly."

Mike began to weaken. He realized his fears were largely irrational, and besides, a horse named Buttercup was a lot more to his liking than one named Hellfire. He was willing to try a few lessons and see how it went. "If Georgina can teach me enough to get the horse to cooperate, fine, but remember, we're talking about hours of standing around. The horse could get too restless for me to handle. You should line up an experienced rider as a backup."

"I'm sure that won't be necessary," Anastasia said. "Georgina taught John, and he was by no means a natural horseman. Isn't that so, darling?"

"I can teach Mike what he'll need to know," Georgina replied. She wasn't sure whether she should welcome the prospect or dread it. The lessons would get her out of the house and give her something to do, but the thought of having Mike to herself for all those hours was far too exciting. When was she going to stop hankering after what she couldn't have?

Jeremy Reade joined them for breakfast the next morning, arriving with dozens of proofs. Georgina looked a little tired in most of them, a little haunted, but so would anyone with a bad case of spring fever. The challenge now was to get a completely different feel in the artwork for the second ad. Georgina had to pretend she'd spotted the Essex man in the distance and convey a mixture of wariness and longing.

She could have done it in her sleep. She felt the same mixture of emotions when she looked at Mike as the Corona woman was supposed to feel for the Essex man. For as long as the session lasted, she permitted herself to use those emotions the same way an actress would have used a tragic event from her past to make herself cry on cue. Things went so well they were finished by lunchtime.

The earl and countess were supposed to be in London for the day, but Georgina arrived back at the house to learn that her father had taken ill and was resting in his room. Sarah felt it was best not to disturb him for a few hours, so Georgina decided to go ahead into lunch, give Mike his riding lesson, and visit the earl in the late afternoon.

About an hour later, down in the stables, she introduced Mike to Buttercup and witnessed the most dubious pair of looks she had ever seen two creatures exchange. Buttercup warmed to Mike after Georgina persuaded him to feed the mare a few pieces of apple, but the reverse was decidedly not the case. "And here I thought football players were fearless," she teased. "What do you expect her to do? Bite you? Kick you? Run off with you?"

"I'm not that rational about it," Mike said. Maybe he had a reason for being scared, but he considered it a pretty dumb reason. "When I was eight or nine, my parents took me to an anti-war demonstration. The crowd got kind of wild and they called in the mounted police to restore order. People were everywhere, running and shouting, and I panicked and ran away from my parents. One of the horses knocked me sideways, but somebody grabbed me before I hit the ground and handed me up to the cop who was riding him.''

"You should have told me that before," Georgina said. "Were you hurt?"

"No, just terrified. It seemed so high off the ground."

"And you were separated from your parents," Georgina pointed out, "so naturally it made a strong impression. We'll take it very slowly—let you get used to Buttercup before you ride her."

Over the next several minutes Mike decided that Buttercup had nothing in common with those huge black police horses. She was docile and friendly, her only apparent vice a habit of nibbling at the local wildflowers as he walked her around the corral. He finally screwed up his courage and climbed into the saddle, then found he kind of liked it. It reminded him of the cowboy shows he'd grown up with. A man felt like a hero on a horse.

They were making their way through the meadow, with Georgina leading the way on a mare named Cinnabar, when Mike saw a large black horse thunder by in the distance. "That's Hellfire," Georgina said. "Alfred—our head stableman—will see he gets the exercise he needs. Don't worry, he'll be ready for you by tomorrow."

At first Mike doubted he'd be ready for Hellfire, but as the lesson proceeded his confidence slowly grew. Georgina kept telling him how well he was doing, and besides, this riding business wasn't so tough. The horse did what he told it to—turn right, turn left, go faster, slow down. In fact, cantering through the meadow was a real kick.

Even so, he was relieved to call it a day by the time Georgina headed back. The orthopedic brace he wore when he exercised could only do so much, and his knee was getting sore from all the posting and gripping. He wanted to grab a quick shower and then ice it down.

"We'll give you another lesson on Buttercup in the morning and try you on Hellfire in the afternoon," Georgina said as they walked into Shanley Hall. "Anastasia was right, you know. You're a natural athlete with excellent instincts for riding. You and Hellfire will do very well together, I promise you."

"I'll hold you to it," Mike said. "If I break my neck and die, I'm going to sue you for all you're worth."

"In that case, you'd best wait till after I'm married." Georgina grinned at him and went off to her room to clean up. Then she headed for her parents' apartment to see how her father was coming along.

It wasn't unusual for the earl to suffer occasional setbacks, but he looked especially tired to Georgina's eyes and his mood seemed subdued to the point of depression. After a fifteen-minute visit she led her mother into the sitting room for a private conversation.

"In all honesty, Mother, I thought you were exaggerating his problems. He seemed to be getting on so well, but today..." Georgina shook her head. "Frankly, I'm worried. Have you thought of scheduling a few more sessions with the psychologist from the hospital?"

"He had some bad news," Sarah said. "It's nothing to worry about. He'll come out of it soon enough."

Georgina wasn't so sure. "What do you mean, bad news? What happened?"

"Have a look at the south tower some time. The entire facade needs repairs. Several estimates came into the office today and they were much higher than we had anticipated."

Sarah paused and smoothed her skirt. Georgina had seldom seen her look so ill at ease. "Actually, I've been meaning to speak to you," she continued. "You know how furious I was with you and Mike yesterday morning, but then your grandmother sat me down and—well, to be honest, she gave me the worst talking-to of my life." The next few sentences came out in a rush. "You must believe me, Georgina, I had no idea how beastly I was being to you and John. I've always—that is, I suppose that even as a girl I was moody. Nothing ever suited me and I complained at the drop of a hat. But really, I *am* proud of you. Both of us are."

Georgina had waited twenty-five years to hear her mother say that. Emotion welled up inside her. "Thank you for telling me. You can't imagine how much it means."

"I think I can." Sarah was almost as pale as her husband now. "Georgina, I know how you adore your grand-mother, but please try to understand . . . I had a miserable childhood—no father and a mother who devoted all her time to business. I suppose that's why I acted as I did—to try to get her attention. Not that I usually succeeded, of course." Sarah paused a moment to compose herself. "They say when you haven't had enough love from your parents you turn around and do the exact same thing to your chil-dren. If I've failed you, I'm sorry."

Georgina wanted to throw her arms around her mother and hug her, but Sarah looked rigid and forbidding. It had been hard for her to explain herself and even harder to apologize. Giving her daughter some physical affection was the hardest thing of all, and quite beyond her.

"All of that's in the past," Georgina said briskly. "It doesn't do any good to dwell on it. Let's just try to under-stand each other better in the future."

Sarah nodded and got up, obviously relieved to have the conversation behind her. "I couldn't agree more, darling. I'll be dining in the apartment with your father tonight, so I won't see you at dinner. Will you stop in to say good-night before you go upstairs?"

"Yes, of course." Georgina gave her mother the usual dutiful kiss and headed toward the back stairway. Maybe she was finally growing up. She no longer felt cheated because of everything she'd never had. You had to take the bad in life with the good.

Her mother had never held her and most likely wouldn't now. She had never said "I love you." They would never talk the way Mike's sisters could probably talk to their mother, and the praise Georgina had always longed for would be as rare as ever.

But the feelings were there—caring and pride and even love—and it was suddenly enough. Georgina was beginning to realize that her parents had always needed her a great deal more than she'd needed them, and that startling insight made all the difference in the world.

Chapter Eleven

Georgina had intended to go straight to her room once she got upstairs, but she found herself stopping in front of Mike's door instead. She suddenly wanted to talk to him, to tell him what she had discovered. It hadn't been a one-way street with her parents after all. If she'd been a dutiful daughter these past few years, it was partly because she'd needed someone to need her. Looking after her parents had made her feel good about herself—like a worthwhile person. Deep down, she must have had some sense of how much she mattered to them, but she'd been so fixed on the outward signs of loving that she had never recognized the emotions underneath.

She gave a light knock, waited for Mike's invitation to come in, and then pushed open the door. "I was talking to my mother..." she began, but then her mother went straight out of her head. Mike was sitting in bed wearing nothing but a pair of gym shorts, reading the newspaper. His left knee was supported by several pillows and wrapped up in some sort of padding. She walked closer for a better look. "What's all that?"

"Ice," he said. "It cuts the swelling."

Georgina sat down on the bed, a little shaken. "Just from a few hours of riding?"

"It's not that bad." He unwrapped the ice bag and put it aside. "It's more of a precaution than anything else."

Georgina stared at his knee, looking at the scars. Obviously he was shading the truth. "Jill once mentioned you'd had serious nerve damage. Roger told me that everything that can go wrong with a joint—ligaments, cartilage, tendons—all of it went wrong with your knee at one time or another. It must get sore and swollen whenever you exercise. That's why you travel with a special ice bag."

Mike didn't enjoy talking about his knee. It brought back unpalatable memories of too many surgeries and too many rehabilitations, and of too many raised hopes that had been smashed by the next injury. "You were saying something about your mother," he reminded Georgina.

Georgina didn't care about her mother. She wanted to touch Mike's knee. His skin was red from the cold, and she wanted to smooth away the pain and warm the angry flesh. She raised her eyes to his thighs, which were so muscular they stretched the fabric of his gym shorts. He couldn't exercise too hard without paying a physical price, but he'd still kept in shape. No, not just in shape—in magnificent shape. She loved looking at him. If he touched her—if he decided he wanted to take her... Her mouth got dry just thinking about it.

Mike leaned back against the pillows and looked at the ceiling. He hated it when Georgina stared that way. Her thoughts were too transparent. If anyone had tried to tell him he could want a woman as much as he wanted her and refuse such an obvious invitation, he would have said they were crazy. He wasn't that much of a gentleman. But there was something so defenseless about Georgina that only a heel would have taken advantage of it.

He sighed and dropped his gaze. When their eyes met, it was like he'd stuck his finger in an electric socket. "I'm a little tired," he said. "Can the conversation wait?"

Georgina felt herself redden. She knew what he was really saying—that he understood what she was thinking but wasn't interested. It was another of his rejections, and, tactful or not, it stung.

She stiffened with embarrassment and stood up. "Of course it can. I'm sorry I disturbed you. I'll see you at dinner. Mother will be keeping Father company in their apartment, so it will just be the three of us." She started to explain about the south tower and how it needed repairs, then realized she was babbling and cut herself off. *You're an earl's daughter,* she reminded herself, *and earls' daughters don't run away from anything.* Smiling politely, she walked out of the room as regally as she could.

She was more careful after that. She made sure her comments at dinner were light and impersonal. When her grandmother retired early, she did the same. And the next morning, when she gave Mike his second riding lesson, she delivered her instructions crisply and left out the gushing praise. Not a minute went by when she didn't miss the closeness they had begun to share, but she told herself it was better that way.

Mike would have agreed if he'd had any idea what she was doing. As far as he could tell, she was punishing him for refusing to make a pass at her. He'd tried to act honorably and what was his reward? A full dose of Georgina as lady of the manor. Only a few weeks before she'd given him hell for daring to touch her, and now she was freezing him out for doing the opposite. The woman didn't know what she wanted.

By Wednesday afternoon her superior attitude had driven him to the brink of his rather limited tolerance. He wanted to knock some of the starch out of her, and not just with words. Five minutes in bed with him and she wouldn't be so snooty.

"You've done an adequate job with Buttercup," she said as they walked to the stables, "but Hellfire will take far more skill to control. He'll challenge you the first time you ride him, but once you've earned his respect, he should do whatever you ask." She proceeded to lecture him about the horse's quirks, stopping every now and then to fire out a question about how he would handle a particular situation. Mike had the feeling he'd get smacked across the knuckles with a riding crop if he gave the wrong answer.

Hellfire and Cinnabar were waiting with one of the grooms. Mike gave his horse a wary look—the stallion reminded him of those enormous black police horses from twenty years before. He was about to check the saddle when Georgina told him to recite everything you were supposed to do before you mounted up. His voice was clipped as he rattled off the answers.

"That's very good," she said. "You can go ahead now."

He folded his arms across his chest and gave her a level look. His patience had just run out. "Thank you for your permission, your ladyship. Are you sure you don't want me to bow to you first?"

Georgina hadn't heard that tone from Mike in weeks. She didn't like it any better now than she had before. "I understand that you're nervous," she said, "but that's no cause to be rude."

"Don't lecture me." He checked out the saddle and bridle. "I'm not one of the local sharecroppers."

She raised her chin. "I never thought you were. The local sharecroppers have far better manners than you do."

Mike was simmering now but told himself to shake it off. Hellfire wasn't Buttercup. He needed to keep his attention on his riding.

Hellfire gave a restless prance at the sudden weight on his back, and Mike firmed up his grip on the reins. If he gave this horse its head it would run away with him. Georgina started toward the corral and he silently did the same.

She put him through his paces for the next hour, barking out orders like a drill sergeant and keeping up a running commentary about everything he was doing wrong. Mike began to get as restless as his horse. Hellfire was meant for speed and freedom, not for trotting around in circles.

Georgina could sense his resentment, but her job was to teach him to ride and she was bloody well going to do it. No wonder the man had started his own advertising agency—he was too bullheaded to follow orders. "Take him to the willow tree and back," she said. "If you can do it properly, we'll go on to the meadow."

Man and horse made a glorious picture, she had to admit that much. Anastasia had been right about stripping off his shirt and putting him on Hellfire. Of course, at the rate he was going, she would probably wring his neck before the day was out and they would need to find a different model.

She watched him with a critical eye but found nothing more to correct. "That was very good," she said. "We can try a canter if you like, but remember, Hellfire is faster and stronger than Buttercup and far more spirited. Keep a firm hand with him. Don't let your concentration wander. Are you ready?"

"If I could run a football eighty yards up the field past four or five guys who were doing their best to level me, I think I can manage to stay on a horse," he said. "Lead the way, your ladyship."

"With all due respect to your no doubt amazing skill on a football field, Mr. Napoli, Hellfire is far more dangerous than a group of boys playing a game. Don't underestimate him." Georgina told herself to leave it at that and get going, but her tongue refused to listen. "And stop calling me 'your ladyship' in that horrible, sarcastic tone. You know I don't like it."

"Stop talking to me like I got tackled without a helmet once too often and I'll be glad to," he retorted.

"It's not my fault that you have a problem taking orders—"

"I've taken a hell of a lot more orders than you ever will. The *problem* is that you're condescending. That English princess routine wears a little thin after a while."

Georgina's heart began to race. Mike's attacks never failed to upset her, but she was also damned annoyed. She'd been professional, not condescending—he'd probably had coaches ten times worse! "The operative word being 'princess' rather than 'prince,'" she said coolly. "Your problem isn't taking orders. It's taking them from a woman."

Mike reluctantly admitted she was right. With Georgina, he wanted to give the orders rather than take them, preferably behind a locked bedroom door. He pictured her in his bed and his body tautened. If the way she'd looked at him yesterday was anything to go by, she'd be a very willing student. How long would it take before his icy English princess was moaning in his arms? How long before she pleaded with him to put both of them out of their misery?

Hellfire started pawing at the ground, obviously sensing Mike's distraction. He cursed himself for an idiot and straightened in the saddle. This was no time to get carried away by fantasies, not unless he wanted to wind up flat on his back.

"Maybe you have a point," he said. "Did I pass the test just now or do we go back to the corral?"

Georgina ignored the edge in his tone. The important thing was that he'd backed down. "I told you, you did very well." She gave Cinnabar a nudge. "Come along."

Fifteen minutes later they were cantering through a back meadow and the earlier tension was almost forgotten. Mike had enjoyed riding Buttercup, but Hellfire was a creature of naked power and thundering excitement. They sped to a gallop and the excitement intensified to blood-racing ecstasy. With Georgina by his side in the bright sunshine, he felt almost omnipotent.

She gradually slowed as they headed into rougher country, and he reluctantly followed suit. A low, hard stirring took hold of his body. Riding was more erotic than he could have imagined. The scenery was so beautiful it took his breath away. There were wildflowers of every conceivable color scattered through the pasture and a wood of graceful birch and larch out ahead. Englishmen, he decided, were bloodless. No man in his right mind would have wasted this setting on hunting foxes if he could have come here with a beautiful woman.

They turned, trotting parallel to the woods now. Mike relaxed his grip, his thoughts skipping between Georgina and the scenery. He wasn't aware of the sudden rustling to his right, so it caught him by surprise when Hellfire jerked to a halt and reared. He wasn't so much panicky as astonished when, a moment later, he found himself flying through the air. He landed with a hard thud that would have been a lot harder if the ground hadn't been softened by the recent rains.

Georgina saw a plump hare bound into the woods just as Hellfire skittered off the opposite way—without Mike. Her first desperate urge was to rush to his side, but she forced herself to stay in the saddle. He was lying on his back, looking a little dazed, but didn't appear to be hurt. She had to teach him to take these incidents in stride or his previous fears would overwhelm him.

She forced herself to sound matter-of-fact. "Are you all right?"

Mike took a deep breath and coughed helplessly. He'd had the wind knocked out of him but nothing seemed to be broken. He took another breath and turned his head. Georgina was sitting on Cinnabar, coolly watching him. He could hear the lecture he was about to get. If he'd been paying attention to his riding, Hellfire never would have thrown him. He would have been able to control the horse and stay in the saddle. Hadn't he listened to a word she'd said?

He mumbled that he was fine and started to get up, but a stabbing pain shot through his left knee, making him wince and freeze. It lasted only a second, but left him even more dazed than before. God, his knee was sore. Why hadn't he noticed it earlier?

Georgina saw the slight hesitation but not the grimace of pain. "Is something the matter?" she asked.

"I said I was fine." Mike snapped out the words without looking at her.

"Then get back on your horse. He hasn't gone far, only about twenty-five yards." She paused. "Falling is a part of riding, Mike. It happens to all of us."

Meaning, Mike supposed, that only a wimp would still be lying on the ground. He flexed his knee and went pale at the pain. He'd definitely pulled something there—probably a tendon.

This time Georgina saw it all—the careful way he bent his knee, the sudden grimace of pain, the whiteness that stole over his face. All she could think about as she ran to his side was that at least it wasn't nerve damage—he wasn't paralyzed. His hand was on his knee as she bent down beside him, apparently probing for damage. Her throat tightened with fear and guilt. She should have realized they had stayed out too long. She should have warned him about the hares in these fields. She should have made sure he was paying attention to his riding instead of indulging in stupid fantasies about him seducing her in the middle of the meadow.

She reached for his knee, needing to be reassured that it was still in one piece. Then she frowned, because there wasn't only warm flesh there, but something foreign and hard. "You wear a brace?" she asked, shocked that he would need one.

His mouth tightened. "A lot of people use them. Go into a professional locker room someday—basketball or football. They're all over the place."

Georgina drew her hand away. She hadn't meant to imply that the brace was distasteful. "I didn't realize that," she said. "Your knee—is it badly injured?"

He shrugged. "I know what to do by now. Rest, ice and heat, pills for the inflammation... I'll be okay."

"But it hurts."

"Yeah, a little." She could see by his face that it hurt a lot. "I should have been paying more attention. It's my own damn fault."

Georgina knew that wasn't so. "I was supposed to be watching you and teaching you. If I was going to bring you along so fast, I should have made a special point of noticing if you got distracted instead of—instead of..." she swallowed hard and made herself go on "...instead of thinking about how lovely it was here and how—how splendid you looked on Hellfire, and how you would look even better tomorrow, without your—your shirt, and how I wanted you to—to—" She closed her eyes for a moment, shaking with reaction. "Oh, God, this is embarrassing."

Until that moment, Mike had been too wrapped up in his own black thoughts to worry about what Georgina might be feeling. Letting himself get thrown was a stupid thing to do and it had put him in a rotten mood. So how had he reacted? By taking it out on Georgina, resenting it when she didn't show enough sympathy and then biting her head off when she asked about the brace. She'd meant well, but he hated the way women always reacted—like he was some kind of wounded animal that needed to be taken care of.

She was staring at the ground now, mortified by the things she'd admitted. Mike wished she were less honest and less vulnerable. He wanted to take her in his arms to reassure her, but knew where it would lead. "Listen to me," he said gently. "It wasn't your fault. You must have told me fifty times to watch what I was doing. You shouldn't have had to tell me again. And as far as the other thing goes..." He paused. "I feel the same way you do, honey. It's stupid to be embarrassed about it. It's chemistry, that's all."

She looked at him, openly skeptical. "You don't have to say that just to make me feel better."

"You think I'm making it up?" He laughed and shook his head. "I'm not that big on gallantry, Georgina. Right now..." His voice trailed off. Throbbing knee or not, he wanted to strip her naked and lay her down in the grass. He wanted to caress and tease her until both of them were on fire with frustration. And then, when neither of them could wait another moment, he wanted to part her thighs and thrust himself deep inside her. "Never mind the specifics," he said. "I wouldn't want to shock you."

He was too late. Georgina was already shocked—shocked that she could have been so blind. When a man looked at a woman the way Mike was looking at her, words became superfluous. The stresses of the past week had battered her so thoroughly that her defenses were utterly spent. She had never felt so helpless before, or so emotionally naked. "But what am I supposed to do?" she asked. "I've never met a man like you before. No one has ever affected me the way you do. It's no use to pretend the opposite—I've tried it and it doesn't work. You only get angry and accuse me of condescending to you. Sometimes I think—"

"Georgina, it doesn't matter..."

"Yes, it does," she insisted. "Sometimes I think I should have an affair with you and get it out of my system. I lie in bed at night and I imagine the two of us—I picture the two of us together. Me, taking my clothes off for you, and you, ordering me to lie down on the bed and then—"

"Dammit, that's enough," Mike groaned. "I get the idea." What did she think he was made of? Ice? He started to get up, felt the same sharp stab of pain as before, and punched the ground in frustration. Goddamn knee.

Georgina just knew he was in agony. His knee was obviously killing him, and she had to start whining about how frustrated she was. What a self-absorbed dolt she'd become!

She bent over him and smoothed back his hair. His face was damp with perspiration. "I'm sorry. I know you're in pain. Should I go for help? My father has a wheelchair up at the house." He didn't move an inch. "Mike? Are you conscious?"

Mike had never been so conscious in his life. Georgina's breasts were grazing his chest and her hair was tickling his neck. Her breath was warm against his face and the scent of her perfume was driving him insane. He opened his eyes, saw her biting her lip in anxiety, and felt a piercing desire that should have sliced him in half, it was that powerful.

He moved his hand to her hair and took a firm but gentle grip. He brought her lips to his open mouth. Then he kissed her, ignoring her initial resistance and thrusting his tongue deep inside her mouth. He didn't want to rush her, but he couldn't help himself. After a week of holding back, he had to have her. He felt a hard satisfaction when she shivered convulsively and put her arms around his neck.

Georgina moaned and pressed herself closer. She'd resisted at first because she was worried about Mike's knee, but all the worry in the world couldn't compete with the probing sensuality of his mouth. Her emotions were running so high that the first thrust of his tongue was like a torch on dry kindling.

The kiss that followed was so intimate and dominating it shattered her instinctive reserve. She couldn't hold anything back—he wasn't letting her. She put her arms around him because she had no choice but to respond—she didn't want to have a choice. When he made her feel this way, when he excited her so much that his body was the only reality, he could do as he pleased with her.

His tongue gentled and began to tease, drawing back to taste her lips. She felt the sharp nip of his teeth and her pulses jumped in anticipation. She widened her lips in invitation, but he kept on teasing. Finally, desperate to have him in her mouth, she slid her tongue past his and kissed him the way he'd been kissing her. He gave a low grunt and took control again, his mouth growing rough with passion as he pulled her more fully on top of him.

The fabric of his jeans was soft and well-worn. It hid nothing from her sensitive flesh—not the hard male contours of his hips or the urgent arousal between. His hands slid down to cup her buttocks, settling her exactly where he wanted her and pressing her so close her loins began to throb. She had never allowed a man to hold her so intimately, but when his hips began to rock in slow, seductive circles, an age-old instinct took over. She arched her body and followed his lead, swaying provocatively. The fire between her legs grew and spread until every inch of her seemed to ache for his touch.

She felt a hazy confusion when he pulled away his mouth and buried it against her neck. His hands were just as abrupt, clasping her hips and gently pushing. She tightened

her arms and refused to move. The contact was too exciting. How could she give it up?

He laughed softly. "You wanna fight? Okay, your ladyship, we'll find out who's stronger." He lifted her up with
no more effort than it would take to lift a child and dumped
her on the ground. She wound up on her side, facing him.

The rejection stung like a lash, but then she saw the quick
wince that crossed his face and understood the reason for it.
"If it hurts too badly—"

"It hurts, all right. What are you going to do about it?"
He started to unbutton her riding jacket, and she realized he
wasn't talking about his knee. He wasn't rejecting her,
either.

"Whatever you want me to," she answered hoarsely.

He pushed aside her jacket and lightly cupped one breast.
She closed her eyes, her heart hammering wildly. He was
exquisitely gentle at first, moving his palm back and forth,
back and forth, skillfully tantalizing her. Her nipples tin-
gled and hardened, announcing how aroused she was. She
gave a helpless moan and threw back her head. Her body
had a will of its own, straining against his hand to increase
the pressure. His touch grew firmer only to playfully lighten
again. He was tormenting her, but in the sweetest way
imaginable.

Watching her, Mike realized the ache in his knee had at
least one benefit. Every time he moved it the wrong way the
stab of pain he felt jerked him back to reality. Georgina was
too responsive, too abandoned. The look on her face would
have tempted a saint. Her softness and submissiveness
mocked at his self-control. If he didn't watch his step, he
was going to move too fast, and he didn't want to do that.
He wanted her to enjoy this as much as he was going to.

He unbuttoned the top button of her blouse and then remembered her earlier confession. "Sit up," he ordered

softly, and smiled to himself. Her fantasies had a lot to recommend them.

Georgina heard the note of command in his voice and opened her eyes. Mike was smiling the wickedest smile she'd ever seen. Her senses were so drugged by desire she could scarcely make sense of what he'd said. "Why do you want me to sit up?" she asked.

"Don't ask questions. Just do it. And then take off your coat."

She did as she was told, then held out the coat. "Do you want it? I mean—what should I do with it?"

He took it out of her hand and tossed it aside. "Now the blouse. Unbutton it for me. Slowly."

She felt herself flush. "You're going to lie there and watch?"

"Isn't that the way it goes in your fantasies? You undress and I watch?"

"Yes, but—"

"So do it."

Georgina looked into her lap and started fumbling with a button. She was shy about showing herself and nervous about what he would do afterward, but somehow that only made it more exciting. When the last button was undone, she pulled off the blouse and reached behind her back for the clasp on her bra.

"Not so fast," he said. He pulled himself up to sit beside her, cursing at the sudden pain. She was concerned about his knee, but then he took her face in his hands and kissed her. Thirty seconds of that deep, hot kiss and her senses were reeling.

"*Now* you can unhook the bra," he teased.

She couldn't even think anymore, only obey one order and wait for the next. She unsnapped the bra and then sat there, trembling. He pulled it off and dropped it on the ground. "I'm supposed to tell you to lie down on the bed now, right?'' He took a nipple between his thumb and forefinger and lazily played with it. She wondered if he had any idea what he was doing to her. ''There's no bed around, sweetheart. Will the grass do?''

Georgina nodded, but he was already pushing her gently onto her back. ''What happens next in that fantasy of yours?''

''We just—you just . . .'' Georgina held out her arms, unable to put it into words. ''You know.''

''We make love? Just like that?'' He eased himself down beside her, giving another of those fleeting but horrible grimaces. This time, though, he stayed motionless for much, much longer. Georgina was torn between worry and desire.

''Shows what you know, your ladyship,'' he finally said. He traced a slow circle on her belly with his fingertip, then slid his hand up to her breast and fondled the nipple. She stared into his eyes, mesmerized by the possessive glitter in them. His mouth came down hard on her lips, giving her so much pleasure with his tongue and teeth that she couldn't keep him in focus anymore and had to close her eyes. It was too new, too overwhelming.

His lips trailed lower, nuzzled her throat, and kept going. She shuddered as his teeth closed over her nipple. How was she going to bear this? Surely she would break apart.

He shifted his weight, muttered a soft, ''Oh, Jesus!'' and froze again. But before Georgina could get a word out, his hand was between her legs and he was stroking the inside of her thigh. His touch was pure torture. First her thighs, then her hips, then her belly, but never the throbbing core of her. And even when he finally found it and caressed it, it was no more than a brush, a whisper. She arched against his hand and moaned his name.

His mouth grew more demanding on her breast, sucking instead of merely tasting. His fingers found the button on her riding pants and unfastened it, then pulled down the zipper. She tensed as he slipped his hand inside her panties and began to explore, silently begging him not to toy with her. It didn't work. Dear God, why wouldn't he touch her where she needed him to? "Mike, please..." She could hardly breathe. "Don't..."

"It's all right. I'll take care of you." He stretched out beside her and found her lips with his mouth. She gave herself up to the kiss, just as she gave herself up to his hand, which caressed her with light, intimate strokes that slowly grew less gentle. He seemed to know exactly what she wanted, driving her higher and higher until the pleasure was so intense she began to fight it just to prolong it. The end was more of a frenzy than a sweet release. She dug her fingers into his back and clung to him, allowing him to touch her until she couldn't bear another instant of it.

He held her for only a few brief seconds afterward, then eased himself away from her. Maybe it was the sudden coldness of the spring air against her bare skin, but reality hit her with a resounding thud. She'd been so drunk with pleasure she'd never once thought about him. Some lover she was!

He was lying on his back, staring at the sky, his expression so blank she had no idea what he was thinking. She sat up, crossing her arms in front of her chest to hide her nakedness. "We don't have to stop," she murmured.

He looked at her, his eyes growing tender. "Yes, we do. Get dressed, honey. Let's get out of here."

"But don't you want to—"

"No."

She thought she understood why. "Does you knee hurt too badly?"

"Not that badly." He smiled wanly. "Not so much I don't wish you were someone else."

Georgina turned her back to him and picked up her bra. None of this made sense. He'd wanted her in the beginning but he didn't anymore. Why not? Why did he wish she were somebody different? What was wrong with her?

The answer tied her stomach in knots. Wretchedly humiliated, she reached for her blouse, slipped it on, and stood up. Dear God, how was she ever going to face him again? How was she going to work with him tomorrow?

"I'll go get the horses," she said. "Will you be able to ride back?"

Mike looked at Georgina's rigid back and knew something was wrong. Sighing, he pulled himself up and ran a tired hand through his hair. He wanted to get some ice on his knee but the knee would have to wait.

"Whatever you're thinking—stop thinking it," he ordered. "Come back here and sit down. We seem to have a talent for misunderstanding each other and I'm not going to let it happen again."

She didn't turn around. "Really, we should be going. People will start to worry."

"Let them. We're going to talk." Mike saw her flinch, realized he was only making things worse, and forced himself to be more patient. "Please, honey. I'm in no shape to chase after you."

Georgina couldn't refuse him when he pleaded with her that way. She walked over and sat down, but couldn't bring herself to look at him. "Tell me what you're so embarrassed about," he coaxed, and then, when she didn't answer, asked, "Do you think you should have stopped me? That you let me go too far?"

Georgina didn't want to make him play guessing games, but to talk about what had happened—she didn't think she could do it. "No," she said. "It's just—I'm not ... I can't, Mike. I know what I did and I'm sorry. Isn't that good enough?"

"Believe me, Georgina, I have no idea what you mean."
He smoothed her hair. "Come on, honey, I'm not a mind
reader. Whatever you think you did, it can't be that bad."

Georgina told herself to stop being such a coward. Besides, the longer she refused to talk, the longer he would
force her to stay. She took a deep breath and blurted everything out. "I was boring and selfish. I turned you off. You
don't even want me to touch you. I say I hate people who
use other people, but then I turn around and do the exact
same thing to somebody I care about. You must be disgusted with me."

She wanted to bolt away but his clipped, "Stay right
where you are!" kept her from doing it. "You weren't boring and you didn't turn me off. You were as sweet and exciting as any woman I've ever been with. I decided I was
going to make love to you, and if it hadn't been for my knee
I would have done it. I don't want to think about what a heel
that makes me, but fortunately for both of us, the pain got
so bad I finally started thinking with my brains instead of
my..." He paused and smiled. "Let's just say I came to my
senses. But only a bastard would have left you hanging at
that point, and I don't like to think of myself in those
terms."

Georgina sat there for a long time, thinking about what
he'd said. If she'd learned one thing about Mike Napoli, it
was that he didn't lie. The attraction was mutual. If he kept
resisting it, it must be because he felt it was the wisest course
of action.

She wasn't so sure anymore. "I've never felt so confused
in my life," she admitted. "It all seemed so simple before. I
would marry a man with money and help out my parents.
They do need help, Mike, and these past few years, they've
also needed *me*. I realized that the other day—and I also
realized I liked being needed. I still want to do as much as I

can for them, but when we're together, none of that seems to matter."

Mike felt guiltier than ever now. He couldn't have made a bigger mess of things if he'd set out to do it deliberately. "I don't want to hurt you," he said, "but if things go any further, I will. I once told you my business was my first priority and I meant it. Both of us know I want you, but I don't have time for you right now. I can't afford the distraction. To grab a free hour in bed whenever I decide I can spare the time—to forget about a real relationship because I'm always chasing off to another meeting..." He shook his head. "That's not for you, Georgina. You'd be miserable with an affair on the run. And you'd also feel guilty every minute, because you were wasting your emotions on me instead of looking for something permanent with a man who could help your parents out."

Georgina picked up a leaf and started to fiddle with it. Honesty was a fine thing, but it could hurt. With very little effort, Mike could have become the most important thing in her world, but she had no such power over him. Tears welled up in her eyes. "If you were successful and rich, and we had met—"

"But I'm not and we didn't. Every dime Rich and I have is tied up in our agency. I can't afford not to work my tail off right now. I don't have time for involvements and I'm not interested in commitments." He tucked a finger under her chin. "Our timing is lousy, Georgina. Let's accept that and leave it at friendship."

Somehow that made it easier—that he thought of her as a friend. Indifference would have killed her. She managed a watery smile and teased, "How about if I find a rich old coot to marry and take you as my lover?"

He smiled back, looking relieved. "I've got a better idea. Let's knock off your grandmother so you can inherit her money. She's the one who got us into this mess in the first place.''

''The creative mind of the advertising genius strikes again,'' Georgina drawled. She stood up and held out her hand to him. He allowed her to help him up, showing no sign of embarrassment about it. *Friends,* she thought. Why did the word have such a hollow sound to it?

Chapter Twelve

Mike checked his watch as he joined Anastasia on the couch in her parlor, hoping their meeting wouldn't take too long. He couldn't afford to spend the whole night here. Conlin & Napoli hadn't functioned nearly so well while he'd been away as everyone had assured him it would, and he'd been working his tail off all week just to keep from falling farther behind.

He opened his portfolio, took out an advance copy of the *New York Times Sunday Magazine* and handed it to Anastasia. The first of the four Essex ads was on pages six and seven. It would appear in a variety of regional and national weeklies over the next several days, with the next three ads scheduled to follow in successive weeks. Anastasia nodded her approval and laid the magazine on the coffee table, still open to Georgina's picture.

The second ad wasn't in print yet, but Mike had a copy in his portfolio. He set it on the table along with three possi-

ble versions of ad number three. Anastasia studied them for
a good ten minutes before announcing she couldn't possibly select the best version of the third ad without choosing
the fourth at the same time. The series had to have a logical
flow to it.

Mike had seven different mock-ups of the fourth ad in his
portfolio, which wasn't that many, considering that Anastasia had started with fifteen. They were running out of
room on the coffee table but he squeezed them in as best he
could. The pictures brought back memories he would have
preferred to forget. The first three weren't so bad—he was
sitting on Hellfire and Georgina was standing in the meadow
looking up at him. But the next four had both of them on
the horse, as if Mike had ridden by and swooped Georgina
up in the saddle. He could remember every damn minute of
that final session. At first, Anastasia had only wanted him
and Georgina to look at each other, but then she'd asked
them to embrace. In the seventh and last photograph he was
cupping Georgina's chin and staring into her eyes as if he
were about to kiss her. It wasn't really Mike's *knee* that had
needed the numbing effects of ice afterward.

He'd made up his mind by then that his days as a chauffeur were over, but the session with Georgina had convinced him to stop dragging his heels about informing
Anastasia. She hadn't put up nearly as much of a fight as
he'd expected, finally conceding that her nephew Nick or
Kirby, her own chauffeur, could drive Georgina around.
Obviously she'd realized she could only push Mike so far—
four or five days away from New York had stretched into
nine, and he had a business to run.

He hadn't seen Georgina all week, and there was no sign
of her tonight, either. He attributed his disappointment to
business—she would have helped Anastasia make up her
mind faster. Anastasia finally eliminated two of the mock-

ups, but at the rate she was going they would be here all night.

"Maybe I should leave them with you," Mike finally suggested. "Show them to Georgina—see what she thinks." He hadn't planned to ask about where she was but the question somehow slipped out. "Is she with Roger LaSalle again tonight?" He'd seen their picture in Thursday's paper, celebrating the Rangers' conference championship at a Manhattan nightclub.

"He's a sweet boy, don't you think?" Anastasia picked up another photograph and set it aside. "Georgie tells me he's been brilliant. She went to Tuesday's game, you know. I expect he'll be demanding a sizable raise."

Mike told himself the guy had everything—money, looks, a career in pro sports and Georgina. Talk about leading a charmed life. "He'll demand it and get it," he agreed.

"Umm. Actually, though, she's at the airport. Kirby took her to meet a friend. She's going to have a drink out there with Jill and her father and then come straight home. She should be back any time now."

Jill as in Jill Eliott, obviously. Mike found himself wanting to see her but doubted the reverse would be true. She probably still hated him.

"I wish I could stay," he said, "but I've got a presentation tomorrow morning at nine and it's only half-finished. I'll call you after lunch to find out what you've decided. Say hello to Georgina for me."

Anastasia ignored him, hardly an unusual course of action for her. "We'll go with the middle picture for the third ad." She removed the other two. "And the fourth . . ." She gathered up two more mock-ups and stacked them on the pile of rejects. "I love the eroticism of this last series of pictures. There's a wonderful chemistry between the two of you and it comes across very nicely on film. I don't want to go too far, but this photo of the two of you almost kissing... But then again, this other one, where you're simply touching her face, has a lovely subtlety to it." She sighed. "It's a difficult choice, Mike. Give me another couple of minutes."

Mike reminded himself that Anastasia was his most important client, and that the sooner he got a decision out of her, the better. If he happened to see Georgina before he left, it was neither here nor there. Certainly that wasn't a reason to stick around.

Even so, his heart started slamming against his rib cage when he heard the front door open and close and then the muffled sound of Georgina's voice: "Grandmother? Are you home?"

"In the parlor, darling," Anastasia called back.

"I've brought a surprise for you." Georgina's voice got louder and clearer as she walked down the hall. "Jill's father had to go out of town at the last minute, so she's come to stay with us for a few days." The two women appeared in the doorway just as Georgina finished speaking.

Mike automatically got to his feet. Jill was smiling as she walked through the door, but the smile turned to white-faced shock the moment she noticed Mike. Anastasia was already speaking to her by then, welcoming her to New York. "You're looking well, dear. I'm so pleased to see you again, and delighted to have you as my guest for as long as you'd like to stay. How's that handsome husband of yours?"

Jill didn't seem to hear. Her eyes were riveted on Mike's face. Mike reddened and looked at the floor, shaken by Jill's anger and by his own wrenching guilt. "What's *he* doing here?" she asked Georgina.

"His agency is doing the advertising for my grandmother's newest line of products," Georgina answered, visibly distressed. "I didn't realize he would be here, Jill. Otherwise I would have warned you."

Anastasia settled back on the couch, fascinated by the sudden drama in the room. "I see you two know each other."

Jill started forward with firm, measured steps. "We certainly do, Mrs. Lindsay."

Mike braced himself for a royal tongue-lashing. Jill was so angry her hands were clenched into fists at her sides. He told himself that whatever she planned to say, it was better to let her say it and get it out of her system. He could apologize to her afterward.

She planted herself in front of him and glared up at him. Her fist shot out so fast Mike barely had time to snap his head to the side. "You filthy bastard!" The fist glanced off his jaw but still packed a powerful wallop. She'd always had a great forehand. Mike stiffened in anticipation of the next blow, but the single punch was apparently enough to satisfy her. "I should have done that six years ago," she said.

Mike stood there silently rubbing his jaw while Jill apologized to Anastasia. "Please excuse my language and my behavior, Mrs. Lindsay. I wouldn't have done it if he hadn't deserved it."

"Think nothing of it," Anastasia said blithely. "You know how I adore a good scene." She looked at Mike and frowned. "You're bleeding, Mike dear. Georgie, fetch him a tissue and bandage before he drips all over my carpet."

"I must have scratched him with my ring. I'm only sorry I didn't break his jaw." Jill reached into her purse and pulled out a crumpled tissue. Then she pushed Mike's hand away from his face and pressed the tissue to the spot that was bleeding. "Here, I'll do it. You'll live, believe me."

That was when Mike realized that Jill hadn't changed a bit in six years. Maybe she was angry, but she was also hopelessly soft-hearted. She dabbed at his face, asking Georgina to bring her some peroxide and cotton to clean it up.

"You don't have to do that," he said. "I know you'd like to kill me."

"Old habits die hard. Here, you hold the tissue." Her lips tightened in disapproval. "You look exhausted. Don't you ever sleep?"

Mike couldn't help but smile. Once a mother hen, always a mother hen. "Not too much. I've been working hard lately."

"Well it shows. Sit down, for Pete's sake. I'm not Queen Victoria. How's your knee?"

"It's fine," Mike replied, settling back on the couch.

"Meaning, I suppose, that you can get around without crutches." Jill's gaze slid to the coffee table. "My God, is that you with Georgina? You're a model, too?"

"Only for Mrs. Lindsay. She wouldn't take no for an answer."

Jill forced back a smile—or tried to. Mike finally relaxed—he could see she was going to forgive him. "I've got to tell you, Napoli, the face may look like hell but the body is as good as ever," she said.

"Yours, too, Eliott. But I forgot—it's not Eliott anymore. It's, uh..."

"Stafford. You knew I'd gotten married?"

"Georgina told me." There was no point avoiding the inevitable—if Mike didn't bring it up, Jill would. "She was pretty hostile to me the first few times we met. Obviously you were the reason, but I didn't find out you two knew each other until we were in England. That's where those photos were taken."

Georgina returned to the parlor just in time to hear what Mike had said. Jill, meanwhile, had picked up the most erotic of the pictures and was studying it intently. "Hmm, yes. I mean, the hostility is just sputtering out of her here." She held up the picture so Georgina could see it. "You were about to push him off the horse when this was taken, right, Georgina?''

Georgina didn't know what to say. She felt as if she'd betrayed her closest friend by caring for Mike so deeply. "Well, uh, Grandmother wanted us to pretend—to try to look at each other in a certain way," she stammered. "Naturally we did our best—"

"To give her what she wanted," Jill finished with a roguish smile. "Obviously it was a great trial for both of you—to *pretend* to be attracted to each other, that is."

She removed the first-aid supplies from Georgina's hands and then sat down beside Mike on the couch and began to dab at his cut. "You should have been strung up by your thumbs and horsewhipped six years ago," she said with a resigned sigh, "but it's still good to see you." She paused, her expression growing solemn. "It took me years to get over what you did, but I finally told myself you must have had a good reason. Did you, Mike?"

"Yes," he answered.

She rolled her eyes. "Well, don't just sit there looking grim about it. Tell me what it was!"

He shook his head. "I can't. I'm sorry."

"But if you could tell Georgina—"

"I didn't."

Jill gave a snort of disbelief. "Do you really expect me to believe that, Georgina? You're the most loyal person I know. You wouldn't even be speaking to the man unless he'd given you an explanation you could accept."

"He said he knew how much he was hurting you but didn't know what else to do. I don't think he felt he had a choice. Maybe that shouldn't have been enough, but it was."

Jill kept dabbling at Mike's face, wrestling with her private frustrations. Finally, slapping on a Band-Aid, she mumbled, "Well, I guess this isn't the time to talk about it.

I shouldn't have brought it up." She looked at Anastasia. "I'm sorry, Mrs. Lindsay. The two of you were working and I barged in here and made a scene—"

"Don't be absurd! It's made my day—to learn Mike has a skeleton in his closet." Anastasia winked at her. "Beyond the fact that his parents weren't married when he was conceived, that is. A little mystery makes a man so much more interesting, don't you agree? Especially if he's been an utter cad at some point in his life. By the way, dear, are you expecting?"

Jill was only in her fourth month and didn't really show, but Georgina wasn't surprised Anastasia had noticed. When it came to how people looked, nothing much got past her.

She was also an expert at smoothing over difficult situations. Perhaps she'd decided they had had enough drama for one night, because she started questioning Jill about her husband and their plans for the future. As they talked, the tension in the room slowly dissipated.

Jill and Mike were awkward with each other at first, but Jill finally broke the ice by asking him how his sister Bianca was. Mike started telling her about Bianca's marriage and two little boys, and before too long they were chatting and joking like best friends. The six-year separation seemed to melt away. Every now and then Mike would look at his watch and say he needed to get going, but he never actually got up. He was apparently enjoying himself too much catching up on old times.

It was close to eleven before he reluctantly brought up the Essex campaign. With only the briefest hesitation, Anastasia pointed to the picture of Mike caressing Georgina's cheek and said it was perfect for ad number four. Mike gave a bemused shake of his head and gathered up the mock-ups. He was about to leave when he looked at Jill uncertainly and then bent down and quickly kissed her on the forehead. Neither of them spoke. They didn't have to. There was a special feeling between the two of them that neither wanted to lose, not ever again.

Georgina and Jill got into bed a few minutes later, but neither was able to sleep. Instead, they lay awake in the darkness and talked with increasing intimacy as the silence and peacefulness of the night gradually cast their spell. The main subject, of course, was Mike Napoli.

Jill found it hard to believe that Mike had told Georgina nothing about why he'd abruptly stopped seeing her, but Georgina convinced her it was true. She explained how traumatized Mike had seemed the day they had spoken about it—as if he was eaten up by remorse. "Obviously he cares about you, Jill. It stuck out all over him tonight. Whatever his reason for cutting you out of his life, it wasn't something so trivial as running away from a love affair. He would have told you how he felt and gone on from there."

Jill admitted she'd reached the same conclusion. "It was after Alan and I had been married for about six months and I'd realized I loved my husband more than I'd ever loved anyone in my life. It took me that long to be objective. It became a sort of game to try to figure Mike out. The reasons I came up with! Impotence was the best one. I decided something dreadful must have happened the last time he hurt himself, but it was impossibly painful for him to talk about so he'd gallantly removed himself from my life. What do you think?"

Georgina laughed softly. "I'm afraid not. If you can believe what they say in the papers, he's had more women than he knows what to do with."

"What does that prove? All those women could be— camouflage."

"They're not, believe me," Georgina said. "He doesn't have any problems in *that* department."

"You sound very sure of that," Jill drawled.

Georgina hesitated. She and Jill were very close, but they had never discussed her relationships with men. There had never been much to discuss.

"Georgina?" Jill prodded.

"Hmm?"

"I saw those pictures of the two of you on the horse, remember? Anyone can see there was something going on. Come on, admit it. You're sleeping with him."

"Of course I'm not. I wrote you about my parents' financial problems and coming to America to find somebody with money—"

"None of which has anything to do with what I asked."

Georgina was quick to correct her. It had everything to do with it, because Mike wasn't remotely suitable, and besides, he was wrapped up in his business and had no time for love affairs. It was true that they were attracted to each other, but they had agreed they were all wrong for each other and shouldn't get involved. Nothing had ever happened.

"Nothing?" Jill asked skeptically.

"Almost nothing," Georgina murmured. "We were out riding one day and he got thrown from his horse and one thing led to another..."

"And now you can say quite unequivocally that every single part of him is in perfect working order, with the possible exception of his left knee, that is."

Georgina felt herself blush. "We were—very close to each other, and I could tell—I could feel..."

"I'll just bet you could!" Jill teased.

"But we were fully clothed. At least, he was. For heaven's sake, Jill, do you expect me to tell you everything?"

"Of course I do," Jill replied. "Come on, Georgina, stop holding out on me. He's the first guy who ever got your clothes off, right? Obviously you wouldn't have let him do it if you weren't crazy about him."

Georgina gave up the fight. She told Jill she had spent the past week trying to pick herself up and get on with her life, but it hadn't worked. She had thrown herself into her job but still thought about Mike constantly. She had tried to forget him by chasing around with Roger LaSalle, but it was hopeless. And now those wretched Essex ads were about to appear and she would have to see the two of them touching each other in God knows how many magazines. It would only keep reminding her of the agonizing session on Hellfire. Yes, she was crazy about him. Yes, he had spoiled her for any other man. And no, she had no idea what to do about it.

Jill didn't, either. "You know how single-minded Mike can be," she said. "Look what happened with me. For some stupid reason he got it into his head that he couldn't be my friend anymore, and that was that. Nothing I could do or say made a difference. Have you ever looked at his left knee, Georgina? Have you seen the scars?"

"Yes, but you'd told me about his surgeries," Georgina said.

"That's just the point. They don't cut you open like that anymore unless there's a major problem. They use a gadget called an arthroscope and sort of thread their way in. Then they fix what needs fixing. Mike had non-arthroscopic surgery three times on that knee. It took him over a year to come back from each of the first two major surgeries. Do you have any idea how much determination that takes? You have to be absolutely pigheaded to convince yourself that, come hell or high water, you're going to play again. Now he's apparently decided that his business has to come first, that he doesn't have time for you, and that he would only hurt you if he got involved with you. It's ridiculous, but what can you really do?" She paused, then added irritably, "The stupid jackass!"

Georgina didn't want to talk about it. It only made her feel angry and helpless. She murmured that she was too tired to think straight anymore and asked Jill about her mother. Had she seen Dina lately? Was she pleased about having a grandchild?

Jill answered that she'd visited Dina in Chicago the previous fall but was no closer to her now than she'd been six years before. Dina had recently gotten married for the third time and had taken to lying about her age. Naturally she was less than thrilled about becoming a grandmother, because it would mean admitting she was closer to fifty than forty.

"This is going to sound awful," Jill went on, "but every time I see my mother I understand a little better why my parents got divorced. Dad once told me it was all his fault— that he was thoughtless and self-centered and unfaithful— but she must have driven him to it. The man I know wouldn't have behaved that way on his own."

"But why should he lie?" Georgina asked. "He probably changed over the years. People can, you know."

"I suppose. He's always saying how grateful he is that I came into his life at a time when he was ready to have me there—that if it had happened before his second wife died he probably would have done everything he could to get rid of me. It's hard to believe, but I guess he knows himself better than I do." Jill rolled onto her stomach and crossed her hands under her chin. "Sometimes I think what happened was part of some grand design. I wanted so desperately to be close to my father in those days, but it never would have happened if I hadn't needed him so much and reached out to him. In a crazy kind of way, Mike did me a favor by dumping me."

Maybe so, but Georgina didn't imagine he'd planned it that way. Nobody could have anticipated that William Eliott would take the daughter he barely knew so completely into his heart and life.

Georgina hadn't seen William in years now, not since her school days in Paris. His company had sent him to the Far East at about the same time as Jill had married, and it was only recently that he had returned to corporate headquarters in New York.

"Perhaps you should introduce Mike to your father, now that they're both in New York," Georgina suggested. "I think they would like each other. It would be a way of finally ending things, of tying up the loose ends for all of you."

"Maybe I'll do that," Jill said. "Dad's always wondered who Mike was. I never did tell him Mike's name. He's always followed college football so I knew he would recognize it, and I had these visions of him going after Mike with a meat cleaver. I'll have to calm him down first, but I guess they can survive lunch together sometime."

Georgina knew it wouldn't be lunch. Anastasia was already curious about what had happened between Jill and Mike and would surely make it her business to find out. Once she sensed the potential drama in a meeting between Mike and William Eliott, she would insist on being their hostess at dinner. As she'd admitted earlier, nothing delighted her so much as the prospect of a good scene.

Chapter Thirteen

If Anastasia had hoped for drama, she got very little. Jill had prepared her father too well, telling him she had said as much to Mike as needed to be said and making him promise to keep his temper. Georgina had never heard William Eliott raise his voice and couldn't imagine him doing so, but Jill claimed he was far more intense than he seemed. He had simply learned to hide it.

He was cool to Mike at first, but Mike was noticeably relieved he was even willing to shake hands. When neither man could find anything to say beyond hello, Jill rushed in to fill the void. "My father played varsity baseball at Harvard, Mike. He always followed the Boston-area teams. When I told him your name he remembered you very well."

William managed a thin smile. "If I'd known who you were six years ago, I would have taken some real satisfaction in what happened to your knee. In fact, I might have wanted to give you a matched set."

"Dad, please," Jill pleaded. "All of that's in the past now, and you promised—"

"I know what I promised. I've said all I plan to say." William's smile got a little less icy. "You were good, though. Explosive on the field. Exciting to watch."

"He still is," Anastasia said with a laugh. "Georgie, go fetch the Essex ads from my study. Mike is going to make me a fortune, William, but you'll see that for yourself in a moment. One look at the campaign he created and I knew he was the only man for the ads, although I must say, if I'd known you at the time I might have changed my mind. That suit is wonderful with your blue eyes. You might be a little more careful about your skin, though. I'll give you some Essex products to take home with you."

Mike saw William's bemused smile and knew exactly how he felt. "Don't take it personally, Mr. Eliott. She does that to everyone. The first time I met her, she told me everything that was wrong with my tailoring."

"Was and still is, unfortunately. Pour me a glass of sherry, Mike. William? Jill? What will you have?"

Jill asked for some wine but William passed, saying his stomach had been acting up a bit lately. Mike wasn't surprised to hear it—William probably worked too hard. He was the senior vice president of a multinational corporation and it went with the territory.

Georgina came back with the final two ads a minute later. "If you want to see Mike suffer," she said to William, "just wait until these ads come out. The model agencies will be calling him day and night. I've been absolutely besieged since the first one appeared on Sunday."

"But what did you expect, darling?" Anastasia asked. "You go club hopping with Roger too often. Naturally the agencies found out who you were and tried to sign you up."

"Just think of the money you would make," Jill said. "Two or three thousand a day, maybe even more."

Georgina gave Anastasia a teasing smile. "Which is twice to three times what you pay me in a month. I think I deserve a raise."

"Both of us know you loathe modeling," Anastasia retorted. "It rather limits your bargaining power."

William promptly offered to teach Georgina the finer points of negotiating, earning himself a reproachful look from Anastasia. "I'd be careful if I were you," she threatened. "I haven't fed you yet."

"The ultimate bribe," William said. "I've heard about the food here. People say it's almost as irresistible as the hostess."

Jill and Georgina exchanged an amused glance. Unless they were very much mistaken, Anastasia and William were flirting with each other. There was a substantial age difference between the two, but if either of them cared it didn't show. Of course, neither did Anastasia's age.

By the time they went in to dinner, there was no question of being mistaken. William had asked Anastasia to lunch the following day and Anastasia had asked William if he cared to use an extra theater ticket she had for Saturday. The two of them seemed to be totally enchanted with each other.

Anastasia was at her best, spinning story after story about her famous grandparents, Nicholas and Nina. When William expressed doubts about the truth of these tales, Anastasia invited him to come to her mother's house some weekend. "All the proof anyone could want is stored in her attic. Photographs, mementoes, old records and diaries— but I don't suppose you read Russian."

"As a matter of fact, I do, a little, anyway. I studied it in college. Name the weekend and I'll be there."

Anastasia said she would check with her mother and get back to him at lunch. "I'm sure she'll want it to be soon, though, because she adores house parties. Naturally you'll

come too, Jill, and you as well, Mike, and I'll have Nicky
bring Rebecca along. We'll have a marvelous time."

Mike's first instinct was to say he'd be too busy, but Rich
was always telling him he worked too hard—that nobody
could be creative sixteen hours a day. The truth was that
they needed another top-drawer copywriter, although God
knew where they would find the money to pay him.

As it happened, the money found them. Two presentations Mike had done on spec earlier that spring resulted in
new accounts, and they were able to lure away one of the
most creative young talents in the business from one of their
competitors. Mike came back from a celebratory lunch with
Rich to find more good news waiting. There was a message
from William Eliott inviting Mike to join him for a game of
racquetball the next day. Mike had no social pretensions,
but he looked forward to playing at William's club. So many
of its members were in a position to hire him.

Although William was a skillful player, he was no match
for Mike in terms of youth and speed. Midway through the
game he was drenched with perspiration and looked tired
and drawn. Mike would have liked to call a halt, but didn't
want to insult the older man's masculinity. The only thing
he could think to do was ease up on his game.

Much to his relief, William shook his head in defeat before another ten minutes had gone by. "It's my damn
stomach again," he grumbled. "I should probably go back
to the doctor, but I'm sick of being thumped and poked and
told to swallow liquids no self-respecting hog would touch.
They never find anything anyway."

The two men started off the court. "If I were a religious
man," William continued, "I would say God was punishing me for my misspent youth. But I'll tell you about that
later."

"Later" turned out to be over dinner. Listening to William talk about his life, Mike decided he must be a re-

formed sinner intent upon showing Mike the error of his ways. The only son of wealthy parents, William had been spoiled rotten from the day he was born. As a college student his main priorities had been women, sports and gambling. His first marriage had been almost a business arrangement—his wife's family had been socially prominent but strapped for money and his family had been the opposite.

"Jill was only four when Dina and I split up," he explained. "I was like most men in those days—my work came first. Jill was usually asleep by the time I got home and I preferred to spend my weekends playing golf or going skiing. I didn't have much of a relationship with my daughter, so when Dina started making it tough for me to see her—saying Jill was sick or taking her out of town at the last minute—I more or less accepted it. Every time I saw her we wound up fighting, so I didn't mind staying away. Dina kept telling me it would be less confusing psychologically for Jill not to see me at all, so when my company asked me to move to the West Coast, I didn't see any reason to refuse. I figured it was enough to send a support check every month. And then I met Galina."

Galina Popova was a Soviet painter who had fought for artistic freedom and been incarcerated in a mental institution for her troubles. By the time she was permitted to emigrate, years of so-called "drug therapy" had left her mentally confused and physically weak. Although her mind and spirit had begun to recover once she'd arrived in the States, her body never had.

"She taught me everything I know," William said. "What courage really means. How precious freedom is. How to love. How to give. I married her and I took care of her, but she was already dying when she got here. When it was over I was so devastated I asked for a transfer back to New York. I needed to get away from the memories. Six months later, Jill phoned me from college and asked if we could get together during Easter vacation. You know the rest.''

Mike nodded. "Jill told me about it.''

"So what happened six years ago?" William asked. "I've been checking you out since Jill told me who you were and nobody has anything bad to say. I was all set to lecture you about the way you treat people, but you're apparently as straight as they come. It doesn't add up.''

Mike had only one option—to make it absolutely clear that he had no intention of discussing the matter. "If I had anything to say I would have said it to Jill,'' he replied.

"You expect me to accept that?" William demanded.

"I don't expect anything." Mike could feel the muscles in the back of his neck knotting up. He didn't want to argue with William Eliott. He liked the man.

William leaned back in his chair, frowning. "Jill is very fond of you. She wants me to help you.''

"And that's why you asked me to dinner?''

"No, dammit, I asked you to dinner because I want to know what happened six years ago!" He pushed away his plate, more irritated than ever. "You can keep your mouth shut, I'll give you that. I suppose it's a good recommendation for doing business in this city, but I still think you owe me an explanation.''

William gave him a hard look, trying to intimidate him into talking, but Mike simply stared back. Finally William sighed and said, "Okay, you win. I've seen your work and I know it's good, but I'd like to get to know you a little better before I mention your agency to any of my friends. We'll have a chance to do that next weekend. You *will* be at Anya Pershing's place, won't you?''

Mike had accepted Anastasia's invitation a few days before. He wanted to spend some time with Jill before she left, and besides, the break would do him good. In fact, he'd given himself every possible reason to go except the one that really mattered—he wanted to see Georgina. In his more honest moments he admitted he was hopelessly infatuated with her, but that was as much as he would permit himself to acknowledge.

He was nervous about seeing her again—afraid he would do something he shouldn't and even more afraid that if he did, she would tell him to take a hike. It was totally unreasonable of him, but he wanted her to be available even though he didn't plan to take advantage of it. He worked late Friday and pretended he wasn't stalling, but he was. By the time Anya Pershing's ancient butler led him into the dining room, the other guests were halfway through dinner.

The teasing look Georgina gave him spelled trouble and he knew it. "Well, well, well," she said, "if it isn't Mr. Napoli! I told you one should never invite the lower classes to house parties, Grandmother. They have such deplorable manners."

Mike ignored the urge to tease her back and apologized to Anastasia and Anya. "I'm sorry. I got tied up at the office."

"I've certainly heard that one before!" Georgina walked over and kissed him hello. "Come meet everyone, darling."

Whatever Georgina was up to, Mike didn't like it. It put thoughts in his head he didn't want to have. Once they were both seated, she introduced him to the guests he didn't know—Nick's sister Melissa, a medical student; their parents, Dr. Cyrus and Marjory Pershing; and Jill's husband Alan.

All through the rest of dinner Georgina spoke to him and looked at him in a warmly familiar way that made him more and more uncomfortable with every passing moment. She more or less dragged him away afterward, ostensibly to show him through the house. Anya's French antiques and Russian objets d'art looked a little out of place in her sprawling Colonial home, but Mike barely noticed the decor. He wasn't only turned on now; he was damn annoyed.

The moment they were out of earshot he backed her against the wall and demanded, "What do you think you're doing?"

Georgina didn't have to ask what he meant. She knew exactly how she was behaving and had convinced herself she had a good reason for it. As for the effect it was having on Mike, she probably should have felt guilty in view of their conversation in England, but instead she was perversely pleased. Let him feel uncomfortable! The stubborn idiot deserved to suffer! He was the one who had decided how things should be, not she, but nothing dictated that she had to play by his rules.

She put her arms around his neck and smiled coyly. "Why, Michael, whatever do you mean?"

He grabbed her hands and forced them to her sides, none too gently. "Cut it out, Georgina. I don't have that much willpower."

She thrust up her chin defiantly. "Did I ask you to have any willpower?"

Mike took a step backward. Georgina had never been aggressive with him before, and it threw him. He didn't want to hurt her, but if she persisted in chasing him, sooner or later he was going to allow himself to get caught. "I'd like to stay the whole weekend," he said, "but I'll leave right now if you don't behave yourself."

Georgina smiled at that. "Behave myself? Do you think of me as a child?"

"You're sure as hell acting like one," he mumbled.

The smile got broader and more wicked. "Then perhaps you should turn me over your knee and spank me."

"Don't tempt me," Mike said, but he was already tempted—miserably tempted. Since his conscience wouldn't allow him to throw her on the nearest bed and strip off her clothes, he did the next best thing. He accused her of having had too much to drink.

"I had exactly two glasses of wine, and please don't glower at me," Georgina replied. She hated it when Mike was critical. She always felt as if she'd committed some unpardonable sin. "Alan Stafford disliked you before he even met you," she went on, "and then, before you arrived, Jill kept going on about you and Alan got more and more jealous. It seemed the easiest way to avoid unpleasantness—to give him the impression that you and I were...together. He's far too fond of me to challenge one of my boyfriends."

"Challenge? As in, *to a fight*?" Mike could hardly take it in. Stafford was half his size. "For God's sake, Georgina, I'd probably kill him if we started trading punches."

"Exactly," she said, openly exasperated. "Given how jealous Alan seems to be, heaven only knows what he'll do."

Mike preferred honest conversations to Georgina's sort of game playing and said so. Georgina thought he'd only be wasting his breath, but he was still determined to try. They returned to the living room to find Anya holding court, surrounded by all sorts of prerevolutionary bric-a-brac. Mike never knew how it happened, but he and Jill wound up in a corner laughing while everyone else was listening to Anya's stories. By the time Mike realized how intimate they must look, it was too late. Alan Stafford was as hostile as an Arctic winter.

An hour later Mike was sitting with him in the library, talking as earnestly as he could about how he and Jill were only friends. Alan was as glacial as ever. He thought Mike was a bastard. He thought Mike was going to hurt Georgina the same way he'd hurt Jill. Nothing Mike could say would have made a difference, except perhaps for the one subject Mike refused to discuss.

Fortunately, the house was full of guests. The weather on Saturday was perfect, and Anya had tennis courts, a swimming pool and a stableful of horses to keep everyone entertained. By mid-afternoon Mike had swum as many laps and played as much tennis as his knee could tolerate, and had gone inside to shower and get some ice. Georgina was still riding when he came back out, but everyone else was sitting around the pool. He pulled over a lounge chair and sat down with the ice. All of the guests looked tired, especially William Eliott. He'd probably played more tennis than he should have.

A drink or two apiece and the atmosphere turned mellow. People began to tell their favorite stories. The butler brought out hors d'oeuvres. Georgina showed up, still dressed in her riding clothes, and Mike remembered the day he'd taken them off. Suddenly he was anything *but* mellow.

"I could sit here all evening," Anastasia said with a yawn, "but if I don't get myself into the shower I'll grow roots." She stood up and held out her hand to William. "Will you scrub my back for me, darling?"

William grinned at her and started to get up. "Best offer I've had all day."

He was halfway out of the chair when he staggered and almost fell. Anastasia took his arm to steady him. "William—"

"I'm all right. Just a little dizzy."

But he wasn't all right. No sooner had he managed to stand than he moaned Anastasia's name and collapsed into her arms. Nick Pershing reached them first, then Alan Stafford. Between the two men, they managed to lay William down on a lounge chair. A second later Cyrus Pershing was at William's side, and Melissa, Cyrus's daughter, was running into the house for his medical bag. William, still unconscious, coughed up some grainy, bloody fluid as Cyrus felt for his pulse.

By the time Melissa came back, Anastasia had called the paramedics and they were on their way. Cyrus did a quick examination and wasn't reassured by what he found. William's pulse was weak and rapid and his blood pressure was dangerously low.

Although William regained consciousness while the paramedics were starting an IV, he was badly disoriented. Cyrus stayed with him, riding in the back of the ambulance, while Jill, Alan and Anastasia followed in Anastasia's car. Cyrus called from the hospital about an hour later to say that internal bleeding was almost certainly the problem, probably from an ulcer that had supposedly healed, and not to wait dinner for them. They would grab a bite in the cafeteria. The next report they got was when Cyrus and the others returned, at about nine that night. William was conscious and coherent but weak from loss of blood.

"He finally admitted that his stomach was much worse than he'd let on," Jill said, "and that he'd been feeling awfully tired. When I think that he could have been alone in his apartment—"

"He wasn't," Alan said. "That's all that matters."

"But if he needs a transfusion—"

"They'll get the blood," Cyrus assured her. "They have a list of people they can call."

"But most of them donated last week, Dr. Pershing. I want to go back to the hospital. I want to be there in case they need me."

"You're pregnant, my dear. *If* William needs a transfusion and *if* no other donor can be found, then we'll reconsider our options." Cyrus patted Jill's hand. "William's blood type is B negative," he explained to the others in the room. "It's very rare. Somebody with the same blood type had open heart surgery last week and used whatever local

blood was available. In William's case, it's a borderline decision as to whether he needs a transfusion. They'll go ahead
if he doesn't improve, but in the meantime, all we can do is
wait.''

Jill barely seemed to hear him. "But I should be at the
hospital in case there's an emergency. I feel so helpless.''

"Your father will be fine," Alan said. "He wouldn't want
you to worry this way, honey. You have to calm down.''

Nothing anyone said seemed to get through to her. She
became more and more agitated until she was pacing rather
than sitting, and since she was pregnant, she wouldn't hear
of taking a sedative or a glass of brandy.

Finally Alan got up and walked over to Mike. "I've never
seen her like this," he said in a low voice. "You two are so
in tune—please, do something. Settle her down.''

Mike had listened to the conversation about a possible
transfusion with bewilderment that had turned slowly into
horror. "That business about giving blood..." he whispered back. "If William's blood type is so rare, what makes
Jill think she can be a donor? I mean, if she has the wrong
blood type, we don't have a problem.''

Jill stopped pacing and glared at him. "I heard that.
What do you think I am, an idiot? Of course I have the same
blood type. With my medical history, do you think I don't
know my blood type?" She brushed away an angry tear.
"And I don't need settling down, Alan. I'm not crazy. He's
my father and I love him. Anyone would be upset.''

Mike felt as if he'd run into a steel wall at top speed. He
was so shaken he could barely think, but somehow he
pushed it all aside and concentrated on Jill. She needed him
right now. She needed the distraction he could provide. He
could fall apart later.

"You *are* crazy," he teased. "You've always been crazy.
Sadistic, too. Did you ever tell your husband what you did
to me when I got home from the hospital and refused to

leave the house?'' He grinned at Alan. ''It wasn't enough to
short-sheet the bed while I was in the bathroom—she had to
stick lumps of Silly Putty under the mattress pad and then
stand there laughing when I kept moving around trying to
get comfortable. She tape-recorded a bunch of the most
boring Sunday radio sermons in history and threatened to
play them over and over until I let her take me to a movie.
She kept changing the television channel to game shows. She
knew I hated game shows.''

''Well, it worked, didn't it!'' Jill said. ''You finally got
your tail out of bed.''

''Only because I wanted to kill you.''

''You were grateful. Admit it.''

''I was too weak to fight you.'' Mike turned back to Alan.
''Did you ever notice how she operates? Nags you and nags
you until she wears you down?''

''I don't,'' Jill said, forgetting about her father for a moment.

''But you do,'' Georgina put in. ''What about that conceited French count you thought was so charming? You
badgered me into accepting a date with him and then I had
to spend an entire performance of *Faust* fighting him off. It
was dreadful.''

Jill smiled. ''I remember that. And to think I was jealous
because he liked you better.''

Mike dragged up another couple of stories from their
college days—the locker-room pranks Jill had talked his
friends into playing; the time his decrepit old car had died
when he was driving her to an important tennis match; the
house she and her friends had rented sight unseen, only to
find that it looked like something from ''The Addams
Family.'' He didn't give her time to worry about her father
and he didn't give himself time to think about her blood
type and what it implied.

Still, it was in the back of his mind, clawing away at him, and when William's doctor called around midnight to say that William's condition had been upgraded to fair and that a transfusion wouldn't be necessary, Mike couldn't get away fast enough. He mumbled something about his knee and escaped to the privacy of his room. All those injuries and surgeries should have taught him to cope with pain, but they hadn't. The foundations of his world had just crumbled, and the pain was like acid on an open wound.

Chapter Fourteen

Georgina could tell Mike was upset, but doubted his knee was the reason. Something had been bothering him all evening. In fact, now that she thought about it, he had looked almost shocked for a time.

She considered following him and asking what was wrong, but decided there wasn't any point. Given how stubborn the wretched man was, he would probably refuse to tell her. One way or another he was going to drive her mad.

Half the time he all but ignored her and the other half he couldn't take his eyes off her. Obviously he wanted the same thing she did, but would he even consider it? Of course not. He'd made up his mind, and that was that. No man on earth was worth the amount of brooding she had done over him.

Worth it or not, he kept her tossing and turning long after she'd gone to bed. Something had shaken him badly, yet he'd pushed it aside and kept Jill entertained. Even Alan had noticed what an effort it took. He had mentioned after Mike left how grateful he was that Mike had stayed to look after Jill despite the pain he seemed to be in.

Of course, that was Mike. Georgina would have been a nervous wreck in England without him. Was it any wonder she adored him?

She was finally dozing off when a soft knock startled her awake again. She groped for the lamp switch and called out a low, "Come in." A moment later Mike opened the door.

She had never used the word *love* to describe her feelings for him, even to herself, but when she saw him standing there looking as if his world had shattered into a million pieces, no other word would do. Her heart ached for him. Whatever was wrong, she wanted to hold him in her arms and comfort him. Of course she loved him.

She moved over a little, making room on the single bed. "Come sit down and tell me about it," she said simply.

Mike had been on his way outside to swim in the pool for a while. That was the way he always handled his problems—by taking refuge in physical activity. But when he'd come to Georgina's door, he'd known he couldn't pass it by. She was the only one he could talk to, the only one he *wanted* to talk to. The pain was too intense to worry about the consequences.

He closed her door and walked to the bed. She'd propped up a pillow against the headboard for him, but there really wasn't room to lie down. He sat down by her waist instead.

The story spilled out more easily than he could have imagined. Maybe that was what happened when you bottled something up for six years. "Bianca was supposed to drive me home after the party, but my father asked me to stay. He said he needed to talk to me."

Georgina understood that he was talking about six years before, explaining what had happened after the party Jill and Bianca had given. "In private, you mean. Just the two of you."

He nodded. "We went into the den. My father put on a record—Billy Joel. I thought that was strange, because he hated pop music. Then I realized he wanted to drown out our conversation. He told me I had to stop seeing Jill, and at first I thought he was joking. We'd been friends for nearly a year by then."

"And he knew about your relationship?" Georgina asked.

"Sure he did. He'd been seeing her in my apartment all summer. When I thought about it later, I realized he must have asked me at least half a dozen times whether I was going to take her out, but he was always very casual about it. He would say something like, 'That little girl from Radcliffe—I think she has a crush on you,' and I would come back with something like, 'Don't be crazy. We're just friends. We spend our time trading medical stories.' Then he would smile and change the subject, but now he was sitting there and telling me I shouldn't see her anymore. So I did what any guy would have done. I told him very respectfully to mind his own business."

"But he didn't," Georgina said.

"That's the understatement of the year." Mike grabbed a magazine from the night table and started to pleat the front cover. He was so lost in the past that Georgina doubted he realized what he was doing. "He went crazy. He lectured me about how I didn't love or respect him, because otherwise I would do what he said. When had he ever tried to run my life? When had he ever been unreasonable? I was a bad son and I was going to send him to an early grave. He went on and on, and the craziest part of all was that he refused to give me a reason. I was supposed to stop seeing Jill just because he said to."

Mike stopped playing with the magazine and stared at the wall. "If my leg hadn't been paralyzed I would have walked out. Instead I started yelling that I was in love with Jill and would never give her up. A second later he told me to shut up and slapped me across the face, really hard. He'd never even spanked me as a kid, not once. I was his favorite child—I'd always known that. I was stunned that he would hit me."

Georgina knew how close Mike's family was, and how old-world. She could understand why he would honor his father's wishes but not why he hadn't given Jill an explanation. "So you stopped seeing her, but why all the mystery about it? Did you promise your father you wouldn't discuss it with her?"

He gave her a pained look. "I thought I was in love with her. I love my father, Georgina, but not to the point of blind obedience. I sat there shaking and didn't say a word. I wouldn't answer him when he spoke to me. He drove me home the next morning and it started all over again, only this time there were reasons. He'd read about Jill in the paper. She was rich. Her family was on the Social Register. They would never accept a Catholic kid with no money who might be crippled for the rest of his life. Jill had been mentioned in the sports pages a few times but I couldn't remember seeing anything personal, and I said so. I asked him how he knew so much about her. Instead of answering, he got angry and started in again about how I was a terrible son and how I was going to ruin my life. I was being torn between two people I loved, and the worst part of all was that I didn't understand why. My father's reasons didn't make sense, but he'd never interfered before so I knew it was important. I didn't know how to handle the situation so I kept it all to myself and gave everyone a hard time. Then, a few days later, my roommate's girlfriend told me Jill and I made a cute couple—that we even looked alike—and it was like the roof had caved in on my head. Jill looked a lot like my sister Ellen, and people were always saying Ellen looked like me—the same blue eyes, the same dark hair, the same kind of solid build.''

Georgina was thunderstruck. ''Dear God, are you telling me Jill is your sister?''

''It was the only explanation that made sense. So I went to my father and told him what I suspected, and he broke down completely. He actually sat there and cried.'' Mike's voice was hoarse with emotion—pain, confusion and anger. ''He told me he and my mother had been separated when Bianca and I were little. The early marriage, the two kids, the pressures of having too little money and living with his in-laws—it had all piled up and he'd started taking his troubles to the local bars. Mom had thrown him out and told him not to come back until he could stay sober, so he'd gone to New York and moved in with a cousin. He'd gotten a job as a guard on a Long Island estate, but the owner was always working and his wife was as bored as she was rich. Within a month they were having an affair. A month after that she was pregnant, and my father was definitely responsible, because the woman's husband had been out of town for almost three weeks. She wasn't especially concerned, though. She said her husband was too wrapped up in business to count back nine months from the baby's birth and realize he hadn't been around.''

''The woman was Dina Eliott,'' Georgina said weakly. ''It's like something out of a soap opera. Of all the incredible things to happen...'' Her voice trailed off in helpless astonishment.

''That's what I thought, but my father was sitting there crying so I knew it must be true. He told me he'd come to his senses a few months later and gone back to Cambridge, but he'd never told my mother about the affair. He was terrified she would find out. He was even more terrified I would sleep with my half sister.''

''But couldn't you have explained—''

''Not without telling Jill that William Eliott wasn't her father.'' Mike shook his head. ''She used to talk about him all the time. You must know what a lousy mother Dina was. If Jill wanted anything at that point in her life, it was to be close to William.''

''And to you. She wanted you.''

''And I wanted her. I thought I was in love with her. She'd pulled me out of the worst depression of my life and I thought I needed her. I didn't even trust myself to keep my hands off her, much less to keep my mouth shut about who her real father was. I'd started something at the party that couldn't be stopped—not when both of us wanted the opposite. Maybe if I could have told her the truth—but I couldn't.''

Georgina understood now. After all, she had lived with Jill for three years. Mike couldn't hold her and kiss her one night and then decide the next morning that he wanted to be buddies again. The same tenacity that had made Jill one of the top tennis players in the country as a schoolgirl would have led her to demand an explanation and press for a love affair. But Mike couldn't explain without shattering her hopes about William Eliott.

She put a gentle hand on his shoulder. ''It must have been awful for you. You both suffered so dreadfully.''

''And for nothing, dammit!'' Mike hurled the magazine to the floor with such force that Georgina flinched. ''I hurt Jill and I hurt myself because I couldn't see any other way out, but none of it had to happen. I jumped to the wrong conclusion and my father sat there crying and convinced me I was right. He lied to me, damn him! I thought I came from a family where love and support and honesty were sacrosanct, but he lied to me so I wouldn't marry Jill. He damn near destroyed two lives, and for what? So that I wouldn't marry too young? So I wouldn't marry a girl who wasn't Catholic?''

Georgina was puzzled at first, but then she figured out why Mike felt his father must have lied. Jill and William Eliott had the same rare blood type—B negative.

"But couldn't another coincidence be involved?" she asked aloud. "If your father is RH negative—"

"He's not. We've gone to donate blood together. We're both O positive."

Biology wasn't Georgina's strong suit, but if she recalled her schoolwork correctly, two RH positive parents could produce an RH negative child if both lacked a certain gene. She asked if it wasn't possible that Dina Eliott and his father could have done so in Jill's case. He conceded that it was but reminded her of how unlikely it would be. After all, both William and Jill were B negative. The odds against that happening at random were so great it was crazy not to think they were father and daughter.

"I suppose," Georgina said, "but I'm sure your father meant well. You were both rather young and from very different backgrounds. Neither family would have approved of the marriage. Perhaps he felt it was doomed to failure and that he was sparing you future pain."

"By lying to me? He knew how I felt about Jill. He could see what it did to me to lose her."

Georgina felt herself pale. It had never occurred to her that any of this might affect her directly, but it did—and very deeply. "You still love her—now that you know it's all right to," she murmured.

Mike was startled by the remark. His father's betrayal was so fundamental, so enormous, that he hadn't been able to think of anything else. Now he did, and told Georgina what he'd realized years ago. "I don't think I ever did, not in the way you mean. Jill was only eighteen. I thought of her as a kid sister. But she'd taken care of me all summer and I was emotionally dependant on her. I wasn't only grateful—I thought she was the finest person I'd ever known. I felt so much for her—tenderness, protectiveness, affection—that it got confused in my mind with falling in love. I needed her, but there was never the kind of crazy physical excitement I feel—" Mike cut himself off before he could say the rest: "When I look at you." He had enough to cope with without confronting his feelings for Georgina. "Never mind," he muttered. "It's not important."

But it was important, at least to Georgina. She could guess what Mike had been about to say and longed to hear still more—that he cared, that they had a future together. Still, he was bleeding inside. He was haunted by the might-have-beens from six years before and devastated by his father's duplicity. It was the wrong time to nag him about their relationship.

She sat up and put her arm around his waist. "Perhaps you should talk to your father. If there's any chance you might be mistaken—"

"It will have to wait." He laughed, but there was no joy in the sound. "This may sound crazy, but he's leaving for the Caribbean on Wednesday and I don't want to do anything to upset him. If it's waited six years, it can wait two more weeks."

Georgina thought that was typical of Mike—sensitive and generous. "I'm glad you came to me," she said. "You're hurting so much and I so want to help." She ran a tender hand across his forehead to brush the hair back from his face.

What followed was pure feminine instinct. She wanted to comfort him. She wanted to be close to him. It was a natural part of loving him. She brushed her mouth across his lips and whispered, "Let me make it better, darling. Let me take care of you."

He flinched away, swore softly, and then pulled her into his arms and kissed her fiercely. She shuddered and gave herself up to the desperate need he seemed to feel, but only seconds later he jerked away as if she'd just caught fire. She clutched at his arm, trying to keep him beside her, but he shrugged away her hand and stood up.

"We've been through all this before," he said. "Nothing's changed."

Everything had changed. Georgina knew she was in love with him now. "But suppose my parents had plenty of money? Suppose your business was better established?"

"They don't and it isn't." Mike sighed, suddenly looking exhausted. "Thank you for listening, Georgina. Please don't talk to Jill about this yet. I want to make sure I have my facts straight first."

Georgina told him she wouldn't think of it, but he was already halfway out the door. She didn't try to stop him again because he was right. Nothing had changed, and until it did, he wasn't going to listen to a word she said.

Mike left the next morning after being so polite to Georgina at breakfast that she could have screamed. William's condition was still the same, so the doctor was keeping him in the hospital another night. Anastasia decided to remain in Connecticut until he was released, as did Jill and Alan, but everyone else left after dinner.

Georgina did a lot of thinking over the next several days and decided she wasn't giving up without a fight. She and Mike cared for each other too deeply to let external problems keep them apart. One way or another, she intended to solve them.

She would have tackled Anastasia on Wednesday, but a much improved William Eliott came to dinner that evening along with Jill and Alan so there was no opportunity for a personal conversation. Although Georgina knew the subject was best handled in the privacy of their home, by Thursday she was so impatient she marched herself into her grandmother's office and plunked herself down across from her desk. Anastasia had about a dozen lipsticks in front of her and was studying the colors intently.

"I've come to talk to you," Georgina announced. "It's important." She paused, wishing her grandmother would stop fussing with the lipsticks and pay her some attention. "I love Mike Napoli and I mean to marry him."

Anastasia picked up a lipstick and held it up to Georgina's face. "Autumn Blaze," she said. "I only wish the color were better on you, because it's going to be very big this fall. I plan to feature it in our ads."

Georgina blinked, wondering if Anastasia had even heard her. "Will you please listen to me? I said—"

"Yes, dear, I heard you and I'm delighted for you—really I am. I'll give you whatever sort of wedding you'd like, either here or in London, or I'll fly in whomever you wish to have present, but the details will have to wait. I'm rather busy just now."

"Not *that* busy!" Georgina snatched away the tube of Autumn Blaze and slid the top on. "How can you be delighted when you've done everything you possibly can to keep us apart? You told me the most dreadful lies about Mike just so I wouldn't get involved with him, and you threatened to fire him if he so much as touched me."

Anastasia didn't bat an eyelash. "Really, Georgina, I thought you were more intelligent. I've thrown the two of you together at every possible opportunity, haven't you realized that by now? I picked Mike out for you ages ago. For one thing, Terry Hall was so exceptionally fond of him, and for another, he's obviously very bright. He was quite taken with your photograph after the first Corona ad with you came out, you know. Terry told me so."

Georgina was speechless for a moment. Now that she thought about it, her grandmother *had* thrown them together a lot, but why hadn't she simply introduced them if she thought they were so right for each other? "But—but— all those stories you made up—"

"And what would you have done if I'd told you how perfect he was and brought him around to the house?" Anastasia demanded. "You were very negative about men when you first came to New York, Georgina. You went on and on about needing to marry a millionaire, but if you ask me, safety was more important to you than money. You wanted someone who wouldn't threaten you. Mike would have scared you witless, and besides, you would have insisted on doing the noble thing and ruling him out because he wasn't wealthy. I know you. The barriers would have gone up and that would have been the end of it. I simply saw to it that you were continually confused and agitated. It's difficult to keep one's defenses in place when one's emotions are constantly in turmoil, wouldn't you agree?"

Georgina sat there, dumbfounded. As usual, Anastasia was right, but she'd never guessed what her grandmother was up to. "Do go on," she finally managed to say. "I can't wait to hear your psychoanalysis of Mike."

"Handsome but spoiled. Charming but a bit of a rake. One look at you and he would have moved in for the kill, so I decided to slow him down and give you a little breathing room. Besides, it's only human nature to want what we believe we can't have. The man has been in absolute agony, especially since England. That was my master stroke, if I do say so myself. I knew Sarah and Anthony would be their usual impossible selves, and that if I sat back and allowed them to pick at you Mike would rush in to protect you. He didn't stand a chance after that. He's besotted with you, poor thing!"

"Is he really!" Georgina was pleased her grandmother thought so, but wasn't so sure it was true. "What a shame he hasn't done anything about it."

For the first time in ages, she had the satisfaction of seeing Anastasia look surprised. Far from having proposed, Georgina explained, Mike refused to even touch her. She told her grandmother the reasons why.

Anastasia gave a delighted chuckle. "Fancy that! The man has a sense of honor. I must say I didn't expect it of him. Tell me, dear, what do you propose to do about it?"

"What do *I* propose to do? You mean *you* don't have a solution?"

"I'm afraid not. I got the two of you together and arranged for you to fall in love. I can't do everything, you know. I'm a busy woman."

As it happened, Georgina had given the problem a great deal of thought. "Very well then, I'll tell you what I propose to do. Mike has been killing himself for months now, soliciting new accounts, and there's no reason for it at all. You know everything that goes on in this city, including who's dissatisfied with their current advertising agency. I want you to tell your friends to consider using Conlin & Napoli. After that it's up to Mike, but you can be of enormous help to him if you want to be."

"Naturally I'd planned to do that," Anastasia said, "and now, if you're quite finished—"

"But I'm not. There's still the problem of Shanley to consider. No matter what you happen to think of my parents, I love them and I intend to help them. Besides, I won't have John inheriting a ramshackle estate and a mass of debts. You're a wealthy woman and there's no earthly reason—"

"Never in a million years!" Anastasia interrupted vehemently. "I'll help John when the time comes, but Sarah and

Anthony aren't getting another dime. I've thrown away too much money on them already."

Georgina couldn't pretend to be surprised. Anastasia had never made any secret of the fact that she considered Sarah to be a spendthrift and Anthony a financial disaster. "I'm only asking you to give me what you will anyway, either in a trust fund or in your will. You're being totally unreasonable."

"I'm an old woman," Anastasia retorted. "I can be unreasonable if I want to be."

Georgina couldn't help but be amused, because Anastasia would have flailed the skin off anyone who dared call her old to her face. She thought resignedly that her grandmother had given her no choice. She would have to resort to the ultimate weapon—blackmail.

She began to get up. "I want you to know that I've enjoyed working for you these past few months, even at the slave wages you've paid me. I shall miss it."

"Miss it?" Anastasia frowned at her. "Sit back down and explain yourself, young lady."

Georgina somehow kept a straight face. "It's very simple, Grandmother. I can earn two to three thousand dollars a day as a model. That's over half a million dollars a year."

Anastasia was scowling by now. "I can multiply, Georgie. Get on with it."

Georgina shrugged. "There's nothing more to say. My father needs an investment of several million dollars to shore up his assets and earn the income to maintain Shanley properly. Given the taxes one has to pay in New York and the frightfully high cost of living here, it will take me years to earn that sort of money as a model. It's a good thing I'm relatively young."

"But you hate modeling," Anastasia reminded her.

"I love my parents," Georgina replied.

"God knows why, except that they've always needed you so desperately."

"Perhaps that's reason enough," Georgina said.

Anastasia sat there looking cross. "You know perfectly well that I want the business to remain in family hands. You also know that Nicky is hopeless when it comes to running anything, and that Melissa won't give up her medical career."

"Perfectly true," Georgina agreed. "You know, when I was helping with Father's affairs, I discovered I had quite a talent for business. It was a surprise, really, because I never expected to be good at that sort of thing. I don't mean to sound conceited, but I'd be brilliant at Corona."

"But you're determined to throw it all away for a modeling career."

"You could always hire somebody to break my arms and legs," Georgina teased.

Anastasia looked very stern. "That is not amusing, Georgina." She picked up a lipstick and started tapping it on the desktop. "You're trying to blackmail me into subsidizing your parents. I won't have it."

"You have no choice," Georgina answered calmly. "I mean to have Mike, but Mike has no money. Since you won't give it to me I shall have to earn it on my own. Of course, if you would like to pay me the same amount in wages that I could earn as a model, that would be all right, too."

"Don't be impertinent. I don't even pay myself that high a salary." Anastasia sat there for the longest time, making Georgina wonder what she could possibly be thinking about. Finally, she said, "Very well, you win, but I refuse to give the money to Anthony directly. He'll only fritter it away on bad investments. Perhaps I can set up some sort of trust fund, with the use of the income restricted to restoration and preservation at Shanley. I suppose Mother would be willing to choose the investments and manage them until John is old enough to do it. The lawyers can work out the details. Will that suit you, milady?''

Georgina gave an ironic bow of her head. ''Indeed, madam. I'll take my leave as soon as we settle the matter of my salary. A thousand a month is hardly adequate now that I'm to marry and move out of your apartment. I won't take a penny under fifty a year.''

''Why, you ungrateful little chit! I should fire you on the spot!'' Despite her harsh words, Anastasia was laughing. ''Not a penny over twenty-five, but I'll remodel a wing of the apartment for you and Mike to live in. I've gotten used to having you around and I'd be horribly lonely without you.''

''That's a lovely offer, Grandmother. Forty-five.''

''Thirty,'' Anastasia said.

''Forty.''

''Thirty-five. That's my final offer. You're a trainee, and I never pay my trainees that much.''

''Very well,'' Georgina said, ''but I must point out that I'm not just any trainee. I'm your granddaughter.''

''You certainly are, darling,'' Anastasia said, and gave Georgina an approving smile.

Chapter Fifteen

The same afternoon, Georgina swept into Mike's office over the protests of his secretary and announced that their problems were solved. Without giving him a chance to get a word in, she explained that, far from objecting to him, Anastasia had picked him out for her. Furthermore, Georgina informed him gleefully, she had more or less blackmailed her grandmother into raising her salary to thirty-five thousand dollars a year and setting up a million-dollar trust fund for Shanley. As far as Conlin & Napoli went, Anastasia's help was a guarantee of success. Their worries were over.

Mike listened to Georgina with a sense of disbelief that grew by turns into mild offense, stiff-necked insult and finally, total outrage. It was bad enough that Anastasia had manipulated him into a state of gut-wrenching physical frustration; now her nutty granddaughter was engaged in rearranging his entire life. Never mind playing Lady Bountiful; Georgina was so imperious she could have given Nicholas II himself a run for his money.

"A million dollars," he mumbled incredulously when Georgina finally shut her mouth. "A million dollars so a pair of not especially productive people can live like royalty in their own private museum. It's obscene."

Georgina reddened a little. She'd assumed Mike would be as happy as she was. "I know you don't like my parents, but Shanley is a part of English history. It deserves to be preserved. My grandmother can well afford it."

"Sure. What's a million bucks to someone like Anastasia Lindsay? Spare change." Mike's jaw tightened. "Hell, if I'd known she was going to snatch me out of the gutter, wave her magic wand and turn me from a frog into a prince, I never would have started my own agency. I mean, why bother working? You're going to inherit a bundle someday. In the meantime we can live off your grandmother and I can earn my keep by learning a bunch of parlor tricks to perform in front of her dinner guests."

Georgina wasn't so carried away by her own cleverness that she failed to notice the sarcasm in Mike's voice. She had evidently offended his pride. She probably should have been more careful about how she had put things, but she'd been so eager to tell him the good news she hadn't bothered about tact.

"We don't have to live with Anastasia if you don't want to," she said. "It's not as though we'll have to worry about money. You'll have so many new accounts your only problem will be expanding fast enough to accommodate them, and we'll also have my salary, of course."

"Of course," Mike repeated. "Thirty-five grand. It's a nice round number, especially for a first job."

At that point Georgina realized that Mike wasn't simply offended—he was exceedingly angry with her. "Did I do something wrong?" she asked, genuinely puzzled. "I know

I've moved rather quickly, but surely you don't object to the outcome. We can be together now. Isn't that what both of us want?''

At that moment, what Mike wanted was to pick up the telephone and hurl it at the nearest wall. Somehow he restrained himself. ''You barge in here, interrupt me while I'm working and tell me you've made all kinds of plans and decisions without bothering to consult me, and I'm supposed to think it's terrific? Dammit, Georgina, this isn't a feudal manor and I'm not one of your vassals. If I want your grandmother's help I'll ask for it myself, and if I ever decide to get married, it won't be to a woman who's so pushy she doesn't even wait for a proposal. Unlike you, I wasn't born with a silver spoon in my mouth. I prefer to work for what I get, not have it handed to me on a silver platter. You'd better believe I object to the outcome, and I object even more strongly to the way you brought it about.''

Georgina simply sat there, stunned by the force of his anger. He'd taken her to task every now and then during the past few months, but never like this. This was a full-blown attack. He sounded as if he hated her. She'd never found it easy to cope with his disapproval, and a part of her wanted to sink through the floor and die.

At the same time, though, she was stung by the injustice of it all. Mike had looked after her in England, and she hadn't ranted and raved about how he was making decisions without consulting her. Was this really so different?

She squared her shoulders and began to defend herself. ''I don't understand why you're so angry. You're always telling me how helpful personal contacts are, so I asked my grandmother to provide them. Nobody's handing you anything on a silver platter. You would still have to impress her friends with your ideas. And what decisions have I made for you? Am I holding a gun to your head and telling you what to do?''

"What could have given me that idea!" he retorted. "Just because you've decided how large an agency I'm going to have, where we'll live, *how* we'll live, and even that I'm going to marry you in the first place, that's no reason to think you're telling me what to do."

The tightness in Georgina's throat warned her that tears weren't far behind. She fought them down and made one last effort to defend herself. "One would think I wanted to torture you. Is it so terrible to live on Fifth Avenue with a chauffeur at your disposal and a wonderful cook and people to do the cleaning and laundry? Is it a hardship to have potential clients calling you day after day? Is the thought of marrying me so distasteful?"

Mike couldn't believe what he was hearing. If Georgina had understood him at all, she couldn't have asked those sort of questions. "All of that's beside the point," he said. "The issue is how the decisions got made in the first place. You and your grandmother are two of a kind. You snap your fingers and expect the world to do your bidding. But I've got a news flash for you. This isn't Imperial Russia and the sun set on the British Empire a long time ago. Nobody runs my business but me. Nobody runs my *life* but me. When I marry, it won't be to a woman who needs cooks and chauffeurs and Fifth Avenue apartments. It will be to someone who would live in a shack with me if that's all I could offer her. Go back to your grandmother and tell her to pick out somebody else for you. Lots of men would jump at the chance to marry you—New York is full of opportunists, Lady Georgina."

"And this office is full of mulish idiots, especially when you're in here by yourself!" Georgina flung herself out of her chair, every inch the earl's daughter. "There's nothing romantic about suffering and struggling, Mr. Napoli, but what's the sense of trying to convince you of that? You think you know everything!"

She turned on her heel and marched out of his office, sailing past his awed secretary. Her boss probably had her cowed, but nobody cowed Lady Georgina Philipps. If Mike didn't appreciate what she'd done, he didn't deserve her.

The pain that hit her only a moment later was so sharp and unexpected she had to stop for a moment to catch her breath. What did it matter whether Mike deserved her or not? The fact was, he didn't want her. He thought she was pushy and spoiled. The thought of marrying her had never crossed his mind. She had made a fool of herself just now.

She blinked back her tears and, head down, hurried toward the elevators. All she wanted at that moment was to get downstairs and out of the building. She groaned in dismay when, out of the corner of her eye, she saw Rich Conlin get off the elevator. She couldn't possibly manage social chitchat right now.

Rich gave her a big smile and asked how she was, but noticed the stricken look on her face before she had a chance to answer. "Is something wrong?" he asked. "You look upset."

Georgina shook her head. "It's nothing. Really, Rich, I've got to be going."

Rich sighed. "Whatever he said or did, forget it. He's been in a lousy mood all week, ever since he got back from Connecticut. I don't dare leave him alone with clients these days—he's in one of his 'I'm not going to suffer fools gladly' phases."

"Including me, obviously." Georgina bit her lip. What an insensitive dolt she'd been! How could she have forgotten what had happened in Connecticut?

Rich put his arm around her. "Hey, are you crying?"

"Trying not to," she admitted. "Please, Rich..."

"Yeah, okay." He let her go, but not before giving her a bracing little pat on the back. "Try not to take him too seriously. You probably caught him at a bad time."

Georgina was spared the necessity of answering by the arrival of the elevator. She couldn't eat a bite of dinner that night, and Anastasia quickly guessed the reason why. But her grandmother took the setback far less seriously than Georgina did. Mike was too proud for his own good, she said, but sooner or later he would come to his senses. In the meantime, Georgina was to go about her business and remember that he was mad about her.

She tried, but every time the phone rang and it wasn't Mike, she died a little inside. Deep down, she'd expected him to call, and when he didn't, she slowly realized he had cause to be angry. Not only had she been insensitive about the hurt he must still be feeling over his father; it had been arrogant and stupid to expect him to swoon in gratitude over the wonderful life she had arranged. He had a bee in his bonnet to begin with about her title and social position, and her failure to consult him must have made him feel she was playing the grand lady of the manor again. It was a mistake she would never repeat.

She was depressed all weekend but tried her best to hide it. On Friday, Anastasia gave a small dinner party for Jill and Alan, who were returning to California the next morning. Naturally she invited Mike, but he claimed he had to work. Obviously he'd decided to avoid her.

Saturday brought a call from Roger LaSalle, whose team had won the Stanley Cup the week before. He and Georgina had continued to see each other, but only as friends. Roger enjoyed having a hot model with a title on his arm and Georgina enjoyed the parties he took her to. He told her he was supposed to go to a reception that night to celebrate the Rangers' victory, but that his date, an actress he was quite smitten with, had gotten sick at the last minute. Georgina agreed to accompany him because it was better than sitting and being miserable, then surprised herself by having a good time. The atmosphere was exciting—lots of celebrities, television cameras everywhere, French champagne and wonderful music. They danced till long past midnight.

She awoke Sunday morning with a bad hangover and a worse case of the blues. Liquor and loud music were only temporary anaesthetics—her quarrel with Mike hurt worse than ever. She told herself to take the bull by the horns and call him, but couldn't bring herself to do it—not in half a dozen tries.

It took her until Monday to finally phone him, and she was shaking with nerves as she waited for him to come on the line. There was at least one advantage to having called his office—she'd had to give her name to his secretary. Having him refuse to speak to her was better than suffering the indignity of being hung up on.

As it happened, he took her call at once, but used such a distant tone that being hung up on would have been less painful. "Yes, Georgina? What can I do for you?"

"I was wondering if you'd like to have lunch today," she said.

There was a measured pause. "I'm afraid not. I'm busy."

"How about tomorrow then?"

"I have an appointment."

Georgina realized he was putting her off but decided to make one last attempt to see him. "I'd really like to talk to you. It doesn't matter when—I'll come by whenever you're free."

"Maybe next week," he answered. "I'll call you."

In other words, Georgina thought as she hung up, don't hold your breath, your ladyship. She swallowed hard, put her head down on her desk, and sobbed out the pain and frustration that had been building since Wednesday afternoon.

* * *

The most difficult part of all was the sense of helplessness she felt. How did you communicate with someone who refused to talk to you? Should she give him a little more time and then phone again? Go to his office and try to see him? Ask her grandmother to speak to him on her behalf? In the end she did none of these things, telling herself the next move would have to come from him.

She was wrong, though. The next move came from Bianca, who called Georgina Wednesday afternoon, totally out of the blue. Without prelude, she announced that Mike hated it when she interfered in his life, which was too bad, because somebody had to straighten him out. "After all," she observed, "he's making such a total mess of it. Tell me, are you involved with Roger LaSalle? We saw you on television the other night, wearing a sexy blue dress and hanging on his arm."

Georgina smiled for the first time in days. "I'm afraid I was a wee bit sloshed. I was hanging on for dear life, trying not to fall flat on my face. Actually, Roger and I are simply friends. I was filling in at the last minute for his newest girlfriend."

"Try telling that to my brother," Bianca said with a giggle. "I thought he would throw something at the TV set when he saw the two of you on the news. You know how he goes all stiff and quiet when he's mad and gets that icy look in his eyes?"

Georgina knew all too well. "I'm afraid so," she replied.

"Well, that's how he looked. Rich told me you came by the office last week and wound up nearly in tears, but Mike wouldn't say a word about why. He's very closemouthed about your relationship." She paused. "If you don't mind my asking, what exactly *is* your relationship?"

Georgina barely knew Bianca Conlin, but she'd liked her the one time they'd met and heard nothing but praise from

Jill about her. Her normal reserve was no match for the desperation she felt about losing Mike forever. Bianca seemed like the only hope in a dismal picture.

She didn't mention what Mike had discovered in Connecticut but poured out her heart about everything else. Bianca responded by confirming most of what Georgina had already guessed. Mike was as stubborn as he was independent. Success was important to him, but only if he could achieve it in his own way. He was a protective older brother who was also a bit of a male chauvinist. He saw it as his duty to take care of the woman he married and support her financially.

"Obviously he's having trouble coming to terms with your money and background," Bianca said. "You're so glamorous and exotic that he probably can't picture you fitting into his world. Tell me the truth, Georgina. Have you ever pushed a shopping cart or scrubbed a floor?"

Georgina admitted she wasn't especially domestic. "I haven't looked after myself since my student days in Paris. To be honest, I don't see any reason to now, but if it's important to Mike, naturally I'll do it. As for scrubbing floors..." She thought about it for a moment. "I've mucked out stables and stripped antique furniture. Both are filthy jobs. Do they count?"

Bianca laughed and said they would have to do. The problem, she mused, was that Mike had never seen Georgina in an ordinary setting, interacting with ordinary people. Why didn't she come up to Cambridge for the weekend? The whole family was getting together to clean out her parents' attic, and it would give Georgina a chance to show Mike that she could get on well with the people he loved. It was bound to make a difference in his attitude.

Georgina had her doubts about whether it was a good idea to spring her presence on an unsuspecting Mike Napoli, but allowed herself to be talked into it. Bianca was going up Friday morning with her two little boys and invited Georgina to ride with her. Rich and Mike wouldn't be leaving until after work, so she would be able to meet the rest of the family first and settle in.

The Napolis' house had originally belonged to Marie's grandparents, but was so well maintained that its age barely showed. It was a large place, with five bedrooms on the second floor. Two of them were occupied by Mike's brother Chris and youngest sister Theresa, who were students and lived at home. Bianca and Rich would be staying in the master bedroom, with their two boys in the room next door. Ellen, Mike's middle sister, had her own apartment but was bunking in with Theresa for the weekend. That left only one bedroom, so Georgina offered to sleep on the couch in the living room.

Bianca told her it wouldn't be necessary—there was a sixth room upstairs. "Dad walled off a section of the attic when Chris was born and put in another bedroom and bathroom, so none of us would have to share. It was Mike's private domain as a kid, but the last time I looked it was crammed with Mom's so-called treasures. Are you up to some moving and cleaning?"

Georgina assumed Bianca meant vacuuming up a bit of dust and clearing out a few cartons, but the room was jammed from floor to ceiling with everything from boxes of old clothing to beat-up furniture and hadn't been cleaned in years. Chris and Theresa got back from school in mid-afternoon and pitched in to help, but it still took until dinnertime to move everything into the attic and scrub away the dust and grime.

Ellen drove up in a pickup just as they were finishing. She had five bags of groceries in the cab along with a stack of pizza boxes. Everyone was both hungry and tired by then, so they sat down at the kitchen table and dug into the food. Georgina was grubby and exhausted but also very happy.

She liked Mike's family. When all of them were done eating, Bianca put the boys to bed and then everybody sat around the table talking, laughing and drinking wine.

That was how Mike first saw Georgina—through the front kitchen window, sitting with Chris and his sisters, holding a glass in her hand and laughing. She was wearing jeans and a Charles and Di T-shirt that was so tacky it was funky, with streaks of dirt on her clothing and dust in her hair. She looked so different from the aristocratic, immaculate woman he was used to that he could hardly believe it was the same person.

Even so, something inside him froze up. What did she want from him? Wasn't Roger LaSalle enough for her? And even more to the point, what was she doing here in the first place?

"Dammit, Rich," he said, "if this is your idea of a joke..."

"Don't look at me. I didn't know she would be here. I detect the fine hand of your oldest sister in this particular turn of events."

Rich was right. Georgina would never show up uninvited, but Bianca wasn't afraid of anything—not even of Mike's wrath when he realized she'd butted into his life. The question was—what did he do now? Ignore Georgina? Order her to leave? Carry her upstairs and make love to her?

Oh, hell, he thought, *where had that one come from?* It wasn't as if he'd forgiven her. Her arrogance was infuriating, she was too damn spoiled to make a decent wife, and she had about as much loyalty as a she-cat in heat. She also looked totally irresistible, smudges and all. How was he going to handle this?

His best course of action, he decided, was to treat her like a casual acquaintance. He would be polite but distant. He and Rich walked into the kitchen to a chorus of greetings, but Georgina didn't say a word. There was no confidence in the smile she gave him—it was strained and uncertain. She took a sip of wine, but her hand was shaking. Their eyes met, but she looked away almost at once, unable to hold his gaze. My God, he thought, what does she think I'm going to do to her? Pick her up by the scruff of her neck and throw her out in the street?

His family had always been demonstrative, so it was automatic to hug Chris and his sisters hello. Then he came to Georgina, who sat there looking so awkward and vulnerable that he instinctively bent down and pecked her on the cheek. Afterward he pulled over a chair, poured himself a glass of wine, and asked Chris and Theresa how school was going.

There was a time when Georgina might have jumped to all sorts of conclusions about Mike's kiss and what it implied, but she'd learned not to second-guess him. He might have forgiven her a little, but if he had, she didn't want to antagonize him all over again by being at all aggressive. She got up from the table, walked over to the oven, and took out a pizza for him and Rich.

Chapter Sixteen

The Napolis' attic was such a disaster that, within ten minutes of getting upstairs, their children forgot about simply throwing away a few chemicals and decided to clean the whole place out. That dilapidated old bridge set—was anyone going to use it again? Those cartons full of bank statements and bills—what was the use of keeping them when the statute of limitations on IRS audits had long ago run out? These tacky plastic dishes, so antique they would probably melt in a modern dishwasher—who would ever want to eat off them? Their mother was supposedly saving all this stuff because one of them might want it someday, but they all agreed that the torn Naugahyde recliner was hopelessly ugly and that nylon sheets from the days before permanent press would never find a home on any of their beds. They saved a few pieces of furniture for the day when Chris and Theresa had their own apartments, but otherwise, unless it had some special sentimental value, out it went, either to the dump or to a nearby second-hand charity store.

The real fun began that afternoon, when the bulk of the serious work had been done and the siblings started delving into their personal histories. Other mothers had taped their children's drawings to the refrigerator for a week and then thrown them away, but Marie had saved every one. She had also saved term papers, athletic trophies, report cards, prom pictures, medical records and every other scrap of paper that had ever crossed her path.

It became a ritual—to open up a carton and then tease each other about the contents...about the awful reports they had done and the homely dates they had had and the silly-looking potholders and lanyards they had made. Mike seemed to get the worst of it, especially when they came across a copy of his birth certificate. They needled him for a good ten minutes about being conceived in sin and continuing along the same path, but finally, tiring of the game, started to trade what they called "Marie stories"—tales about the lectures she was always giving them, most of them on the subject of sex.

"I've never admitted this before," Rich said with a sly smile, "but it took me months to get Bianca to sleep with me—and that was *after* we were married!"

Bianca rolled her eyes. "Just because I was a little nervous on our wedding night..."

"A little nervous!" Rich gave a hoot of laughter and launched into a story about multiple attacks of hunger, a bath so long it should have been listed in the *Guinness Book of World Records*, and a mysterious ailment not unlike African sleeping sickness.

When he was finished, Bianca accused him of making the whole thing up and changed the subject to dinner. "Let's draw straws. Whoever loses has to go for Chinese food."

Mike stood up, stretching his arms wearily above his head. "I'll do it. What do you guys want?"

Georgina didn't care what she ate, only that she would finally have a chance to get Mike alone. As soon as everyone had agreed on what to order, she walked to his side and offered to keep him company. "You won't have to worry about parking that way. I'll wait with the car while you go inside for the food."

Mike didn't bother to argue. He knew Georgina wanted to talk to him and was resigned to hearing her out. It was only polite, even though nothing she could say would make any difference. After all, she'd been waited on hand and foot from the day she was born and expected to live a certain way. The minute he dropped his guard, the minute she knew he'd forgiven her, she would probably start trying to run his life again. Facts were facts, no matter how much he wanted her or how well he got along with his family.

The speech she made in the car was pretty much what he'd expected—an apology for presuming more than she had any right to and a promise it wouldn't happen again. If she'd charged ahead like a bull in a china shop, it was only because she'd been so eager for them to be together. She was sorry she'd forgotten how upset he was over his father—her excitement about solving their problems had blinded her. She understood he was angry, but surely he still cared for her. Couldn't they start over again?

When Georgina looked at Mike in that earnest, uncertain way, he found it hard to refuse her a thing. It was just as well he was driving, because he was sorely tempted to forget about common sense and take her in his arms. And that wouldn't solve anything.

"I've got a lot on my mind right now," he said. "Let's put things on hold for the rest of the weekend. We can talk again in New York."

She looked into her lap, visibly disappointed. "Is that a brush-off or do you really mean it?"

Mike was grateful the restaurant was just ahead. He didn't want to get sucked into a conversation about their relationship. "I mean we'll talk. Whether you realize it or not, starting over again isn't an option. Things have gone too far. If we keep seeing each other we're going to have to get engaged, and I don't want to do that." He double-parked in front of the restaurant and got out of the car, deliberately cutting off any reply she might make.

Georgina took a deep breath and tried to steady her nerves. Maybe Mike had a reason to feel pressured, what with Anastasia setting up a million-dollar trust fund just so they could be together. Even more to the point, he was sure to feel obligated to marry her if he took her to bed, which he certainly would if they continued to see each other. What was she supposed to do now?

She thought about suggesting a no-strings affair but knew it would make her miserable. She could always give up and go home, but she'd never been a quitter. That left only one option—to go on as before, trying to show him she wasn't the spoiled shrew he thought she was.

When he got back to the car with the food, she gave an appreciative sniff and started telling him about Jill's endless quest in Paris for what she considered to be good ethnic restaurants. Between Jill's pedestrian taste in food and Georgina's talent for storytelling, she had him laughing out loud by the time they got home. There was a moment just before they got out of the car when he looked into her eyes and abruptly stopped smiling, and she was sure he was going to kiss her. She stared back, her heart racing out of control, but instead of taking her in his arms he grabbed the sack of food and turned away. Neither of them spoke as they walked into the house.

After dinner, everybody trooped back up to the attic. The most fascinating cartons of all—the ones containing mementos of their parents' and grandparents' days—still remained to be opened.

Much to everyone's amazement, there were some real treasures in those cartons, buried along with the likes of Frank Napoli's high school letter jacket and Marie's eighth-grade diary. Old comic books and baseball cards, electric trains, a collection of miniature dolls—the stuff was worth thousands by now.

"Maybe we shouldn't have been so quick to toss away the plastic dishes," Bianca said, and reached for the next carton. "They might be priceless antiques some day." She opened the carton, then gave a bemused shake of her head. It contained everything from ticket stubs to prom dance cards. "Will you look at this? Mom must have kept souvenirs from every date she ever had."

The contents were all the more unexpected because Marie Vitulli and Frank Napoli had had to watch their money carefully as kids and save up for special occasions. Yet here, packed away in this carton, were indications of an entirely different life—playbills from musicals bound for Broadway, matchbooks from expensive restaurants, Boston Pops concert programs.

Ellen said what all of them were thinking. "My God, there must have been other guys—guys with the money to afford all this. These cards—are all of them from Dad?"

They were. Frank had given Marie dozens of them over the years, for birthdays, Christmases and Valentine's Days. If there *had* been other men in her life, they apparently hadn't been the literary type.

The carton was almost empty now. Bianca picked up a tattered manila folder from the bottom and opened it up. The yellowed pieces of paper inside looked like legal docu-

ments, so she handed them to Theresa, the future lawyer in
the family, to inspect.

"They're adoption agency forms from about thirty years
ago," Theresa said, and then teased her brother, "Just
think, Mike, we almost got rid of you. If Dad hadn't come
charging to the rescue, you might have wound up with a
pair of Philadelphia bluebloods for parents. Tough luck,
huh?"

Only scattered pieces of paper remained in the carton.
Mike grinned at Theresa as he picked up the next one and
turned it over. It was a very early baby picture of him in his
mother's arms, taken in the hospital. Beneath it were several sheets of a doctor's stationery—a doctor in Philadelphia. In a scrawled hand, he had jotted down Mike's age at
the top of each page—from one week to seven months—and
then his height, weight, inoculations and other details from
each of his visits. But the name listed on these well-baby
check-ups wasn't Michael Napoli. It was Michael Vitulli.

Puzzled, Mike picked up the final piece of paper in the
carton and unfolded it. It was a birth certificate, but not
another copy of the one they had come across earlier. On
this one, his name was listed as Michael Anthony Vitulli,
and his father was listed as unknown.

"This is totally incredible," Bianca said to Mike. "They
must not have been married when you were born, because
if Dad had tracked Mom down by then, she would have
been willing to give his name to the authorities. What do you
want to bet that they celebrated their twenty-ninth anniversary last month and not their thirtieth?"

Mike felt as if he'd been socked in the groin by a heavy-
weight boxer. "Keep digging, Bianca. Whatever happened,
it's probably somewhere in these cartons." He managed a
weak smile and got up. "I think I need a beer."

Chris and his sisters started teasing him about taking his sudden status as a bastard too hard, but Georgina had seen the shock in his eyes as he walked out of the attic and knew that the date of his parents' marriage wasn't what had upset him. She picked up a handful of the cards Frank had given Marie and started checking through the dates and inscriptions. The one from the Valentine's Day before Mike's birth read, *I'll always love you. I'll be here when you want me. I'll wait forever. Love, Frank.* He'd written it because he still loved her even though she was involved with somebody else—somebody who could afford expensive dates, somebody who had gotten her pregnant, somebody who had ultimately refused to take responsibility for their child.

Badly shaken, she put the card in her pocket and went downstairs to find Mike. He was sitting in the den, reading an encyclopedia article about blood. Georgina stared at the table he was studying—*Exclusions of Paternity on the ABO System*. His finger was under the pairing *Type A X Type B*, but Frank Napoli was Type O, as was Mike. His mother was obviously Type A, and he was checking to see what offspring she might produce with a man who was Type B. Was Type O one of the possibilities? The answer was yes.

She silently handed Mike the Valentine's card. He read it, and then, grim-faced, put it aside. "It's been bothering me all this time—how out of character it was for my father to lie to me about Jill just to split us up. That's part of what made me so angry—that he could teach me to judge people as individuals and then act like such a hypocrite."

Georgina sat down on the arm of his chair. "I can understand why he did it. He was protecting your mother from what you might think of her if you learned the truth. And he loved you so much—you told me you were his favorite child. It takes an extraordinary man to forget that a child is another man's natural son and love him exactly as his own.

He must have been afraid that if you found out the truth, your feelings for him would change."

Mike knew all that but it didn't lessen the rage in his gut. All those years, all those lies... He closed the encyclopedia with a hard snap. "Do I look like him?" he asked Georgina.

"Like William?" She studied his face for a moment. "A little, I suppose. Your eyes are the same shade of blue, and your build is about the same, but I wouldn't say there's a striking resemblance. William and your father are rather alike, at least judging from the photographs I've seen."

"Yeah," Mike muttered. "William and my father. Only he's not my father."

"He is in every way that counts," Georgina said gently.

Mike stood up. "I'm not in the mood for platitudes. I've got to get out of here. Tell everyone I went for a walk, okay?"

Georgina let him go. She understood how traumatic it must be to suddenly learn that the man you had loved and respected all your life had not only lied to you about something terribly important but wasn't your biological father at all. She longed to comfort him, but recognized that if he didn't want her company, there was nothing she could do to help.

She spent the rest of the evening in the attic, going through cartons with Mike's brothers and sisters. Although they never came across a marriage license, they did find evidence that Marie and Frank's wedding had taken place in the May after Mike's birth. Marie's cousin in Philadelphia had written her a letter early that June, addressing it to "Marie Napoli" and sending it to the Vitullis' house in Cambridge—to this house. She told Marie to put the past behind her, reminded her that Frank had always loved her, and said she was sure they would be happy now that they were married. Georgina was the only one in the room who understood the real meaning of that letter, but it wasn't her place to explain. Mike would have to tell his family the truth, assuming he would even want to.

It was almost midnight by then and Mike had been gone for hours. His brothers and sisters didn't seem concerned—they said he had a habit of going off by himself when he needed to think. Georgina tried to follow their lead and put him out of her mind, but she was too worried to succeed.

She slept fitfully, awakened by every little nighttime rustle and creak. It seemed to take forever before she heard what she'd been waiting for—the sound of the front door opening and closing and the tread of Mike's footfalls on the steps. She listened to him walk through the hallway and start up the attic steps, then heard a sudden, frightening thud above her. It was followed by utter silence.

Bolting out of bed, she ran to the attic steps to find out what had happened. Mike was sitting in a heap about halfway up, apparently unhurt. She hadn't even reached him when she realized he'd been drinking—his eyes had a peculiar glaze and the air was heavy with the smell of liquor.

Mike hadn't just "been drinking"—he had so much liquor in him that everything seemed a little hazy, except maybe for Georgina in her flimsy nightgown. Apparently she'd come to help him, so he staggered to his feet and put his arm around her shoulders for balance. His body stirred at the feel of her bare skin under his hand, so he absently slid his palm under her nightgown and cupped her breast. She felt so soft and desirable that he decided to kiss the nipple, but vaguely remembered there was a reason he shouldn't do that. Oh, yeah. The Napoli family code. The girls stayed pure until their wedding nights and the boys didn't contribute to a nice girl's corruption. What a crock. If his mother had listened to her own lectures and not tarted around with a rich Harvard boy, he never would have been born.

Besides, he wasn't a Napoli—he didn't have to live by their code. When he got to the top of the steps he pulled Georgina around and pushed her spaghetti straps off her shoulders. The nightgown fell to her waist, revealing full, firm breasts with puckered, erect nipples. He bent his head, intending to kiss them, but she was tugging at his arm to pull him into his room so he had to stop. No problem there. The bedroom was definitely a better place for this sort of thing than the hallway.

She closed the door once they got inside, pulling her nightgown back into place as he stripped off his shirt. "You need to go to sleep," she said. "You barely know what you're doing."

Mike sat down on the bed, a little confused. God, she was beautiful. His whole body throbbed with the need to have her. "But I want to sleep with you," he said.

"I know you do, darling, but this isn't a good time." She walked to the bed, knelt down by his feet, and started to remove his shoes. "Let's just get these off. That's it. Now take off your jeans, and we'll get you into bed. You'll be asleep in no time."

Mike pulled off the jeans as she turned back the covers, then obediently slid between the sheets. He felt achingly lonely in that double bed, isolated and abandoned. He had nobody anymore, only a father who wasn't really his father and a mother who had lived a lie and a brother and three sisters who thought he was somebody he wasn't. The pain was excruciating, unendurable. He looked at Georgina, saw the gentle concern in her eyes, and thought, *She's the only one who waited up, the only one who cared. Nobody else gave a damn.* It didn't occur to him that nobody else knew what was wrong.

He hadn't cried in years, not since that final injury, but suddenly he was shaking uncontrollably and fighting a feeling of suffocation. He gulped for air. His eyes began to burn. So did his chest. He sobbed, a hoarse, dry bark of a sound, and felt tears in the back of his eyes.

His misery was like a knife through Georgina's heart. She couldn't bear to see him suffer so much, so she got into bed and gathered him into her arms. Smoothing his hair and stroking his back, she said the sorts of things she'd said to John when he had hurt himself as a child. "It's all right, darling, I'll take care of you. I won't ever leave you. There's no need to cry."

His sobs tapered off and he relaxed in her arms. Then, all of a sudden, she wasn't the only one stroking and caressing. If she was surprised to feel his hand massaging her hip through her sheer nightgown, she was even more surprised when he started tugging at the fabric to push it out of the way. The lips that had been buried against her neck like a hurting child's started to nip and kiss like a very virile man's. Georgina knew she should stop him but couldn't bring herself to do it. He seemed to want her so very badly, and she loved him so very much.

She realized how aroused he was when he cupped her naked buttocks and pulled her hard against him; the only thing between them was the soft cotton of his briefs. As always, the touch of his mouth and hands caused a lightning bolt of excitement to race along her veins, but she was also a little nervous. He'd always been teasing and gentle in the past, but now he was hurried and a bit rough.

His lips finally found her mouth, kissing her with such desperate urgency that fear gave way to understanding. It wasn't just that he wanted her physically. He also needed her emotionally, needed the comfort and temporary oblivion that lovemaking could provide. She realized it wasn't going to be wonderful, not with all the liquor he had in him, but didn't really care. This was for him, not her.

He tore his mouth away, rolled onto his back, and yanked off his briefs. Georgina went into his arms quickly and willingly when he reached for her again, but she also whispered a gentle plea. "Please, not so fast. Hold me for a little while first."

"Oh, God." He shuddered and turned away from her. "What in hell am I doing? I'm sorry."

Georgina snuggled up behind him and nuzzled his neck. "It's all right. You don't have to stop."

"I do." He took a deep, convulsive breath. "But sweet Jesus, I don't want to. I don't want to but I have to."

There it is again, Georgina thought impatiently. Her blasted virginity and his stupid sense of honor! What was she supposed to do, offer herself to the first man on the street so Mike would feel free to touch her? It was ridiculous.

She ran her finger down his side and teased his hip and thigh. "I'm not as innocent as you seem to think." As if to prove it, she slid her hand between his legs and fondled him intimately. The hot strength of him made her feel feminine and powerful at the same time.

His initial start of surprise gave way to a thick-tongued, "But who— In England I was so sure... Was it LaSalle? Did you go to bed with LaSalle?"

Georgina made her fingers even more provocative. "Does it really matter?"

"No. Don't stop." He moaned and pressed himself against her hand. "Please, don't stop. Touch me harder."

She did as he asked, only to be pulled on top of him within seconds. She fitted herself against his hips and responded to his movements, unconcerned with her own pleasure. His lips were frantic, his hands clumsy with excitement. Between the liquor and the way she'd touched him, he had no self-control left. She forced herself not to tense up. She loved him so much at that moment she would have done anything to comfort him.

She flinched in shock and pain at the first hard thrust of his body, then took a deep breath and arched against him to invite a second. She bit her lip. Dear God, she hadn't expected it to hurt so much. The pain finally stopped after a few more times, and it was over very soon after that. She wanted to move away then, to have a few moments of privacy, but he was holding her too tightly. It seemed to take forever for him to catch his breath and loosen his grip.

Georgina expected gratitude and tenderness after that, but what she got was a furious tongue-lashing. Mike lifted her off him, sat up in bed, and turned on the lamp with an angry yank on the cord. "Dammit, Georgina, why did you lie to me? How could you have done it?"

Georgina couldn't have been any more hurt if he'd slapped her across the face. She sat up, pulling the covers almost to her chin in self-defense. "You wanted me and I wanted to give myself. Does anything else matter?"

"Of course it matters," he said. "Now I feel guilty as hell—but I suppose that was what you wanted."

"Of course it wasn't what I wanted," Georgina flared back. "It never even occurred to me that you would be able to tell—not after all those years of horseback riding."

"Horseback riding? You actually expect me to believe a line like that?" He looked at her with a mixture of disgust and skepticism. "I'll tell you what you *really* thought. You thought I'd feel obligated to marry you once I realized I was taking a virgin to bed. Well, forget that. I'm not going to get trapped."

Georgina was past feeling hurt now—she was so stung by the injustice of his accusations that she wanted to thrash him senseless. "Why, you rude, egotistical lout! What makes you think I would even have you? I slept with you because you cried in my arms and seemed to need me desperately. All I wanted was to comfort you. You're so bloody drunk I knew I wasn't going to enjoy it, but I was stupid enough not to care. I just wanted to be with you, and since my virginity so obviously disqualified me, I let you think I had slept with someone else. The thought of marriage never crossed my mind."

She could tell he wasn't listening. The expression on his face didn't change a bit. "And suppose you're pregnant? Then what happens? I'm not going to do the same thing my father did. I'm not going to run out on my child."

"If William Eliott was even half as arrogant and conceited as you are, it's little wonder your mother moved to Philadelphia," Georgina said, and began groping under the covers for her nightgown.

She finally found it and pulled it on, but when she started to get up, Mike grabbed her wrist to stop her. "If you're pregnant I want to hear about it. We'll have to get married."

Georgina pulled her arm away, totally out of patience with him. "If you think I'm going to get down on my hands and knees and thank you for that, you're crazy. I don't know why I even bother with you. Here your mother had the courage to go off on her own and keep you to raise when she had no prospect of a husband and when the world was bound to call her filthy names, and you have the nerve to get drunk about it. Your father—your *real* father, Frank Napoli—has loved you with all his heart from the time you were a tiny baby and you drink yourself into a stupor because he had the sheer nerve to be human—to lie to protect himself and your mother. Most of the people I know would get down on their knees and thank God if they had parents even half as wonderful as yours—including me. But of course, you're not interested in anything *I* have to say. After all, I committed the unpardonable sin of wanting to be with you and trying to do something about it instead of crying about how the fates were against us. And then, as if that weren't bad enough, I loved you so much I decided not to stop you when you started pawing me. Believe me, it's not an experience I would care to repeat. You can save your bloody marriage proposal, Mr. Napoli, because I wouldn't accept it even if I were expecting triplets!''

He blinked at her, looking as if his brain were too suffused with alcohol for mere words to penetrate. ''Oh, what's the use,'' Georgina muttered, and scrambled off the bed. The only thing worse than a drunken fool was a woman who tried to talk sense to him.

Chapter Seventeen

Mike was gone by the time Georgina woke up. He didn't try to see her or call her once she was back in New York, but on Monday afternoon a dozen red roses arrived at her office with a card reading simply, *I'm sorry. Mike.*

Sorry for what? she wondered. For behaving like a childish idiot and drinking himself into a stupor? For mauling her in bed? For insulting her sense of honor to such a degree that she still gnashed her teeth whenever she thought of it? She closed the box of roses and tossed it in the trash.

It took her another day to remember why she'd fallen in love with him in the first place—because he'd been so gentle and protective in England. She was still angry, but she probably wouldn't have thrown away his roses if he'd sent her another dozen. Besides, her conscience had begun to bother her. She had known since Sunday night that she wasn't pregnant but hadn't seen fit to tell him.

Since she hadn't received the apology she felt she deserved—*I'm sorry. Mike*, hardly sufficed—she wasn't about to phone him. She decided to write him instead, and send the note to his office via messenger. The letter was more sarcastic than good breeding would have allowed, but Georgina didn't care. She wanted him to know how angry she was.

Mike's secretary handed him the note when he returned from having lunch with a client. He realized it must be from Georgina because the Corona logo was on the stationery. He already knew he was a fool, a swine and a gutless wimp, so nothing she could say would be all that bad.

There was no salutation, only a blunt, *You'll be relieved to learn that you won't have to sacrifice your precious freedom in the name of paternal responsibility. I'm not pregnant. Georgina*. Mike winced, feeling no relief at all. He reached for the phone, hesitated, then cursed himself for a coward. He kept putting off the call on the theory that she needed time to cool down, but it was a rationalization. He felt guilty and insecure—that was the real truth of it.

He dialed her number, gave her name to the switchboard operator, and waited nervously. She came on the line with a crisp, "Georgina Philipps speaking."

"This is Mike," he said. "I got your note." The dead silence on the other end told him she wasn't going to reply, so he continued, "I, uh, I had too much to drink Saturday night. I guess you know that." There was still no answer, so he decided to try throwing himself on her sense of compassion. "I had such a bad headache Sunday morning I ran out of aspirin trying to kill it. On the way home, I was so nauseous I had to keep stopping the car to—well, I suppose you get the general picture."

"There's justice in the world after all," she said, not sounding the least bit compassionate.

"Yeah, right." He cleared his throat, thinking, *Strike 1, Napoli*. "Did you get my flowers?"

"I threw them away," she said.

Strike 2. She was still furious with him. "Uh, Georgina—I want you to know, I wasn't so drunk I didn't think about what you said after we—" What? Made love? It was hardly the right term. "On Saturday night," he corrected. "You were right about my parents—they're both terrific. I'm lucky to have them. It's just—I was in shock. I needed time to get used to the idea. I didn't intend to start drinking, but I came to a bar, and then another, and another, and somehow I stopped in at every one of them."

"I'm sure the publicans of Cambridge were most appreciative," she said. For the first time, Mike caught something other than hostility in her voice—maybe even a hint of amusement.

"I suppose," he said. "Look, I'm not trying to make excuses for what I did, but I want you to understand... I was very drunk that night. I hadn't slept with anyone in months because you were the only one I wanted, and then I got the idea you'd been to bed with LaSalle and I was jealous as hell. I realize I went a little crazy—that I lost control of myself. And afterward—afterward I acted like a pig. I felt guilty about not stopping and even guiltier about hurting you. Instead of being angry at myself, I took it out on you. I'm sorry."

He heard her sigh deeply. "Your guilt was misplaced. I didn't care about the pain. Your words hurt far more. They were very unfair."

Mike knew that. Georgina might have stormed in and tried to take over his life, but she wasn't manipulative. Dishonesty and deceit were alien to her. "I guess it was easier for me to lash out at you than to deal with your feelings for me," he admitted. "I only wish I could take back everything that happened."

"Yes, well, it's over and done with and best forgotten."
She was suddenly all business. "You have my word, it won't
affect your contract with us. If that's all, I really should get
back to work."

"I'd like us to be friends," Mike said.

"I don't think so," she answered softly. "It would be too
painful. Goodbye, Mike."

"Georgina, wait—"

He was too late. There was nothing on the other end of
the line but silence—she had hung up. He gently replaced
the receiver and stared at his office door. In addition to
everything else, now he felt depressed and confused.

Nothing was going the way he wanted it to. He had an
important presentation later in the week and hated the ideas
he'd come up with. He needed to talk to William Eliott if he
was ever to lay the past to rest, but William was in Paris on
business and wouldn't be back till Friday. Worst of all, he
couldn't decide what to do about Georgina. He only knew
that the thought of never seeing her again made him break
out in a cold sweat. Every time he'd needed her, she'd been
there for him, but it wasn't the same as with Jill. He felt a
consuming passion for her that words like *lust* and *chemistry* didn't begin to explain. If this was love, it was the pits.

Georgina, meanwhile, was staring at her phone and telling herself not to pick it up. Was there really any point in
having a casual friendship with Mike just so she could see
him once in a while? She thought not. A one-way relationship was no relationship at all. *Good phrase, that,* she
thought, and jotted it down on an index card. Then she
added the words *love* and *commitment* for good measure.

During the next several days she was like a dieter who
steps on the scale whenever she's tempted to eat something
she shouldn't. Mike Napoli was sheer poison. She had to
stay away from him. Every time she felt herself weaken she

took out the index card and read what she had written. It kept her from calling him.

By Friday she was sure the worst was over, but the sound of his voice on the other end of the phone told her she was wrong. A simple, "How are you doing?" spoken in a warm, sexy way and the index card might have been in London for all the good it did.

"I'm fine," she said coolly, "but very busy."

"Can you get away for a few hours?" he asked. "I'm having lunch with William Eliott today. I'd like you to be there."

Her heart started to race wildly. Was he really asking her to join him for one of the most intimate conversations of his life? And if so, why?

"Do you plan to talk to him about your mother?" she asked.

"Yes."

"And you want me there as a sort of buffer?"

It was a long couple of seconds before he answered, but when he did, his voice was husky with emotion. "I miss you like crazy, honey. I want you in my life. Don't say no."

Georgina looked at the index card. "I love you, Mike, but if you don't feel the same way—"

"Of course I feel the same way, but both of us know there are problems. You might not like my solutions. I thought we could talk this afternoon—after lunch." He paused. "I'll pick you up at eleven. Okay?"

Georgina said she would meet him out front, feeling such a confusing mixture of joy and anxiety that work became impossible. He loved her. Dear God, he actually loved her! It was intoxicating, exhilarating. But what was all that talk about problems? She thought she had solved their problems.

He pulled up in a taxi exactly at eleven and greeted her with a peck on the forehead. She wanted to put her arms around him and kiss him properly, but he seemed so preoccupied that she took his hand instead and gave it a reassuring squeeze. William's office was in lower Manhattan and the traffic was even heavier than usual, but they hardly talked during the lengthy ride downtown.

William was openly puzzled about the reason for Mike's visit but still a gracious, relaxed host. "You said you wanted to speak to me privately so I arranged for us to use the conference room. My secretary will get us some sandwiches." He opened the door and gestured to his left. "It's right this way."

Mike looked more preoccupied than ever as they seated themselves at the table. "I'm not sure how to begin," he said, "except to tell you I don't want anything from you. When this is over, we never have to see each other again."

William smiled at him. "Okay, Mike, you've got me hanging on the edge of my chair. What's this all about?"

Mike opened his briefcase and took out a picture of him and his mother. Georgina recognized it at once—it was the photo from the hospital in Philadelphia. "My mother's maiden name was Marie Vitulli. I was born October 25, 1957. Six years ago my father told me that Jill was my half-sister. He claimed he'd had an affair with your first wife during a time when he was separated from my mother. I think he twisted around the facts, but not the essential truth. Jill and I *are* related, but not through Frank Napoli. Through you."

William looked at the picture and then stared at Mike. The color had drained from his face. "I'll be damned," he said hoarsely. "Marie Vitulli."

"You knew she was pregnant?" Mike asked.

He nodded. "I gave her the name of a doctor in New York and five hundred dollars in cash." His face went from white to dull red. "Jesus, that sounds terrible—to tell you I gave your mother money to have you aborted—but I did, and she took it. I never saw her again. I assumed she'd gone through with the abortion, but she must have used the money for medical expenses."

"She went to her cousin's house in Philadelphia. As far as I can figure out, my father caught up with her when I was about seven months old and talked her into marrying him. I didn't know about any of this until last weekend, when I found some papers in my parents' attic." Mike took back the picture. "You must have really snowed her—a rich Harvard guy paying attention to a little townie. My mother saves things—playbills, matchbooks, concert programs. I'll say this much for you. You took her out in style."

William got even redder. "I once told you, I wasn't a nice person in those days. Your mother was the prettiest girl I'd ever seen and I was determined to get her into bed, but I wasn't about to tie myself down with a wife and kid when I was only twenty—especially not to a wife who was still in high school and who was from the wrong kind of family."

"So you paid her off and walked out," Mike said.

"That's about the size of it," William admitted.

Georgina could sense the leashed fury in Mike. He looked as if he wanted to break William's jaw, and William was sitting there in such quiet shame that he probably would have let him do it. Trying to defuse the situation, she gently asked William how he and Marie had met. At a movie, he mumbled. He'd seen her there with her girlfriend and asked her for her phone number. And where had they gone on their first date? To the theater, he replied, and told her the name of the play. Before too long she had him reminiscing about Marie with such obvious emotion that even Mike was forced to recognize it. At least William had genuinely cared for his mother, even if in the end he'd been too shallow and selfish to stand by her and face up to his responsibilities.

Eventually William started asking Mike some questions—about his childhood, about his father, and most of all, about Marie. They talked for a good hour and a half, until William had to leave for his next appointment. He walked Mike and Georgina to the elevators, asking Mike if he planned to talk to Jill and nodding in satisfaction when Mike said yes.

"It will mean a lot to her to finally understand what happened. She'll be thrilled to find out she has a brother." He looked at the floor. "I'm thrilled to find out I have a son, especially such a fine one."

The two men shook hands, a gesture that was more of a beginning than an ending. Georgina sensed that William would have welcomed an embrace, but Mike wasn't ready for that yet. He didn't seem angry anymore, but obviously needed more time before he could forgive William completely.

Afterward, in the elevator, she admitted she was relieved they hadn't come to blows. "I think you can add something to each other's lives eventually. Besides, to be shamefully selfish about it, William and my grandmother are inseparable these days and it would be awkward if she had to keep the two of you apart."

"Knowing Anastasia, she would do the exact opposite," Mike said. "Think how much a fistfight or two would liven up her dinner parties."

Georgina smiled. "Then you don't mind if I tell her?"

He shrugged. "If you don't, he will."

As they stepped out of the elevator, Georgina asked him what he planned to tell his parents. "I'm sure Anastasia will want William at our wedding," she said. "But it would be a terrible shock to your mother to suddenly see him if she doesn't know you've learned the truth. And even if she does know, she might feel uncomfortable if he were there. Perhaps he shouldn't come. Then again, there are bound to be other family occasions—christenings and so on. Lord, what a tangle!"

Mike didn't know whether to laugh or groan. Not only did Georgina have them married; she had already turned them into parents. Her presumption was incredible, but he was too relieved to mind.

It had meant a lot to him to learn that William and his mother had cared for one another—that he hadn't been the product of one of a series of one-night stands. Even more important, William seemed proud of him and eager to continue the relationship. Mike needed more time before he would want to do the same, but for the first time in weeks, he felt a sense of peace.

"I don't believe in family secrets," he said. "You wind up tripping over your own lies. I'll talk to my parents as soon as they get back from the Caribbean. And as far as William coming to the wedding goes, a lot can change in a year."

She gave him a bewildered look. "What do you mean, in a year?"

"We'll talk about it on the way to my apartment." He flagged down a cab and helped her inside.

Mike had given the matter a great deal of thought and reached what he considered sensible conclusions. He loved Georgina, but he wasn't about to live off her or her grandmother. At the same time, he recognized that she would be miserable in his tiny studio apartment. The obvious solution was to get married in a year or so, by which time he should be able to give her at least a few of the luxuries she was used to.

Georgina listened to these so-called solutions with a growing sense of disbelief. A proper little wife would have held her tongue, but his ideas were so ludicrous she immediately began to argue. Anastasia had offered to buy them a co-op as a wedding present, but her grandmother really preferred that they live with her. Her apartment was so enormous that privacy wouldn't be a problem, but if it really galled Mike to accept anything from Anastasia, even as a wedding gift, they didn't have to. Georgina's salary would pay for a bigger place.

The more Georgina talked, the more she despaired of making any headway. Mike wouldn't admit what a chauvinist he was being to insist that he wasn't going to marry her until he could support her in the style he'd decided she required. He kept insisting that only a gigolo would live off his wife's money. It didn't even do any good to point out that if the positions had been reversed and *she* had been the one struggling to establish a business, she wouldn't have hesitated to marry him and let him help her. He loved her, he said, but his self-respect had to come first.

By the time they reached his building, she was telling herself to give in to the inevitable. "All right, then, we'll live in your apartment until you can afford a bigger place and I'll cook and clean and put all my money in the bank. I don't really care so long as we can be together."

"You won't say that once you've seen the place," he answered.

Georgina understood his strategy the moment she walked in the door. Not only was the place tiny; it was in shambles. The sofa bed he slept on was still pulled out, with last night's rumpled sheets and blankets on top. The desk in the corner was covered with papers from an account he was working on and there were all sorts of research materials piled up on the floor nearby. She found dirty dishes in the kitchen sink, a messy bathroom, and drawers and closets that were crammed with his belongings. He lived, in short, like a typical bachelor. Even tidied up, the place would have been claustrophobic.

Mike saw the expression on Georgina's face and told himself that the old saw about one picture being worth a thousand words was right. He doubted she would argue with him anymore.

He'd stopped in at Tiffany's that morning and had a velvet jewelry case in his pocket. He took it out, opened it up, and slipped the sapphire and diamond ring inside onto her finger. It fit perfectly—Anastasia had told him the size.

"It's lovely," Georgina said, "but far too large. You shouldn't have spent so much."

"It was purely self-serving." Mike took a step backward. Now that he'd made his point about the apartment, he wanted to get her out of here. There was no use tormenting himself with what he couldn't have. "I want other men to notice it, especially Roger LaSalle."

"He's just a friend, although I suppose it amused him to make you jealous." She smiled and started forward. "Isn't a kiss customary in these circumstances?"

Mike had hoped to avoid that particular topic, at least until they were safely outside, but with Georgina holding out her arms it wasn't going to be possible. He caught hold of her wrists and placed them at her sides. "Let's wait till we're married, sweetheart. You weren't cut out for an affair."

"Good heavens, for an entire year?" She giggled. "You can't be serious. Besides, it's not an affair if we're engaged."

"It damn well is. You're the kind of woman who needs the security of marriage to enjoy making love. I don't want you to spend the next year worrying about an accidental pregnancy."

"Ah, I see!" Georgina was still grinning. "You think you traumatized me so severely last Saturday night that I'll be terrified to sleep with you now."

Mike felt himself redden. "You said it wasn't an experience you cared to repeat, and I don't blame you. I practically took you by force. It won't kill me to wait."

Georgina had earnestly tried to go along with what Mike wanted, but this latest wrinkle of his exasperated her so thoroughly that every bit of her aristocratic stubbornness came charging to the fore. The man's ideas were absurd. They should be married as soon as possible and move into someplace bigger than a postage stamp. In the meantime, they should certainly become lovers. She longed for the emotional intimacy that lovemaking would bring, not to mention the physical ecstasy.

All was fair in love and war, she decided, even a little subterfuge. She closed her eyes and rubbed her temples. "I have a frightful headache," she said meekly. "Could you get me a couple of aspirins before we go?"

While he was in the bathroom fetching the pills she slipped off her shoes, jacket and skirt. She was unbuttoning her blouse when he reappeared in the living room.

He was startled at first, then displeased. "I meant what I said, Georgina. Put your clothes back on."

"I just wanted to lie down for a little while," she explained, sounding for all the world as if the pain were simply excruciating. "Could you fetch me an ice bag? It might help."

He turned into Florence Nightingale so fast she had to bite her lip to keep from laughing. After giving her the pills and some water, he straightened up the bed and hurried off to the kitchen. She was sitting up in bed when he got back, with the covers pulled to her waist. She wasn't wearing a bra, just a silk camisole designed to make a man want to remove it.

She leaned back, put the ice bag on her head, and closed her eyes. "Can you reach the back of my neck? The muscles are so tight..."

Naturally he couldn't refuse, even though it meant sitting close beside her and bending over her supposedly pain-racked body. His fingers felt so wonderful that she sighed with pleasure. After several minutes she opened her eyes and smiled. He was staring at the way her nipples jutted against the camisole, his face a study in frustration.

She figured she had him where she wanted him, so she put the ice bag aside, twined her arms around his neck, and purred, "I'm burning up, darling. Can you do anything to lower my temperature?"

It took him a moment, but he suddenly realized he'd been had. "You never had a headache. You're trying to get me into bed."

"Mea culpa. Stop being so stubborn and make love to me. I know you're dying to."

She slid her hand across his thigh, but he was off the bed and across the room before she had a chance to caress him. He looked so disapproving she decided it was pointless to mince words. He needed some hard truths.

"I think your ideas are idiotic," she said, "and if you could put aside your macho arrogance and incredible chauvinism for even a minute, you would have to agree. Lots of women work and contribute to the family income these days—even your own sister before the children were born. There's no reason for us not to marry, live comfortably, and make love to each other all night long if we want to. Now stop being stubborn and come to bed."

He was so angry that one of the veins in the side of his neck had begun to throb. "Don't try to manipulate me, Georgina. I told you to get dressed. We're leaving."

"Is that an order?" she demanded.

"You're damn right, and for once in your life you're going to obey."

So it had turned into a contest of wills, had it? In that case, Georgina decided, the man didn't stand a chance. After all, she had always known how to demolish his self-control.

She swung her legs over the side of the bed and gave a sexy, catlike stretch. "If money is the problem, perhaps you could moonlight. You weren't a bad chauffeur, you know, although you *were* impossibly impertinent. Perhaps my grandmother would be willing to employ you again.''

He didn't say a word, just folded his arms across his chest and waited.

Georgina wriggled out of her half slip, twisting provocatively to give him a good look at her panties and garter belt. ''Ah, but I'd forgotten. You lower-class types can be frightfully proud about what sort of work you'll accept.'' She unhooked one stocking and peeled it down, then did the same with the other. ''How about being a gamekeeper on my great-grandmother's estate? If you behave yourself and remember your proper place, perhaps I'll allow you to play Mellors to my Lady Chatterley. Would you enjoy that, darling? Would you enjoy teaching a refined lady of quality how an earthy peasant like you makes love?''

He shook his head. ''Forget it, Georgina. You're not going to get a rise out of me.''

''It seems I already have,'' she said with a pointed stare at his belt.

Mike conceded how right she was. He was itching to grab her and both of them knew it. She might even be right about the other stuff—whether he should take her to bed, whether he'd acted like too much of a male chauvinist—but if he gave in now, he would never be able to control her. The lady was a handful and a half.

She removed her garter belt and stood up, taunting him with the beauty of her body. ''Of course, if you expect me to keep you around, you'll have to learn how to please me. First of all, you'll have to be available whenever I want you. And you'll have to learn to obey my orders with a little more enthusiasm.'' She walked toward him. ''I could train you as my personal servant. Teach you how to fetch me drinks... unzip my dress... draw my bath... scrub my back.''

Mike's resolve began to weaken when she draped the garter belt over his shoulder. He thought about leaving the apartment, but she would still be there when he got back. The temperature in the room seemed to soar. "Teach you how to kiss my breasts," she continued huskily, smiling up at him. "How to carry me to bed. How to move inside of me. I wouldn't tolerate any disobedience, you know. I can be a harsh taskmistress. I'm sure you wouldn't want to offend me and get on the wrong end of my riding crop."

She hadn't even touched Mike yet but he was burning up. He wanted to tease her until she was submissive in his arms and begging to be taken. And then he wanted to make her eat every damn word she'd said. "And *you* wouldn't want to get on the wrong end of my palm," he drawled. "Stop trying to seduce me, Lady Georgina, before I throw you face down on that bed and give you the spanking you deserve."

Her smile got wider. "That seems to be a favorite threat of yours. I dare you to carry it out."

Mike stood there, dying to take her up on it. He was simply going to have to accept his own limits. Nothing on God's green earth was going to stop him from having her. He'd never wanted a woman even half this much—she was like a tropical fever in his blood.

"The trouble with servants," he said, "is that sometimes they rebel, and when they do, the upper classes are lucky to escape with their beautiful hides intact."

Georgina darted away before Mike could grab her, determined to tease him for as long as she could. When he ran after her and caught her around the waist, she wiggled and clawed for all she was worth. She fully expected him to drag her to the bed, but not what came next—he pulled her across his knees and turned her onto her stomach.

He wouldn't, she thought—but he did, bringing his open palm down on the fullest part of her buttocks for a sharp little slap that was wildly erotic. She shuddered helplessly, but kept on resisting. All she got for her troubles was more punishment—if you could call anything so arousing punishment.

As she lay there, panting to catch her breath, he slid his hand under her panties and caressed her bare bottom. "Ready to give up yet?" he asked.

She was more than ready. "Yes."

"And you'll do whatever I tell you to?"

She hesitated. "What if I say no?"

"I have ways of changing your mind." He caressed her with a skillful delicacy that destroyed any thought of resistance. Then he turned her over, sat her on his lap, and kissed her with hot, deep thrusts of his tongue and left her clinging to him in mindless need. Finally satisfied, he put her away from him with almost stunning arrogance and smiled the smuggest smile she had ever seen. "I believe we were discussing taking orders—who gives them and who takes them. Since you didn't like the one about leaving, we'll try something different. Stand up and take off the rest of your clothes."

Georgina's mouth went dry. She'd never undressed completely for a man unless she counted Saturday night, but that had been in a pitch-black room. If Mike wanted to see her, though, she wouldn't refuse. She hesitantly stood up, and, blushing, pulled off her camisole top. Then she stepped out of her bikini panties.

Since she wasn't looking at him, she heard rather than saw him get up. "Now me," he said. "Undress me, sweetheart."

Georgina nodded and reached for his tie. She'd never felt so clumsy in her whole life. Not only was her hand shaking; her whole body was trembling. In the beginning her desire outweighed her nervousness, but by the time she got his jacket and shirt off, panic had begun to set in. Suppose he went too fast again? Suppose there was another disaster?

He kicked off his shoes and put her hand on his belt. She found out exactly how much he wanted her as she fumbled with the buckle, and the knowledge made her more panicky than ever. He stood there smiling while she removed his pants and briefs, but all she could think about was Saturday night, and how much it had hurt. It was even worse when he took her hand and pressed it against his belly. She stroked him the way he wanted her to, but there was no pleasure in it for her. The memories were too vivid.

He lifted her into his arms and carried her to the bed. "In a few minutes," he said, stretching out beside her, "you're going to take back every word you said. No more master and servant, your ladyship, except in bed. We're going to be equals from now on. We'll make our decisions together, even if it means I have to admit I've been a bit of a chauvinist. If you stop trying to run my life, I might even be willing to take your goddamn money."

Georgina was so astonished she almost forgot to be frightened. Mike nuzzled her neck, murmuring, "You don't play fair. I can't say no to you when you look at me that way—like you're terrified I'm going to hurt you again. And since I can't seem to keep my hands off you…" He brushed his mouth across her lips. "Nobody ever died of pleasure, but I'm going to take you as close as I can."

He was as good as his word. Georgina thought nothing could be more exquisitely exciting than the deft touch of his hands on her body, but that was only because she had never experienced his mouth. He explored every inch of her, sometimes gently, sometimes with shattering arrogance, and teased her outrageously, arousing her to fever pitch only to slow her down again. She wanted to touch him back but he kept twisting out of reach, and she had to be content with caressing his back and shoulders.

Finally, he brought her so close to the edge that the withdrawal that followed was sheer torture. "Mike, please—I can't stand it..."

"*You* can't stand it?" He laughed softly. "How do you think *I* feel?" He slid on top of her and gently parted her thighs. The intimacy was electrifying, but she couldn't help tensing up. "Relax," he murmured. "If you don't like it, we don't have to do it again. We can just mess around for the next fifty years."

There was no pain this time, only searing, intoxicating pleasure. Georgina tried to hold back, but it was impossible. In the end she was gripping him with both her arms and legs, urging him to go deeper and faster and harder until both of them lost control and exploded.

Afterward, when they had finally caught their breath and were lying in each other's arms, he smiled and asked whether he'd atoned for his sins of Saturday night. Both of them knew he had, but his question provided too good an opportunity to pass up.

"You were beastly," she said. "It's going to take more than a quick roll in the hay to make me forgive you." She traced a figure eight on his chest. "I wasn't cut out to be a mistress, darling, even an engaged one."

"Umm," he said.

"So let's get married."

Mike had seen this coming, but it didn't matter. He knew when he was beaten. "You're too damn good in bed," he grumbled. "Both of us know I'm never going to be able to keep away from you, and since the prospect of sleeping alone at night suddenly has absolutely no appeal..." He shrugged. "I would never ask you to live in sin, so I suppose marriage is the only alternative. You set the date."

Georgina grinned triumphantly. "Good heavens, I would have seduced you ages ago if I'd known how tractable it was going to make you." She paused, still working away at his chest with her fingers. "This place really is rather small, darling. I love you to distraction and naturally I'll do whatever you like, but I'm afraid I'm a rotten cook and a worse housekeeper. And Grandmother would be frightfully lonely rattling around in that huge apartment of hers." She caressed his belly. "Really, we would be doing her a kindness to live with her. She isn't one to interfere, you know. She's much too busy leading her own life."

Mike closed his eyes, enjoying the touch of her hand, which had wandered a little lower. "If she hadn't interfered, you wouldn't be here right now, driving me crazy with whatever it is you're doing."

She giggled. "I'm seducing you again. What do you say? If it doesn't work out, we'll move. I promise not to argue. Not a single word."

When she put it that way, refusing didn't seem reasonable. "Maybe. We would have to pay our share of the bills, though."

"Yes, darling." She nibbled on his ear.

"And if I feel there's too little privacy—"

"Absolutely."

"And if she interferes at all—"

"Whatever you say. You're the boss." She nibbled her way to his lips and teased them open with her tongue. "There's an old saying, my love. Why marry a poor girl when you can have a rich one? I won't cause you any problems, I swear it. After all, I was raised to be a wife and mother. I'm really extremely submissive."

"In a pig's eye," Mike muttered, and pulled her on top of him. He had the sinking feeling he was hitching himself to another Anastasia Lindsay, but at the moment he didn't care. So what if Conlin & Napoli would be a creative and financial success long before he'd dreamed possible? He could stomach that. And living on Fifth Avenue with a cook and a chauffeur wouldn't be so odious, as long as he was sure he was pulling his financial weight. He mentally corrected himself. As long as he and Georgina were. She was right about his being a male chauvinist, but he promised himself he would change. He loved Georgina and he wanted her to be happy. She was good for him. If it hadn't been for her, he might have been dead drunk right now, still wallowing in self-pity over his father's supposed betrayal. Anyone as strong-willed as he was obviously needed a strong woman to match him.

He lifted her breast to his mouth and sucked the nipple. It was becoming increasingly hard to think, what with Georgina wriggling around on top of him. "Have I mentioned how much I love you?" he asked thickly.

Georgina closed her eyes and let her desire for him wash over her like a warm, lovely bath. "Yes. I love you, too. I never knew it was possible to be so happy."

Life was almost unbearably sweet. She and Mike were going to make a wonderful team. He was the perfect man, except of course for his tailoring, and she would see to that first thing Monday morning.

Silhouette Special Edition

COMING NEXT MONTH

#391 SOME WARM HUNGER—Bay Matthews

Once, Jessie Harper had put her career first and had turned down
Bodie Lattimer's marriage offer. Years later, she was a first-rate horse trainer, a
loving mother, yet an unfulfilled woman. Then Bodie came back to town....

#392 ALL THINGS CONSIDERED—Debbie Macomber

When her long-absent husband reappeared, Lanni Matthiessen was
understandably wary. Judd soon proved mature, manly, worthy of her love. But
with the fates—and his father—against them, could she keep Judd by her side?

#393 CHASE THE WIND—Rebecca Swan

Suffocated by urban life, Justine Fleming fled to rural Washington. Though
high-powered Blair Sutherland needed her country comforts, his fast-track
moves were taking her breath away!

#394 SNOWBOUND—Lisa Jackson

As teacher Bethany Mills reluctantly helped private eye Brett Hanson track
down her criminal ex-husband, they forged a most uneasy alliance—until a
blizzard trapped them in an avalanche of desire.

#395 TREASURES OF THE HEART—Anne Lacey

Lane Hartleigh wouldn't stand by and watch brawny demolitions expert
Graham Randall destroy her beloved ancestral home. Against all odds she'd
defend her treasure, but against Graham, could she defend her heart?

#396 CARVED IN STONE—Kathleen Eagle

Weary of being typecast, actor Sky Hunter retreated to the Rockies. Battling the
elements, he had his chance to play hero to novelist Elaina Delacourte. But he
soon learned that truth is far less predictable than fiction!

AVAILABLE NOW:

#385 FORBIDDEN FRUIT
Brooke Hastings

#386 MANDREGO
Tracy Sinclair

#387 THE MIDNIGHT HOUR
Jude O'Neill

#388 THE BABY TRAP
Carole Halston

#389 THE SUN ALWAYS RISES
Judith Daniels

#390 THE FAIRY TALE GIRL
Ann Major

ATTRACTIVE, SPACE SAVING BOOK RACK

Display your most prized novels on this handsome and sturdy book rack. The hand-rubbed walnut finish will blend into your library decor with quiet elegance, providing a practical organizer for your favorite hard-or soft-covered books.

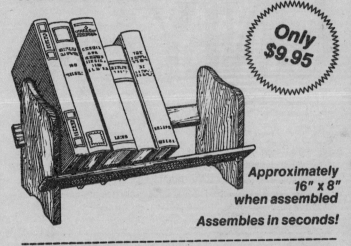

Only $9.95

Approximately 16" x 8" when assembled

Assembles in seconds!

To order, rush your name, address and zip code, along with a check or money order for $10.70* ($9.95 plus 75¢ postage and handling) payable to *Silhouette Books.*

Silhouette Books
Book Rack Offer
901 Fuhrmann Blvd.
P.O. Box 1325
Buffalo, NY 14269-1325

Offer not available in Canada.

*New York residents add appropriate sales tax.

BKR-2R

JULIE ELLIS

author of the bestselling
Rich Is Best rivals the likes of
Judith Krantz and Belva Plain with

THE ONLY SIN

It sweeps through the glamorous cities of Paris, London, New York and Hollywood. It captures life at the turn of the century and moves to the present day. *The Only Sin* is the triumphant story of Lilli Landau's rise to power, wealth and international fame in the sensational fast-paced world of cosmetics.
